KU-615-233

For Val.

Proof-reader, copy-editor, unpaid agent, publicist, events manager, wife, lover, and best friend, with all my love and admiration.

OLDHAM METRO LIBRARY SERVICE	
A3463806X	
Bertrams	13/05/2015
CRI	£16.50
CRO	

Acknowledgments

My thanks to those who have helped me as I wrote *Silent as the Grave*.

In particular, to Sir Thomas Ingilby Bt, for giving me an insight as to how an ancient castle works. Mulgrave Castle may bear some resemblance to Ripley Castle, but the Rowe ancestry doesn't have anything in common with the Ingilby family – at least I hope not!

I would also like to thank Tony (No Show) Rowe of Springwood Royals Cricket Club in New South Wales, Australia. Tony's auction bid to be named as a character in *Silent as the Grave* helped provide much-needed funds for victims of the devastating Australian bushfires. His generosity reflects the true meaning of the 'Spirit of Cricket.' I hope I have done him justice.

My thanks to Hazel Cushion and the team at Accent Press for their hard work and professionalism. I am especially grateful to Greg Rees, whose meticulous editing went far beyond correcting my punctuation and grammar.

Finally, to my wife Val, for the countless hours she spent getting the manuscript into order.

Chapter One

I picked up the report and studied it once more. I thought of the man who had written it a hundred years ago. How difficult must it have been for poor Inspector Cummins to conduct a proper investigation? In those days the landed gentry wielded great power and influence. What chance did a mere police officer stand when set against such a family, if they had something to hide? And they did have something to hide; I had felt that from the first time I read the document.

I concentrated again on the passages of the report I had been sent and felt certain that some, if not all, of the five people mentioned in the document had suffered a ghastly fate; that they had in fact been murdered. I felt a strong sense of sympathy with Cummins and wondered if he had felt as I did about the people who had mysteriously vanished. Now it was to be my turn. Now I had been asked to go to Mulgrave Castle. Now I had been asked to investigate the disappearances. If it had been difficult for Cummins; how much more of a task would it be for me, so much longer after the events?

I had just one advantage over Cummins. It was the Rowe family themselves who had asked me to go; they who had begged me to try to discover the truth.

The document was headed, 'Extract from the report of Inspector Cummins to the Chief Constable of The North Riding of Yorkshire Constabulary, 1880.

'My Lord,

In accordance with your instructions I have carried out detailed investigations into recent and historical disappearances at, and in the environs of, Mulgrave Castle. The results of the enquiries, such as they are, I set out below. Much of what I have to report is, regrettably, hearsay and local gossip, as can only be expected given the passage of time, and this is, as I am sure your Lordship must be well aware, a poor substitute for factual evidence. In order to maintain a sense of order I have separated the events into chronological sequence.

Lady Elizabeth Rowe, disappearance in 1679

Accounts of the event have, I regret to report, become garbled and distorted, and during the course of my investigations I heard not one but several versions of this story, of the disappearance of Lady Elizabeth, ranging from the mundane to the outlandishly gothic. Nonetheless, I will set them down in the second part of this paper. First however, I will outline the facts that are incontestable.

Lady Elizabeth vanished during the month of December. Correspondence charting her absence from social events in the area, and that of her supposed paramour, would lead one to the conclusion that the date of her disappearance was between the 27th December and the 31st day of the same month.

There is little to gainsay the probability that local rumour, both at the time and since, was incorrect when it insinuated that Lady Elizabeth and Sir Robert Mainwaring were involved in a romantic liaison. The diary of Lady Elizabeth's maid, Fanny Hardcastle – which has by some mysterious means found its way back into the possession of the Rowe family – would tend to confirm this. I examined the document and quote from it verbatim. Unfortunately, the girl, although in possession of some rudimentary

2

elements of education, could not be considered to possess high standards of literacy. Such being the case, and as the volume is written on some poor-quality paper and the wretched girl forbore to put a date to any of the entries, its accuracy is questionable at best. However, for good or ill, here is what she recorded.

"On Friday, my Lady was wont to visit with Sir Robt. She took greyt care of her toilette before setting out and was gone an unconsionabel time. On her return she was towsled in the hair and had high colour to her cheeks. There was sum disturbing of her robes and she bade me address her apearance as soon as may be. I asked her what had made her so disarayed in her getting out and she told me but to take care of her and ask not things that were not my consern.

Sunday. Sir Tomas to London for a week with Friends. No sooner had he gone than my Lady was away to Sir Robt. She was gone the night and only back for brakefast just on Monday. I did not ask whear she was for the night as she has been moste forthrite in telling me to look to my own matters not hers. But I have the laundryng of her attire so I can see for myself and have no doubt what is about. Poor Sir Tomas I dread to think what will happen if finds owt.

Wednesday. Matters are getting wurse. Sir Robt. came for dinner and stay'd the night in my Ladys bedchamber. I herd so much noise and disturbing that I could scarce sleep, as my room is close to my Lady. What will become of all this I wonder.

Tuesday. Sir Tomas back from London. Much distress and raised voises. Later I went to my Lady but she was not in her bedchambre, neither her attire nor her toilette things. I to Sir Tomas and told him I thought my Lady gone. He with me to her bedchamber. When he hath seen what I said were truth he cast him on my Ladys bed sobbing and weeping much.

Two weeks and no news of my Lady. Sir Tomas distrort and wanders the Castle between tymes and sets out to search for her, always returning much sadd'ned. He has taken to sleeping in my Ladys chambre and I hear him passing up and down for much of the night, oft times crying out for her."

That concludes the maid's account, such as it is. In those days there was no authority to which a missing person could be reported, so independent verification of the facts is difficult. Local rumour at the time, no doubt much embroidered since, was that Lady Elizabeth and Sir Robert had eloped to the Continent of Europe. No trace of the missing couple was ever discovered, although it is said that Sir Thomas spent much time, effort, and indeed money searching for them. Certainly no remains were ever found that would tend to suggest that anything of a more sinister nature had transpired.

Two years after the disappearance, Sir Thomas travelled to Italy to look for his errant wife. It was a fruitless search, and it is said that he was so depressed by this failure that he took his own life, and was discovered in his wife's bedchamber having hanged himself with the sheets from her bed. The estate passed to his son, Sir Matthew, then only eleven years of age, and that concludes the sparse facts about Lady Elizabeth's disappearance.

Of the local rumour, there seems to be a consensus that the Continent was where the eloping couple ended up, although there is also a tale that the couple never left England, indeed never left Mulgrave. This story, totally without foundation in fact so far as I can judge, and in passing allows for much rustic embellishment of a lewd nature, suggests that Sir Thomas discovered the couple in a compromising situation. The story imputes Sir Thomas, maddened by jealousy, did away with his wife and her lover and buried their remains in the grounds of Mulgrave. Alternatively, he weighted the corpses and

4

dropped them into the lake in front of the Castle. Accompanying either version is the tale of ghostly appearances, of Lady Elizabeth, her lover Sir Robert Mainwaring, and indeed of Sir Thomas himself, told with great relish by any of the local inhabitants one may question regarding the matter. So many and so frequent are these ghostly manifestations that it must be difficult at certain times to walk the Castle and grounds without being hemmed about by a considerable gathering of apparitions ...

In conclusion, my Lord, after the passage of so much time, and with not a shred of evidence to the contrary, I must report that the most likely explanation for the disappearance of Lady Elizabeth Rowe was indeed that she eloped, possibly to Europe, with Sir Robert Mainwaring.

Sir Richard Rowe, disappearance in 1779

Sir Richard Rowe inherited the baronetcy when only two years old. Curiously, it was as a consequence of the birth of his younger brother, Hugo, later Sir Hugo. Their father had celebrated the happy event of the birth of his younger son rather too well, and had done so it widely throughout the county. He was returning home, intoxicated, according to reports to such an extent that he had to ride being unable to walk, when he suffered a fall over the cliff at Stark Ghyll. Both horse and rider perished.

The two boys were raised by their mother, Lady Hester, under the guardianship of her brother, the Hon. Aubrey Makepeace. Much has been recorded of his reportedly notorious life-style, and I would venture to suggest that a less suitable prospect for the position of guardian it would be difficult to find.

That much is fact, but as in the case of Lady Elizabeth, the remainder is based on hearsay and supposition. Of the two boys, Sir Richard inherited from his father an athletic turn of mind, and was adept at most sporting activities. He was accounted an exceptional shot at game for one so young, and was reportedly a fine runner, accomplished oarsman, excellent at all ball games, and was a strong and powerful swimmer. This last I consider to be of some significance. In contrast, Sir Hugo was of a vain and weak character, much addicted to gambling and the attractions offered in London and other cities of a like nature. It is said he won and lost a fortune several times over before his untimely death from what is reputed to have been a disease contracted by his indulgence in keeping company with ladies whose virtue was of the easy persuasion. Fortunately for the Rowe estate, much of the money he might have otherwise squandered at the gaming tables had been secured by his father in entails that were unable to be broken. Certainly Sir Hugo's young widow had more than sufficient to console her whilst supervising the upbringing of her son Sir Mark, a lively and robust six-year-old who inherited none of his father's vices.

In the disappearance of Sir Richard, I find myself in somewhat of a quandary in reconciling the known facts and rumours with the boy's disposition and abilities. Sir Richard was seventeen years of age when he disappeared, was accounted to be of greater than average intelligence, and was also reportedly of a calm and level-headed nature. Despite this, he embarked on a course of action that appears rash and foolhardy, more in character with his younger brother. On the morning of the last day of the year, with snow laying on the ground, for anyone, no matter how strong and talented a swimmer to undertake a swim in a fresh-water lake in these latitudes is unthinkably foolish. Nonetheless, this was reportedly Sir Richard's stated ambition that morning.

When the boy failed to appear for luncheon enquiries elicited from Sir Hugo that his brother had stated this intention to him over breakfast. A search was immediately organized, tracks were discovered in the snow leading to the lake, and at the water's edge a pair of boots, a robe, and towels belonging to the young baronet were soon found. The lake was not frozen over, and a boat was launched. Later, the lake was dragged, but no trace of Sir Richard's body was ever discovered. I would venture to suggest the searches would have been rudimentary by modern standards, notwithstanding that I am puzzled that these events occurred at all.

Gossip regarding the incident follows remarkably similar lines to that surrounding the disappearance of Lady Elizabeth one hundred years earlier. In the case of Sir Richard, the story revolves around the supposed jealousy felt by Sir Hugo towards his talented sibling and the younger boy's desire for the title and the fortune attached to it. The story goes on to postulate the theory that Sir Hugo murdered his brother and concealed the body. Methods of murder and concealment vary according to the person relating the story. None of the tales have any basis in fact, although I do consider there to be many inconsistencies and unexplained irregularities in the story of Sir Richard's disappearance.

Reading the evidence of the Coroner's enquiry which was held in 1787 to establish presumption of death, I am led to the belief that many questions that should have been raised were not, possibly owing to the awe in which that official held the Rowe family, and out of respect for the grief of the dead boy's mother. The verdict was, perhaps inevitably, one of death by misadventure, although there was little by way of evidence to suggest this above all other possibilities.

It is perhaps inevitable that the wildest of stories, some of them involving a degree of superstition, should have surfaced in the light of recent events. Nevertheless, I feel there is much in the tale of Sir Richard's disappearance *that would have excited my interest had I been called upon to investigate it at the time it happened. In short, my Lord, I am far from satisfied that the full tale of the death of Sir Richard Rowe has been told.*

Lady Amelia Rowe, 1879

   As in the case of Lady Elizabeth, the disappearance of Lady Amelia, wife of Sir Frederick Rowe, is complete; mystifyingly so. Despite the most exhaustive enquiries absolutely no trace of the missing lady has been found. Prior to her vanishing there was much gossip and speculation regarding her friendship with the Honourable Ralph Aston. I am sure your Lordship is aware that Mr Aston has acquired a reputation for a reckless and somewhat rakish style of living, and has been rumoured to have enjoyed romantic links with a string of beautiful young ladies. I have to report that similarly thorough enquiries as to Mr Aston's whereabouts have yielded not one iota more in the way of success than the ones relating to Lady Amelia.

   It is, my Lord, well known that Lady Amelia and Sir Frederick lead separate lives. From eye-witness accounts and other circumstantial evidence I have little doubt that Lady Amelia   and Mr Aston are lovers, and that at some point between Christmas and New Year, taking advantage of Sir Frederick's prolonged absence on a deer-stalking holiday in Scotland, the pair eloped. The fact that we have discovered no trace of their whereabouts I count as less than significant, for, if the situation is as I believe it to be, they would make every effort to avoid discovery, and if a person is determined enough to vanish, then vanish they will.

   Sir Frederick's attitude to my enquiries would tend to bear out my supposition that nothing more sinister than a romantic entanglement is the order of the day here. Sir Frederick has been cooperative, in a disinterested sort of way, and his main grievance about Lady Amelia seems to be her lack of consideration in causing my investigation to be made at this time, thus interrupting the opening days of the shooting season.

In short, unless compelling evidence to the contrary comes to light, I believe that the disappearance of Lady Amelia and Mr Aston to be no more sinister than the flight of illicit lovers.

Conclusion.

I have, at your Lordship's behest, spent much time investigating this disappearance, as well as those previously of Sir Richard and Lady Elizabeth. Whilst I consider it to be a singular coincidence that all three events took place between Christmas Day and New Year's Day, and equally remarkable that the events are separated by exactly one hundred-years, I have found no evidence of a connecting factor, apart from the superstitious tales of family curses and similar nonsense peddled by the locals. Superstition is a part of country life; indeed it seems to me to be fostered in part to enrich an otherwise dull existence. However much these tales might enliven a quiet evening at local hostelries I fear that without any basis in fact they must remain purely speculation, entertaining though they might be.

Lacking any contrary evidence I regret that these mysteries, if indeed they are mysterious, must remain so, for I can find no justification to recommend commitment of further resources to this matter until and unless further evidence emerges that would shed further light on them.

I remain, my Lord, your most Humble and Obedient Servant,

Albert Arthur Cummins, Inspector of Police, North Riding Of Yorkshire Constabulary.

This 24th *Day of September in the year of our Lord, 1880.'*

I put the document aside and thought about the contents. Somewhere within the house or grounds of Mulgrave Castle I was convinced there was evidence of anything up to five murders. That night I had a strange dream. I dreamed I was in some part of the castle. I knew there were others there with me. I could neither hear them nor see them but I sensed their presence.

It was cold; but they had long since ceased to feel either heat or cold.

It was dark; but they had long since lost the power to see.

It was silent – as silent as the grave.

Chapter Two

December 1979

I've never considered myself lucky with women. Mind you, I'm not that good at cards either. Even when I was a minor 'celebrity' – dreadful word – I couldn't claim women were actually falling over themselves to get to me. Not that I'd have been interested anyway; for by then I was married, some would have said securely married, but such are the stresses and strains placed on a marriage by both Georgina's profession and my own that security is a lot to hope for.

I had started out in the way many journalists do, as a junior reporter on a local newspaper. In my case this was in Yorkshire. At that time local radio stations were a novelty that had not reached as far north as the River Trent, let alone the Swale, but by the time they did someone must have seen something promising about my style of news presentation because I was invited to become a 'stringer' for our local, fledgling broadcaster.

As the network was in its infancy there was little sign that it would survive to adulthood, but it did, and as it grew I found my services more and more in demand. Eventually, I was offered a staff position, and from radio I transferred seamlessly to regional television almost before I had chance to realize where my career was heading. Local had become national and I was heading for London.

It was only after that; when one or two people began glancing at me in the street with an 'I know your face' expression that I began to understand how far I had come. Once again I was lucky; I was in the right place at the right time and was offered a post as a foreign correspondent. I had little hesitation in accepting, for I knew it was a golden opportunity to broaden my experience and knowledge, to travel; to reach a more senior position in the news business. All in all there was so much to recommend it; little in the way of disadvantages. I was twenty-seven years old, single, an only child, and both my parents were dead. There was nothing to keep me in England.

Of course any thoughts that I would become a star overnight were soon banished. This was achieved courtesy of the city of Lisbon. Don't get me wrong; Lisbon is a beautiful city, full of friendly, charming, and courteous people. From a news reporter's view, though, none of those facts is a recommendation. During my time there little happened. So little that I was reminded of my early days on the staff of the local paper; covering weddings, cricket matches, and village fetes. Lisbon is just like that, only on a bigger scale – and without the cricket.

From there I was moved to Paris and saw a bit more action; then I was recalled to London and told of my new posting. A week later I boarded a jet at Heathrow. I was about to begin one of a foreign correspondent's dream jobs. I was heading for New York.

Two minutes after I had taken my seat, I started fiddling with my safety belt, and my action caused me to inadvertently grope a young woman who was bending to take the seat alongside mine. Scarlet with embarrassment, I apologized for what was a pure accident.

She turned and gave me an icy stare that melted rapidly into a warm smile. 'I've heard of some different ways of introducing oneself, but that's a new one,' she laughed.

She sat down and held a hand out. 'Hi, I'm Georgina Dale,' she told me but of course by then I had already recognized her.

'I know that,' I smiled as I shook hands. 'I'd have to be a hermit not to.'

'You're not a hermit, then?'

'No, I'm certainly not a hermit, and your face is everywhere – films, TV, cosmetics commercials.'

'I was just thinking your face is familiar too.'

'Sorry, I should have introduced myself properly; I'm Adam Bailey.'

'That's it! I thought I recognized your voice,' she told me.

'I'm surprised you have time to watch news bulletins; and recognizing my voice, that's something else again.'

'What you must remember is that I'm an actress. In our business the voice is much more important than the face.'

I smiled at a stray, private thought.

'What is it?' Georgina challenged me.

'Nothing much. I was just thinking about the way I introduced myself; I'd say the bottom was quite important too.'

She laughed. 'Was it deliberate?'

'I wish I could say it was. It would have been if I'd thought of it in time!'

Six months later we were married. We bought an apartment and settled down and for the first couple of years things were great. It was only after we'd been in New York eighteen months or so that gradually; imperceptibly, Georgina's work began to get less and less frequent. At first she had been flooded with offers; then the flood became a trickle; eventually, it dried up completely. It was at that moment, with the most inopportune piece of timing imaginable, that my employers decided I was the man to be sent to cover the war in Ethiopia.

I have no way of judging if matters would have turned out differently had I stayed in New York. In my job you didn't have a choice. Actually, I suppose that's incorrect; you do have a choice – accept the posting, or join the dole queue.

I had been in Ethiopia six months covering the war from the insurgent's point of view; which for the most part meant hiding out in mountain passes. There I would be subjected to strafing missions from fighters on an almost daily basis. During the evenings, I would be subjected to lectures about the deeds of glorious but long dead warriors and boasts about what the current generation were about to do to their enemies. I'm still not sure whether I preferred the bombing.

Then I got wounded; by pure chance. The injury came courtesy of a ricochet from a rifle. By the time I was able to reach neutral territory and get decent hospital treatment I was in pretty bad shape. After I'd recovered slightly, to the extent that the nursing staff had stopped trying to guess when I was going to peg out, I received a visitor.

He was a young, inexperienced, and highly nervous official from the British Embassy. It was, in all probability, the first time he'd been charged with delivering bad news. That didn't matter; because the sort of news he brought couldn't be told well no matter who did the telling. It was from his stumbling, embarrassed delivery that I learned that Georgina had committed suicide.

In some people it is loneliness that breeds depression. In others the depressive state is brought about by rejection; the feeling of failure. Georgina had been beset by both. My regret at leaving her, at not being there when she needed me, brought about a burden of guilt that added to my grief. It was a black and dreadful emotion I felt then, one that I have felt in a greater or lesser degree ever since; that I will probably continue to feel for the rest of my life.

As soon as I was well enough to travel, I returned to New York. A sympathetic NYPD sergeant told me all he knew; much more than I wanted to know. Georgina had taken a cocktail of drugs washed down by a bottle of vodka, walked out of the apartment on to the balcony, and kept on going until she hit the sidewalk fifteen storeys below.

Once I had straightened up my affairs and sold the apartment, I returned to England. I refused any further assignments and resigned rather than embarrass my employers. After a few weeks in London I decided cities were no longer for me. I caught a train north and finished up in my native Yorkshire. A week later I bought a tiny cottage, moved in, and settled down to my new career as a writer.

I published one factual account of my experiences in Ethiopia under the title *War in the Hills*. This was the only volume to appear in my own name. For the thrillers that followed I chose a pen name, much to the despair of my agent who bemoaned the loss of marketing opportunities. By then I was uninterested in celebrity status. I just wanted to be left alone to write. I suppose it was as much a form of escapism for me to write the books, as for other people to read them. Gradually, my face, my voice, and my name became less and less well known; which suited me perfectly.

I settled into my semi-reclusive bachelor existence. Nothing I did constituted a commitment, either to me, or from me; and that also suited me just fine. The occasional insidious notion that I was merely existing rather than living was one I was easily able to dismiss.

As I said earlier, I've never thought of myself as a ladies' man. Although prior to my marriage there had been one or two youthful flings, I had only become involved in one serious romantic relationship. Harriet Samuels had been introduced to me during my first year at university. She had recently arrived, as had I, and was looking for somewhere to live. She explained at our first meeting that the bed-sitter she was in was located over the noisiest nightclub in the northern hemisphere, and that as the racket was keeping her awake until the small hours of the morning she was constantly falling asleep during lectures.

I pointed out the advantages of this, as the majority of the lectures I attended seemed to be designed as a cure for insomnia. Harriet acknowledged my point but clinched the debate by telling me how she had missed a full lecture dealing with social unrest in Lower Saxony during the Middle Ages. Convinced by the power of this reasoning and her distress at missing out on so pivotal a discourse, I allowed her to share my flat, share the rent payments, share the cooking, share the cleaning and washing; and, for a glorious period of over two years up to and during our Finals, to share my bed. She did point out that this was having a similar effect on her sleep pattern as the nightclub had, but I was well aware by then that she could have slept through all the lectures in her final year and still walked away with a good degree. She accepted my argument, and later accepted the degree.

Our separation was as inevitable as our affair had been improbable. Harriet and I belonged in different worlds, socially speaking at least. Harriet's parents were wealthy. Her father was a very successful businessman, her mother a GP at a private clinic. My father was a clergyman, my mother a primary school teacher. The difference between us was best illustrated by our modes of transport. Harriet arrived for lectures in a Porsche, while I arrived on a bicycle – if I could borrow one, that is.

It was a long time before I worked out that if Harriet's parents could afford to buy her a Porsche they could afford far more than the rent she was contributing to our flat. I challenged Harriet about this one night. She grinned and agreed. 'Daddy wanted to rent a flat for me in a really nice area, but I refused.' She snuggled down alongside me and began caressing me.

My last question before desire overcame me was, 'Why did you refuse?'

Harriet smiled. 'Because I'd already met you, silly.'

Like I said, I'm no ladies' man. Sometimes I need to have things spelt out for me.

After we left university it was inevitable we should drift apart. There was no great parting scene, no high emotion and drama, just a slow, gradual process of increasing neglect. A couple of years later, I read of Harriet's wedding to a prominent member of an old aristocratic family. I looked at the pictures without a trace of regret. Sir Anthony Rowe, the lucky groom, looked to be a pleasant type, and Harriet was obviously in love with him. I wished her all the luck in her marriage as I turned the pages of the magazine. I thought when I closed it I was closing a chapter of my life for ever.

That was pretty much the way of things until a few weeks before Christmas. It was the greyest of grey days. One of those December days when the mist and low cloud prevent the light from penetrating the house. No rain as such, but dampness in every particle of air, every fibre of being. The year was winding down to its weary conclusion, not with a bang, not even with a whimper, but with a sullen and gloomy silence.

Christmas, formerly just a speck on the horizon, was galloping ever nearer, like a rider whose horse has bolted and is in headlong, uncontrollable flight. I had given no thought to the festive season. Not that I had any particular reason for disliking it; likewise, though, I had little cause to celebrate it. The mail was one of the reasons I found Christmas distasteful. As the celebration drew nearer the postman's arrival got later and later as he struggled to deliver an ever increasing quantity of cards, advertisements, and junk mail. That particular day there were five cards, a bill, and a letter. Three of the cards were from people in the village. Obviously, posting the cards they could have delivered by hand was their way of doing their bit to keep the village post office from going out of business. It'd need more than their efforts if that was the extent of their support.

The other two cards weren't for me but for the cottage's previous owners. I'd no idea where they'd moved to, so there was no chance of me forwarding them on. I'd been in the cottage two years so the senders had obviously taken the address from an old list. That led me to speculate how long people kept sending cards to dead acquaintances. What happened to the cards? Did the Royal Mail know more than the rest of us? Had they a forwarding address for dead people? I dismissed the idea as ludicrous; if that were the case the junk mail wouldn't keep arriving. I turned my attention to the letter. The postmark was York, which meant it could have been from a host of places nowhere near the city itself; the handwriting vaguely familiar.

I stared at the envelope, teasing myself by trying to guess who the sender was. I'd have been there well past Easter before I got it right. In the end curiosity got the better of me and I opened it up. I turned to the signature and gasped in surprise. I know Christmas is a time for remembering old friends but it was over fifteen years since I had seen Harriet Samuels. Correction: Lady Harriet Rowe, as she now was. I groped my way to a seat in the lounge and began to read the letter.

Dear Adam,

> *I wonder, will it seem as strange to you getting this letter as it does for me to write it? After all these years of being out of touch I wouldn't be surprised if you tossed it in the bin.*
>
> *In case you haven't, I'll continue. The thing is, Tony and I would like your help. I don't know if you have plans for Christmas but in case you don't,*

we'd like you to come and spend it at Mulgrave Castle with us. It will be quite a party; all our family will be here and some friends as well so it should be quite a shindig. Please ring me to let me know if you would like to join us. The house party will go through until the New Year.

Yours with fondest wishes and memories,
Harriet.

There was a long postscript to the letter in which Harriet described the problem she and her husband needed my help with, and it was the postscript that decided me. The letter itself had gone a fair way to persuading me; I had no plans and I would love to see Harriet again. Let me be honest: I defy any man *not* to feel as I did when he has had a relationship with a woman such as I had with Harriet. But it was the story she told that hooked me in the end. I knew it would take too long for me to write back in time; I would have to phone my acceptance.

'Mulgrave Castle,' the voice was male; well spoken.

'May I speak to Lady Harriet please?'

'I'm afraid she's not here today. Who's calling?'

'It's Adam Bailey; to whom I speaking, please?'

'Hello, Adam. Tony Rowe here, I take it you've got Harriet's letter?'

'Yes, it arrived a few minutes ago.'

'Good God, the post gets worse! We posted that nearly a fortnight ago; we'd almost given up on you. Did Harriet get the address wrong?'

'No, it was right, even down to the postcode. It made me wonder where she got it from.'

'Ah, that was Harriet being clever. Pulled a few strings, got it from your publishers, you know, from the book you did about the Ethiopian war.'

'Smart of her,' I agreed. 'Well, if the invitation's still open, I'd be glad to accept.'

'That's great news. I'll tell Harriet the minute she gets back. She's gone off Christmas shopping. I can't stand it myself.'

'I know exactly how you feel.' A bond was in the process of forming.

'Right, so we can expect you Christmas Eve; I'll look forward to meeting you.'

'Likewise, it will be a treat for me too. I was thinking it might be a solitary Christmas this year.'

'Can't have that.' I was warming to Rowe with every word. 'Nobody should be alone at Christmas. It doesn't seem right.'

Chapter Three

Snow was falling heavily throughout the county as I headed north. Big flakes were reflected in the headlights of the car as they drifted lazily down, aimless with the lack of wind to drive them. Conditions were good on the main roads, but as I considered the remote location of Mulgrave Castle and the potential dangers of untreated minor country lanes I was thankful for the four-wheel drive capabilities of my Range Rover. As soon as I turned off the main road I noticed the deterioration. Where seconds earlier I'd been travelling on black tarmac, glistening where the grit had melted the falling snow, I was now on a white surface, the snow crunching under the tyres as the big engine thrust the vehicle forward. The weather was deteriorating, the snow whirling ever thicker and faster in the headlights. I added the spotlights and increased the tempo of the wipers. Soon every passing landmark was shrouded in snow; trees were coated, their lighter limbs already bending as the snow accumulated on them. I still had over thirty miles to travel on these minor roads before I reached the village of Mulgrave, then a further five to the castle itself. With the steady obscuring of signposts and any other identification I was glad of the map I'd thought to put in the car. Without it, I'd have been well and truly lost.

The snow had reached blizzard conditions, and my pace had dropped to a crawl when I eventually entered a village my map had informed me was Mulgrave. I realized with some surprise that I hadn't seen another vehicle since leaving the main road. If the snow continued much longer the roads would be impassable, and Mulgrave Castle would be cut off from the outside world. I chuckled aloud at my thoughts. The weather was turning the scenario into one reminiscent of a country house mystery. Eat your heart out, Agatha Christie.

It was with some relief that I saw the solid stone lodge picked out in the beams of my lights. I knew from Harriet's letter that this was occupied by their resident cook and her husband, who also worked at the castle, and that the gates would be opened ready for my arrival. I swung past the lodge and headed between an avenue of trees down a long drive over half-a-mile long, which opened into a wide gravel sweep. In spite of the ever-thickening snow I could hear the gravel crunching on my tyres. The sound was muted by the snow, however, and my arrival would have gone unnoticed. I sat for a moment after switching the ignition off; admiring the front façade of the house. I was mildly surprised when the massive front door swung open and a figure came hurrying out towards me. I climbed out of the car.

'Adam,' the figure hailed me. 'Hi, I'm Tony Rowe; let me give you a hand in with your bags.' We reached the sanctuary of the building. 'It's a pleasure to meet you, Adam, I'm sorry you must have had such a rotten journey getting here.' Tony put down the case he had carried in for me and as we shook hands I glanced up at the sound of her voice.

'You haven't told him it isn't over with yet, then?' Harriet was standing on the half landing, where the broad staircase turned at right-angles midway to the first floor. She walked gracefully down the shallow flight and I could see the years had been kind to her. The beautiful girl had become a lovely woman. 'Hello, Adam,' she smiled warmly.

I shook her hand and kissed her with due formality on one cheek. 'Harriet, you look lovelier than ever,' I greeted her. 'It's wonderful to see you again. Thank you so much for inviting me. What was it you meant about it not being over with?'

Rowe cleared his throat nervously. 'I was about to ask you a favour when Harriet interrupted. We have a bit of a crisis over the transport, you see. My BMW has decided to malfunction, I can't get a spark out of it, and my estate manager's borrowed the Land Rover to go off to Scotland for Christmas and the Hogmanay holiday. To be honest we haven't another vehicle capable of tackling these roads in the snow,' he paused and Harriet took over.

'My sister Eve and Tony's business partner Edgar Beaumont are at Netherdale railway station. They both caught the morning train up from London and got as far as Netherdale and they can't get any further. Eve rang me just before you got here. I tried to tell her we couldn't guarantee to be able to collect her, but without much success to be honest. Eve told me they couldn't find a taxi driver prepared to venture out of town and demanded we send someone to pick them up. Eve can be a bit like that, I'm afraid. Then we saw you arrive in your Range Rover and it seemed like an answer to our prayers.'

'Eve's a bloody bad tempered, spoilt idiot, that's what she is.'

'Tony's right,' she confessed reluctantly. 'Eve can be difficult.' (I heard a muttered aside of, 'Impossible more like,' from Tony.) 'So if you don't feel up to tackling those roads again, Adam, just say so. Don't feel obligated; Eve and Edgar can book into The Golden Bear or somewhere in Netherdale and keep each other company until the weather clears. They're well enough matched in some ways.'

'Don't worry; I don't mind going to pick them up. The Range Rover should be able to cope if I take it steady.'

I declined their offer that one of them should accompany me. 'No, it's fine, you're far too busy. I'll manage on my own.'

Harriet insisted I had a coffee before I left, so it was twenty minutes later when I set off. Despite my bold words to Tony and Harriet, I had serious reservations about the journey ahead. There was no sign of the snow abating and road conditions were worsening all the time.

I had almost reached the junction with the Netherdale ring road when a bumping vibration told me the Range Rover had picked up a puncture. I slowed gingerly to a halt and put on my hazard lights. The action was a reflex one; I had little expectation of their being any traffic as I hadn't seen another vehicle since leaving Mulgrave Castle. I swore a bit – no, to be fair, I swore a lot – then got out to inspect the damage. The rear wheel on the driver's side was the culprit. The snow, driven by a strong north-easterly wind, was driving almost horizontally into my face. I cursed Bing Crosby and Irving Berlin for wishing a 'White Christmas' upon the world and started to rectify the problem.

I unloaded the jack and the spare wheel. Changing a wheel is not my idea of fun at the best of times. This certainly was *not* the best of times. The operation must have taken in excess of half an hour, during which I got cold and wet, then colder and wetter. The biggest problem I faced was that when I had put the car in for servicing a few weeks earlier, the mechanic had used an air-powered wheel-brace to tighten the wheel nuts. This is a far more efficient device than a hand-operated one; the problem is it makes the nuts virtually impossible to remove by hand. I was forced to undo them one at a time, removing the jack and edging the car forward between each removal to get the next nut in a position where I could bring my full weight to bear by standing on the brace. When my foot slipped from the brace and the tool scratched my shin, I almost gave up.

But eventually, and with considerably more swearing, I completed the repair, replaced the punctured wheel in the boot, and let down the jack. When I had secured everything I climbed back into the car and started the engine. Although I was now sheltered from the weather I was cold, wet, dirty, and weary. My temper was not at its best either. I thought briefly about the couple waiting at the station. No doubt they'd have the refuge of a warm, well-lit coffee bar. I sat for five minutes or so, allowing the car heater to alleviate the numbness in my hands and feet. The heater did its best, but the difference it made was negligible.

The station yard was almost in darkness when I arrived some twenty-five minutes later. Obviously I had miscalculated. There would be no more trains stopping there before Boxing Day and the station staff had been ordered to save on electricity.

The car headlights picked out two figures huddled against the meagre protection offered by the wall of the building. Through the myriad of snowflakes dancing across the beam I could just make out that they were a man and a woman. Obviously these were my passengers. I pulled to a halt alongside them and climbed stiffly out. I was about to greet them when the woman spoke, 'Where the bloody hell do you think you've been? Do you realize how long we've been waiting here freezing to death? Put the cases in the boot and get us to the Castle, pronto. Just you wait until my sister hears about this.' She swept past me and climbed into the back of the car.

I turned to her companion; half hoping for a warmer reception. 'You should have been here an hour ago. You'll be lucky if you've still got a job once I speak to Sir Anthony, you're a bloody disgrace.'

With that he joined the woman in the back of the car; my car. I walked angrily across to where they'd left their baggage. There were two suitcases and a hold-all. I examined these; then returned and opened the back of the Range Rover. The wind was driving the snow directly towards the back of the vehicle. I carried each case to the car individually, taking my time and being careful not to slip on the treacherous surface; then dumped them unceremoniously into the boot. I dragged the process out as long as I could justify and felt better for it. It was mean and petty, true enough; but I enjoyed it. When I had finished, I slammed the boot viciously; then the driver's door with equal venom; apologising silently to the car as I did so; then set off back towards the castle.

Whether the two of them had run out of conversation during their long wait or not I wasn't sure; and to be honest I didn't care much. They neither spoke to me nor to each other and that suited me fine. My attention was concentrated wholly on the road conditions which had deteriorated from appalling to ghastly since my previous journey. In parts the road was virtually impassable. For any other vehicle it would have been, but it is those conditions that a Range Rover is built for. Not for the first time did I say a silent prayer of thanks to the manufacturers and applaud the wisdom of my choice.

It took more than an hour before I saw the welcoming light of the lodge ahead. The snow; that had started as fine pellets was now a mass of large flakes falling in whirling, gyrating confusion. As I pulled to a halt outside the main entrance to the castle the woman broke the silence. If I had hoped that the warmth of the car would have mellowed her mood or even that I might get a word of thanks for my efforts on their behalf I was in for a rude shock. 'Take the car round to the courtyard; unload our bags, and bring them to our rooms,' she ordered me in an abrupt tone. 'Your slackness has already made us late for dinner. By the time we've changed, the rest of the party will probably be onto the dessert course.'

She waited for her companion to get out then slammed the door in a bad-tempered manner behind them and stalked across towards the steps in front of the entrance. I watched her and the man trudging behind her. 'And a Merry fucking Christmas to you as well,' I muttered. I took considerable pleasure in seeing the man slip off the bottom step and deposit his fat arse in a snowdrift. It was the nearest to a bit of fun I'd had all day. My faith in natural justice restored, I drove round the end of the building and found my way to the courtyard at the rear. I parked as close to the door as I could and lifted their cases out of the boot before depositing them inside the nearby entrance. I locked the car and entered the castle, following the long corridor towards the sound of voices and the smell of cooking. I entered the kitchen; a huge room that at first glance seemed to be constructed purely from stainless steel.

To my surprise, Harriet was there, chatting with a slim, good-looking woman who I guessed to be in her late thirties; and who by her clothing seemed to be the cook. Harriet glanced across when I opened the door, 'Adam, thank goodness you're back safely. We were beginning to worry that you might have had an accident or got stuck in the snow.' She examined me closely and exclaimed, 'Your hands are filthy, what happened?'

'I had a puncture on the way there,' I told her ruefully. 'That's what delayed me.'

'But where are Eve and Edgar?'

I grinned. 'They've gone off to their rooms and are probably waiting for your chauffeur to deliver their luggage so they can change for dinner.'

'Our chauffeur ... but we haven't got a chauffeur,' Harriet said in astonishment. 'He left us last month to go and work in America.'

'I think they were under the impression I was the replacement.'

'Oh dear.' Harriet began to giggle. 'But didn't you explain; didn't you tell them who you are?'

'I wasn't really given very much of an opportunity,' I confessed.

'Oh, I see. Don't tell me, let me guess; Eve was in one of her moods? Was she very unpleasant?'

'At the station she was extremely unpleasant; after that neither of them spoke a word to me until they got here.'

'Just wait until I have a word with her, she'll feel the rough edge of my tongue. I love my sister dearly but she can be a real bitch sometimes. Politeness forbids me to tell you what Tony reckons she needs but you can guess. Something you could give her but I couldn't.'

A stifled chuckle reminded us we weren't alone. 'I'm sorry, Polly,' Harriet said. 'I should have introduced you. Adam, meet Polly Jardine: a maestro in the kitchen and my closest friend and confidante. Polly, this is Adam Bailey; he used to be famous.'

As we shook hands, Harriet leaned over to Polly and told her confidentially, 'Adam was a TV reporter but I knew him long before that. We were at university together. I seduced him and he's never looked back since.'

'Harriet,' I told her sternly, 'stop trying to embarrass me in front of your friends. It didn't work years ago and it won't work now. Shouldn't I make a move to get those cases up to the rooms?'

'No you jolly well shouldn't. If Eve and Edgar want them they can come down and get them. I can't wait to give Eve a piece of my mind.'

'No, please don't do that,' I contradicted her, 'let me have the pleasure.' I paused, struck by something in her expression. 'You don't *like* Beaumont, do you?'

'No, I do *not*,' Harriet said emphatically. 'Neither does Tony. Beaumont's father was originally Tony's partner, and ever since he died Tony's been trying to get Edgar to sell his share in the business. The trouble is, Beaumont knows he's onto a good thing so he sits tight. Tony's in a bit of a cleft stick. If he wants to get shut of Beaumont he'd have to engineer things so the company loses money. That wouldn't do us any good. The only reason we've invited him is so that Tony can try to persuade him again.'

'He might be tempted if you keep arranging accidents like the one he just had.' I told Harriet and Polly about Beaumont's fall.

'I wish I'd seen that. Never mind, I'm going to enjoy watching you deal with Eve instead. I'd better warn Tony and his mother not to give the game away. Come on, let me show you your room.'

'Harriet,' Polly called after us as we turned to leave the kitchen, 'what time do you want me to serve the first course?'

'We'll be ready as soon as Adam is, better ask him.' Harriet glanced at me.

'I don't want to put you out, Polly.' I smiled at her. 'Would half an hour be asking too much?'

'Of course not, no problem at all,' Polly reassured me. 'It's been a pleasure to meet you; especially after everything Harriet's told me about you.'

'What did that final remark mean?' I asked as I followed Harriet down the corridor.

Harriet grinned. 'I should have warned you, Adam, had I been given the chance, that Polly is a dreadful tease.'

If I was to comply with the deadline I had promised Polly I would achieve, I scarcely had time to appreciate the luxury of my room. I had a quick shower, shaved, and was dressed but by the time I reached the ground floor the rest of the party had assembled in the dining hall. Tony had been deputed to meet me and guide me in the right direction. He met me at the foot of the staircase. 'The entire rabble has gathered at the trough,' he told me cheerfully. 'When the butler summoned them they rushed through like a herd of Gadarene swine.'

29

The dining hall was a fitting chamber for a castle. It positively reeked of Mediaeval England. Was it, I wondered fleetingly, a genuine relic of the past, or had it been left over after the castle had been rented to an over-zealous Hollywood film director. From the stone flags on the floor to the vaulted ceiling supported by massive oak beams, from the panelled walls to the immense fireplace where a couple of trees were blazing fiercely upon a hearth that had been blackened by centuries of use, the whole room looked more like a film set than an eating place.

The centrepiece of the room was the dining table and this matched the antiquity and noble proportions of the rest of the room. It was comfortably larger than a full sized snooker table and of similar dimensions. I stared around in awe. 'This is magnificent,' I breathed.

Tony laughed. 'Yes, I reckon all it needs is Douglas Fairbanks and Errol Flynn duelling with swords and we've got the lot.'

He indicated a space halfway down one side of the table and wandered off to take his place at the head. Harriet tried to introduce me but was barely able to make herself heard over the hubbub of a dozen conversations. 'This is Adam, everyone,' she cried out then gave up the unequal contest.

I took my seat and looked around. The room should have looked crowded but such was its size the party of eighteen gathered round the dining table merely seemed a comfortable number. As I looked along the table I was pleased to see Edgar Beaumont was far enough from me to make conversation impossible. I could not see my other anti-social passenger at first. To my immediate right was a friendly looking young girl, of fourteen or fifteen, I guessed. She smiled. 'Hi, I'm Samantha Rowe, but everyone calls me Sammy.'

'Hello, Sammy,' I smiled, 'I'm Adam Bailey, and everyone calls me Adam.'

Sammy thought about my statement for a second. 'I don't think you can shorten Adam much,' she said a trifle wistfully, 'except perhaps to "Ad", and that doesn't seem right.'

'No I guess not,' I laughed. 'Maybe I got away lightly then.' I glanced to my left and had to check myself from saying 'Oh, no,' out loud.

I ought to have guessed from Harriet's mischievous grin after she had shown me to my room that she was up to something. 'I have to leave you to it,' she'd told me. 'I must see to the seating arrangements for dinner.'

As I contemplated Eve, my immediate neighbour at the table I reflected ruefully on Harriet's misplaced sense of humour. Not that Eve was less than easy on the eye. She would, I guessed, be ten years or so younger than Harriet, with very similar features and a very attractive figure. Her greatest asset however was a stunning mop of red-gold hair that framed her undoubtedly beautiful face. I'd caught a couple of glimpses of that face in the rear view mirror of the Range Rover. Then; huddled inside a hooded anorak and wearing a surly frown it had done the owner less than justice. Now it looked much better with a pleasant smile on display.

She turned to face me and the similarity with Harriet was enhanced, if it weren't for the hair they'd pass for identical twins, I thought. 'Hello, I'm Eve Samuels,' she told me, her voice low, husky and very attractive in a smoky cocktail lounge sort of way.

'Yes, I know.' My reply was curt.

'I didn't catch your name when Harriet introduced you,' Eve said.

'Adam,' I told her. As Sammy had said you can't shorten it more than that.

'Adam what?' Eve was no quitter, I'd grant her that.

'Bailey.' I wasn't going to let her off the hook that easily.

'Pleased to meet you, Adam. And don't worry, you don't have to be at all shy with me.'

I looked at her in surprise. 'Harriet's my older sister,' she explained kindly. 'She likes to manage people. She told me I had to make an effort to ensure you were OK. She said you were really nice but quite shy because of your speech problem. Actually that's rather strange because looking at you I wouldn't have put you down as a shy person.'

I looked down the table to where Harriet was watching with what I could only describe as a triumphant smirk on her face. I scowled at her and the smirk became a grin. 'I'm afraid your sister's been playing a joke on you. I'm not at all shy. I don't have a speech problem, so you don't have to bother trying to be nice to me. After all, it must be quite a strain for you.' The insult was by no means a subtle one but I was beyond subtlety.

Eve gasped with shock. 'That was bloody rude,' she hissed. 'And I was thinking how nice you looked. When I first saw you I thought I recognized you; thought you looked pleasant. It just shows how wrong you can be.'

'Not necessarily,' I told her in as brusque a manner as I could. 'You may have seen my face on television, or on the cover of one of my books.' I paused before adding, 'Or of course you could remember it from when you were riding in my Range Rover this afternoon.'

There was a long painful silence before Eve said in a puzzled tone, 'I'm sorry, I don't understand.'

'You might get a better grasp of things if you allow people to explain before you go off half-cocked,' I told her. 'Take this afternoon, for example. If you'd waited and been a bit less hot-headed I might have had chance to explain that I'd arrived here after a lousy journey, and then; because there was a crisis over transport, I'd turned straight round and driven back to Netherdale to collect you and that fat pillock over there. I might also have had chance to explain that the delay was due to the Range Rover having a puncture halfway between here and Netherdale, which meant I had to change the wheel in a blizzard.' I paused and added, 'You would have learned all that this afternoon if you hadn't been so bloody rude; bloody bad-mannered, bloody arrogant, and bloody ungrateful.'

As a conversation stopper my little speech was a resounding success. Eve turned away and sat with her head down contemplating her plate. I looked at Sammy on my right. 'Help me out, Sammy,' I asked her. 'I'm a stranger in town, who are these guys?'

Sammy grinned. 'They're nearly all family,' she confided. 'Mummy and Daddy you know, then there are my brother Charlie and my twin sister Becky, Daddy's cousins and their broods, and my Grandma,' she gestured to a slim lady on Harriet's right.'

'OK, Sammy, that'll do for now, I'm sure I'll get introduced properly after dinner. I think I'd probably get indigestion if I tried to remember them all whilst I'm eating.'

As I spoke, I glanced to my left, the movement involuntary. Eve was still staring at her plate and to my horror I saw a tear fall from her cheek onto her napkin. I felt ashamed. I knew I'd gone over the top and let my own temper flow unchecked, much as Eve had earlier. I couldn't bear the enmity. I touched her arm and whispered, 'I'm sorry, I shouldn't have said all that, but you made me very angry.'

Eve thrust her chair back and with a sudden movement got up and left the table. She almost collided with the stately figure of the butler, who was entering with the soup. Harriet made to rise and follow her sister but I waved her back to her seat. 'My job,' I told her as I followed Eve out of the room.

I caught up with her at the top of the stairs. 'Eve,' I

called, 'wait a minute.'

She paused and as I reached her I grasped her arms and turned her to face me. The tears she had shed in the dining hall had become a torrent. I shook her arm slightly. 'Please don't cry,' I pleaded. 'Look, we got off on the wrong foot, that's all. You made me angry but I've no excuse for saying what I did. Now, how about we call it quits and try again. It is Christmas after all.'

I'm not sure quite what I expected as a response, perhaps it's as well otherwise I wouldn't have been on my guard. Eve took a half pace back and swung a resounding slap that was aimed at my face. I saw it coming and blocked it with a hand on her wrist. Immediately, she became a scratching virago. 'Nobody speaks to me like that,' she snarled, trying desperately to free herself, but my hold was firm.

I resorted to the only weapon in my armoury. I jerked her roughly towards me and kissed her. She struggled wildly at first, but I was much stronger and she eventually became more quiescent. I should have known better. Suddenly, she was kissing me passionately and I felt the thrill of a woman's close contact for the first time in years. I closed my eyes. She drew away briefly. The punch was delivered with a strength I didn't suspect she possessed. The force and the shock sent me backwards.

I staggered winded; the eye she had punched watering slightly. I saw Eve disappear into the nearest bedroom. I reached the door and pushed it open before she had chance to lock it. She turned and I saw the alarm in her eyes. 'Now can we call it quits?' I asked.

'Why should I?'

'Because if you don't, I'll keep you here until you agree and then neither of us will get any dinner. I don't know about you but I'm famished.'

She looked at me for a long moment. 'I think you're going to have a black eye by morning,' she told me complacently.

I glanced in the mirror briefly and shrugged. 'Worth it, I reckon.' I remembered her kiss.

I could tell by the glint in her eyes that she did too. There was another emotion lurking there, but I was unable to recognize it. I waited whilst she tidied her hair and redid her make-up then offered my arm to escort her downstairs.

By the time dinner was over we were, if not the best of pals, at least friendly enough to hold a polite conversation.

Chapter Four

The meal was a protracted one and once it was over the younger children were packed off to bed, no doubt to dream of the presents they would open the next morning. After they had gone I was introduced to some of the other adult members of the party: Tony's mother Lady Charlotte, his cousins Russell Rowe and Colin Drake, and their wives.

Sammy, who had attached herself to me as personal tutor, guide, and chaperone informed me that the butler, whose name was Rathbone but whom everyone called Ollie, was the only staff member who actually lived in the castle itself. I laboured under the misapprehension that the butler's nickname was a shortened form of Oliver. It was Boxing Day before I discovered that Mr and Mrs Rathbone senior had given their son the magnificently ridiculous Christian name of Ollerenshaw.

It was Sammy who enlightened me about another of her mother's practical jokes. 'So where does Polly live?' I asked in all innocence.

Sammy looked surprised. 'In London,' she told me.

At that point the lady in question entered the room. Gone were the chef's whites and she looked quite stunning in tan and fawn top and beige slacks. 'I think Harriet's been pulling my leg about you,' I told her.

'In what way?'

'She led me to believe you were the castle's chef,' I confessed ruefully.

Polly smiled. 'It wasn't a total fib,' she told me. 'I am a professional chef, just not at the castle. I own several restaurants in London.

'How do you manage to get time off over Christmas?'

'Quite simple really. I'm the boss!'

'So what brings you here and gets you working on Christmas Eve?' I asked.

'Harriet and I were at school together and we've been friends ever since. I was abroad when you and Harriet were at university together, that's why we never met, but I've heard a lot about you.'

'I remember; Harriet used to get postcards from you, sent from all over the world.'

'That's right, so when Harriet learned I was free she invited me for Christmas. I suggested the temporary appointment. Cathy Marsh is Harriet's regular cook, she lives at the Lodge with her husband and their daughter. Her husband's Tony's gardener and their daughter works in the castle as well. I agreed to stand in for Cathy tonight so they could have their Christmas dinner. Cathy will take care of tomorrow's big meal but a party of this size takes some catering for so I'll give her a hand.'

Tony had disappeared for the snooker room with his cousins and Beaumont, Eve had already retired to bed pleading a headache, and I was beginning to feel the effects of the day, so I wished my hostess goodnight and went off to my room to complete my unpacking.

I had only been in the room five minutes when there was a knock at the door. It was Lady Charlotte, Tony's mother. 'Forgive the intrusion, Adam, but I wanted a word with you in private.'

'Please, come in, Lady Charlotte. I was only hanging my clothes up.'

'Can we dispense with the Lady bit, Adam? I'm Charlotte to my friends.'

'Thank you. So what's the problem, Charlotte?'

'That's the thing, I'm not exactly sure,' she told me frankly, 'but I just wanted to talk to you about the reason behind your visit.'

'You mean the family curse idea?'

'Yes, to be honest I wasn't particularly in favour of the idea to begin with, but that was before I met you.' She smiled disarmingly. 'It's always more difficult when you don't know the person under discussion isn't it?'

I smiled. 'Sometimes it can work the other way, but generally I agree.'

'Anyway, I thought it was a bad idea. To me it seemed like raking over the past to no good end and I was worried what the effect would be on Tony. Well, to be fair, on both Tony and Harriet.'

'Do you know anything about the supposed family curse?' I asked.

'No more than anyone else, 'Charlotte admitted. 'I just wanted to be sure that if you did unearth anything startling you would handle it tactfully, if you follow my meaning.'

'I'll do my best to, but there's no guarantee I'll find anything out; no guarantee there's anything to be found out,' I told her.

'In one sense I hope there is nothing,' Charlotte agreed, 'but then again it would be helpful if the whole thing was cleared up once and for all. It's bad enough having Tony worried sick about it without that being passed onto the children as well. I'm going now, but thanks for listening, Adam. I'm reassured you'll do the right thing.'

I was still wondering about Charlotte's motive for the visit five minutes after she had gone. My musings were interrupted by another tap on the door. I opened it to find Harriet standing there. She looked, if not exactly nervous, then certainly a trifle flustered. She walked past me into the room. 'I just thought I'd come and see if you were comfortable and had everything you need.'

'Yes thank you, Harriet,' I sat in one of the armchairs

by the window, 'the room's very comfortable and I've everything I need.'

'Good, that's great. Look, I'm sorry for Eve's behaviour earlier. She isn't often like that, no matter what Tony says about her. She's had a rough time recently and she's always been a bit on the fiery side. What happened between you two when you left the dining room?'

'Harriet, that's not really for me to say,' I replied, diplomatically.

'Well, whatever it was, you must have made an impression because she was asking all sorts of questions about you later. She didn't realize you and I had been together once.'

'Harriet,' I said gently, 'what's the real reason for this visit? You didn't come here to talk about Eve, did you?'

'No I don't suppose I did. To be honest I'm not really sure why I did come,' her face was suddenly twisted with an emotion I was unable to fathom. 'The thing is, I thought it would be easy having you here, after all it's been a long time since we were together, but then when I saw you again I realized it isn't easy; it isn't easy at all.'

'Whose idea was it to invite me?' I asked, ignoring the pointed message behind her words. There was danger enough in one of us going along that route, far more so if both of us travelled down memory lane.

'I'm not sure, to be honest,' Harriet confessed. 'If I remember rightly, it was a discussion about the family curse one weekend when all the family was here that started it, and someone mentioned your name, that's all. Tony took up the idea and I went along with it.'

'Are you and Tony happy?' I asked bluntly.

'Oh, yes,' Harriet responded. 'At least we were until recently. Tony won't say anything but I know he's dreadfully worried about the family curse, and especially now, thinking of what might happen with it being one hundred years since the last time it struck. The legend

40

never used to bother him, but ever since his father died he seems more and more preoccupied with it – even more so at this time of year. Last Christmas was hell for the two of us, and this year we felt we had to do *something*.'

'In that case, I think the sooner you leave my bedroom the better it would be for all of us,' I suggested.

Harriet stared at me and I saw a look in her eyes that was as clear a danger signal as could be. Then it passed and she smiled. 'Old flames don't always die, do they?'

'Not unless someone acts firmly to put them out,' I replied.

She walked over to the door. I made to open it for her but she stopped me. She kissed me and there was nothing platonic in the kiss. 'What if we don't want them put out?' she whispered; then she was gone.

After Harriet left I thought about what she'd said. Was Tony's concern a reaction to it being a hundred years since the curse – if one existed – had manifested itself? Or was there a more sinister underlying cause? Could it be that someone had deliberately stoked the fires of his anxiety?

I was still pondering this disturbing notion, and wondering how to set about the task I'd been set, when there was yet another knock at the door. I was beginning to consider suggesting to Tony that he should fit a revolving door to the room. I'm not quite certain who I expected to be standing there, but certainly not the visitor in question.

'I thought you might like to share a nightcap with me.' She had a bottle of malt whisky in one hand and a couple of glasses in the other.

I smiled. 'Why not? It's like Piccadilly Circus in here anyway, so I couldn't get to sleep if I tried.'

I opened the door wide and she followed me in, heeling the door neatly to a close. We walked over to the armchairs and she poured us a generous measure each from the bottle. 'Is this how you wind down after a busy day?' I asked.

'Not as a rule,' Polly said, 'we're usually too knackered.'

'It must be bloody hard work. No wonder you're so slim.'

She laughed. 'Skinny, you mean.'

'No, I certainly wouldn't call you skinny. All the curves seem to be just in the right places.'

She raised her eyebrows at the compliment. 'I see; the way to Adam Bailey's heart is through a glass of malt, is it?'

'No, not really,' I smiled.

'What was the Piccadilly Circus remark all about?'

'Oh just that you're the third woman to visit me since I came up to go to bed. I'm thinking of selling tickets for tomorrow night.'

'Who were the others?' Polly asked, her tone elaborately casual.

'Charlotte first, then Harriet.' I saw no reason to lie.

'Harriet? That was a bit dangerous, wasn't it?'

'I'm sure Tony wouldn't have minded.'

'That's not what I meant and you know it,' Polly retorted.

'What then?' I challenged her.

'I mean it's dangerous enough you just being at the castle in the first place, let alone entertaining Harriet in your bedroom.'

'You are going to explain that remark, I trust.'

Possibly my tone was colder than I intended for Polly reddened slightly with annoyance. 'OK since you insist on having it spelt out for you. In the first place I don't know what your feelings are for Harriet after all this time, but I do know she still finds you very attractive.'

'Has she said anything to you about that?'

'No she hasn't, but I could tell by the way she was looking at you in the sitting room. What about you, are you still carrying a torch for her?'

42

'No, Polly, I'm not,' I replied honestly. 'I know Harriet's still a very attractive woman but that's all over with.'

'Thank goodness for that,' she said softly.

I glanced at her and saw again that slightly heightened colour. 'Leaving that aside,' she continued, 'I reckon you were foolish to accept the invitation.'

'Why do you say that?'

'I don't believe in the family curse business as such, but there are other factors at work here. For one thing, Tony's a wealthy man, extremely wealthy, and that can breed all sorts of emotions in others around him. Jealousy for one. Think of it this way, suppose the so-called curse was to strike again in a similar way as it has twice already. Who do you think would be the likeliest victims? I suggest it would probably be Harriet and her lover, don't you?' She held up a hand to still my protest. 'I know you're not lovers, but how do you think your presence here would be viewed by the outside world? It's no secret that you and Harriet once had a passionate affair. Who would believe there was an innocent purpose behind this visit?'

'But that's not true and you know it,' I protested.

Polly gave me a long pitying look. 'Do I? Do I really know that? I'm as close to Harriet as anyone apart from Tony but I couldn't swear hand on heart you aren't still lovers. The way she speaks about you, the way she looks at you; it could so easily be interpreted that way. Think about it as you would if you were still a reporter. Think about some of the cynics who have to write copy for the gutter press that's sensational enough to keep their circulation up. What do you think they'd make of this situation? Think about it, then convince me your motives are pure. Didn't one little corner of your mind think "Well, if I got chance and it was on offer, why not?" Didn't it?'

'Polly, you have got an extremely dirty mind,' I told her. 'You know those so-called facts are nowhere near the truth.'

'Yes I do, and yes I have got a dirty mind – but no more than a reporter would have.'

She poured us both another drink. 'So what do you intend to do about it?'

'Do about what?' I asked her. 'Your dirty mind?'

Polly grinned. 'We'll come to that later. No, I mean about the curse.'

'I was going to dig about a bit and see what I can find out.'

'Now that sounds like a plan you've thought through in great depth,' the sarcasm was bitingly obvious.

'I couldn't really do much until I got here and had a look at the layout of the place and assessed the situation,' I said defensively.

'Do you realize why Tony and Harriet are so worried? Has Harriet or Charlotte said anything to you?' Polly asked.

'No, apart from the obvious reason, the curse, that's all anyone's said to me.'

'Yes, I understand that, but has nobody mentioned what's behind the curse, what really frightens them?'

'I don't understand.'

Polly took a hefty slug from her glass of malt. I watched admiringly as she knocked it back with accomplished ease. 'So no one's mentioned it. No wonder you're not able to make any plans.' Polly leaned forward. 'Adam, the reason they're so worried is the fear that Tony might have inherited the strain of insanity that has run through the Rowe family for countless generations.'

'What? I've heard nothing about that. How do you know?'

'Harriet let it slip one night when she was staying at my flat. She'd had a drop too much red wine and the truth came out along with it. They haven't mentioned it to you?'

I shook my head. 'I'm not surprised,' Polly said. 'They

keep it very quiet. I wouldn't mention that you know about it to Tony or Harriet if I was you; they're very touchy on the subject.'

'Who do I ask then? Do you know the facts?'

Polly shook her head. 'I know just what I've told you, no more. If you wanted to find out I reckon Charlotte would be your best bet.'

'Charlotte?' I said in considerable surprise, 'are you sure?'

'Pretty much. She knows everything there is to know about what goes on here, for all she plays the genteel lady. I bet she came here tonight to vet you. She's desperate to get the curse business done with for good.'

We finished our drinks and I walked over to the door with her. She turned to face me her back against the wood panelling. She looked very attractive, and that wasn't just the effect of the whisky. I leaned over to kiss her and there was nothing but raw passion in the way she returned my kiss. As we separated breathlessly a few minutes later Polly said, 'Of course if you really want to protect yourself from the curse the best way is to take another lover instead of Harriet.'

'I thought you didn't believe in the curse?'

'I don't,' she admitted. 'It was the best excuse I could come up with. Goodnight, Adam.'

Little did either of us know that, as we joked about it, the Rowe family curse had already claimed another victim.

Chapter Five

I woke up early on Christmas morning. It was not excitement that roused me but the light reflecting from the snow outside. I'd forgotten to close the curtains after Polly left and was suffering the consequences. I decided a shower might alleviate the mild hangover that had resulted from the generous measures of malt whisky. It took a while but it worked. As I shaved, I examined the damage inflicted by Eve. The eye had a slight discolouration round it, barely noticeable unless one was looking for it, and my cheek was a little tender from the slap. Elsewhere was also a little tender, but I'd live.

I returned to the bedroom from the en-suite shower room to discover that the failure to close the curtains hadn't been my only sin of omission. It also seemed that I'd failed to lock my door. During my absence, someone, whether clad in a red suit or not, had sneaked into my room and left a Christmas present on the four-poster bed.

I stared at the parcel in surprise. Discounting Santa Claus, I wondered who had been abroad at this early hour and who had taken the trouble to wrap me a present and deliver it? Who had been bold enough or knowledgeable enough to take advantage of my temporary absence? I could make a guess at the contents for the wrapping paper had been formed into the shape of a bottle. There were two attachments to the silver paper round the bottle. One was a small gift tag in matching silver, the other a sprig of mistletoe. In my short stay at Mulgrave Castle it appeared

I had acquired an admirer. I examined the gift tag. The greeting read, *Happy Christmas, Adam. From ??*

I have to admit I was more than half-convinced it would contain malt whisky, so I was mildly surprised to find instead that I had been given a very expensive-looking bottle of claret. However, I had absolutely no idea who the present was from.

I dressed slowly, pausing once or twice to stare at the bottle and the gift tag. I admit that I was still baffled and intrigued when I was ready to face the undoubted racket and chaos of Christmas morning in the company of a castle-full of youngsters.

Before I left my room I stared out at the snowbound scene surrounding the castle. No Christmas card could have bettered the sight. Although snow had ceased to fall sometime during the night, the sky was heavy with the promise of more; as if we needed more. I was surprised to see how much had fallen since I had arrived back at the castle early the previous evening. The Range Rover's tyre tracks had been completely filled in since I had driven up to the main entrance and round to the courtyard behind the castle. It didn't need a road traffic report to guess that Mulgrave Castle was completely cut off from the outside world. Not that it should be a cause for concern as I had little doubt that the castle was self-sufficient. Despite the obvious age of the building, it was reasonably warm. The improvements Tony Rowe and his recent predecessors had made ensured it was also as comfortable as a decent hotel.

Breakfast on Christmas morning was a riotous meal. It was an extended affair, punctuated by the undoubted amusement caused when each of the younger occupants opened a present. The noise of children demonstrating various examples of the latest toys and games was a constant background.

I received only one present to add to the mystery gift I'd left upstairs. This one was from Tony and Harriet, as the label announced. It contained a book entitled *A Man Alone*. This proved to be a recipe book designed for use by single males. I thanked Tony, for Harriet was not within earshot at the time. In fact Christmas morning was marked by the female inhabitants of the castle queuing up to avoid me. I expected to be ignored by Eve after our disagreement the previous night. I wasn't totally surprised that Harriet was keeping her distance, but I couldn't fathom out why Charlotte was steering clear of me, and Polly's desertion was a severe blow to my masculine pride.

It was scant consolation that the males were slightly more forthcoming. I was greeted enthusiastically by Tony; whose good humour in the face of the provocative nature of the antics of his offspring was commendable. Both his cousins, Russell and Colin, seemed a little more sociable than I might have expected from my fleeting encounter with them the previous evening.

Such was the confusion of the morning that it was almost noon before the absence of one of the party was noticed. I glanced across the dining table; the natural focal point for all activity and noticed the vacant chair. 'Beaumont seems to be having a long lie-in,' I remarked to Tony who happened to be passing at that moment. Tony paused from defending himself from the attentions of his son and heir. Charles, known to one and all as Charlie, who seemed bent on getting an early inheritance judging by the vigour with which he was attacking his father with a plastic sword. The most junior member of the household declared a temporary truce and father and son followed my gaze. 'That's a surprise,' Tony agreed. 'You haven't done him in with this lethal weapon, have you, Charlie?'

His son denied the charge vehemently. 'Perhaps the forces of evil got him during the night,' he suggested hopefully.

'We should be so lucky,' Tony said dourly. 'I suppose I'd better go and see if he's all right.'

A few minutes later, when Sammy, about the only female in the castle who was prepared to come anywhere near me, was attempting to damage my hearing by playing the outpourings of a heavy metal group into my ear from her brand new portable cassette player, I was given a welcome distraction by a tap on my shoulder. I removed the earpiece thankfully. 'Can we have a word in private, Adam? Outside if you don't mind.'

I followed Tony into the hall. Much to my surprise I was accompanied, and by the most unlikely of companions at that. Eve, who had overheard Tony's request, followed me out of the dining hall. 'Is there a problem?' I asked when we reached the sitting room.

Tony frowned forbiddingly at his sister-in-law. He obviously underestimated Eve badly. 'Go on, Tony,' she encouraged him, 'spit it out, whatever it is.'

Tony shrugged his shoulders in acceptance. 'Beaumont's not in his room,' he told us reluctantly, 'What's more, his bed hasn't been slept in.'

I cleared my throat. The next question was a delicate one. 'I don't suppose there's any chance he might have stayed in another room, is there?' I couldn't avoid a sideways glance at Eve as I spoke.

Her cheeks flushed with annoyance and her eyes sparkled as she replied, 'I don't know what you're looking at me for; I wouldn't let him near my room. I detest the man.'

'I don't think there's the slightest chance he slept elsewhere,' the haste with which Tony intervened suggested he thought Eve might be about to do me violence.

At this point Harriet appeared, to demand what was going on and why she had been left to entertain a collection of hyperactive adolescents without the support of her nearest and dearest. As her glance merely took in her husband and sister I assumed I was off that list, which was a mild relief. Tony explained the situation. 'Has anyone searched his room thoroughly?' Harriet asked. 'I realize he's not in it, but there might be some clue as to where he's disappeared to.'

'Good idea, Harriet,' Tony agreed, 'Adam and I will go have a look now.'

'I'll come with you,' Eve volunteered.

I wasn't sure who was more surprised, Tony or me. Perhaps I should explain at this point that I make no pretences to being a detective. I had been a crime reporter for two years but there is a world of difference between detecting crime and reporting it. I say this in my own defence for I failed to grasp the significance of what I saw, or rather failed to see in Beaumont's room until a good while later. Not that it would have made any difference to Beaumont by then. About the only bright thing I did was to suggest to Tony that he lock Beaumont's door after we left the room. 'I'm not saying there is something wrong,' I attempted to reassure him, 'just a precaution.'

I could see by their expressions that neither Tony nor Eve was reassured. When we returned to the dining hall Tony took command and addressed the gathering. He explained what had happened and began organizing a search party. It takes something really special to divert children's attention on Christmas morning. A game of hide-and-seek with the possibility of finding a corpse is as effective a method as I've seen. I suppose to them it was merely another party game; an attraction staged for their benefit. The adults were markedly less enthusiastic. I wondered if this was from a fear of the sinister implications behind his disappearance or merely an indication of Beaumont's unpopularity.

Tony left Harriet to delegate different areas of the castle to various guests. Much to my disappointment, Polly was assigned the top floor together with the twins, Sammy and Becky, whilst I was given the ground floor along with

Charlie and Eve. We set off, with Charlie acting as our tour guide. We searched all the family rooms first, the sitting room, the dining hall, the sun room, the breakfast room, Tony's study, the library, the snooker room, and then began inspecting the working quarters. We passed quickly through the kitchen, where Cathy Marsh was in the throes of the final preparations for the Christmas dinner and looked in the gun room, the scullery, the coal and log stores, the wine cellar, and the laundry.

In the laundry there was another door apart from the one we used. 'Where does that lead?' I asked Charlie.

'Nowhere much; there's a corridor leading to the garden. All there is down there is a toilet. We only use that door in summer.'

'We'd better check it, nevertheless.'

The toilet was empty; the outside door was securely locked and bolted. As I turned from inspecting this I noticed a small puddle on the tiled floor of the corridor. I bent to examine it. 'What is it, Adam?' It was the first time Eve had spoken directly to me since the previous night.

I looked up at her. Her face registered no more than mild curiosity. 'It's water,' I told her, 'but what puzzles me is where it's come from.'

I traced my finger through the small pool of water and towards the centre met with a little resistance. I looked all round, at the floor, the walls, and the ceiling, then I glanced back at the door checking that the bolts were securely in place. 'This water,' I told my companions, 'is melted snow. Someone has been outside and returned with snow on their shoes that they've stamped here to get rid of it.'

It was then that my mind went back to Beaumont's room and to what I had failed to notice there. I looked up again. 'Eve, think back to yesterday evening. When I dropped you at the front entrance, did Beaumont go straight to his room?'

She thought for a minute. 'Yes,' she said slowly, 'we stopped for a moment to say hello to Tony. He told us which rooms we were in and we went straight upstairs. I was miffed because you'd been allocated the room I usually get, when Russell Rowe and that dreadful wife of his haven't claimed it, that is. I stopped to protest, but Tony said you were the guest of honour. He'd already told Russell the same. I spent a couple of minutes talking to Tony but Beaumont stalked straight off up to his room. Why, is it important?'

'It might be. Can you remember if he took his coat off before he went to his room?'

'No, definitely not; I'd have remembered because I was still laughing at him falling in the snowdrift and the back of his coat was wet through.'

I smiled. 'Yes, I enjoyed that too.'

'You still haven't explained why you think it might be important.'

'If he didn't leave his coat downstairs, why isn't it in his room?'

'Isn't it, are you sure? Now you mention it I don't recall seeing it when we looked just now. So what does that mean?'

'It may mean he left the building sometime last night. If not, where's his coat vanished to?'

'But that's mad,' Eve objected. 'Nobody in their right mind would have gone outside in that foul weather. There was a blizzard raging outside.'

I looked at her. 'I remember last night very well, there was a blizzard raging outside and a virago raging inside.'

She reddened angrily and for a moment I thought she was about to go for me again, then her expression softened. 'I regret that,' she confessed. 'Your face still looks a bit on the pink side, does it hurt?'

I stood up and smiled at her. 'Not much, it was a bit tender shaving this morning.'

'What do you think happened to Beaumont? Do you really believe he went out in the snow?'

'I want to hear what the others have to report. If they've found no trace of him there is another, far more serious fact to consider.'

'Go on, Sherlock, tell us.'

'If Beaumont left the castle via that door and there's no trace of him within the building, can we assume that he didn't come back in?'

'Yes, I suppose so. I fail to grasp the significance though.'

'I do,' Charlie said suddenly. 'If Beaumont didn't come back in, who did? Who left the snowy puddle on the floor and who bolted the door?'

'Well done, Charlie,' I told him.

'You mean somebody else followed him outside?' Eve asked.

'Or arranged to meet him outside, perhaps he had an assignation?'

'Not another one! I thought you'd cornered that market.'

I stared at her. 'What does that remark mean?'

'I was referring to the string of females you had traipsing in and out of your room half the night.'

'I thought you went to bed early with a headache; or was that all pretence?'

'There's more than one reason for a woman to feign a headache,' she told me. 'Anyway, what about Beaumont?'

'You tell me, he's your friend not mine.'

'He's no friend of mine,' Eve denied hotly. 'Give me credit for a bit better taste than that. I can't stand him. One of the reasons I was so angry was I'd had to put up with the creep for so long.'

'Sorry, I thought you and he were an item.'

Eve shuddered. 'Perish the thought. Anyway, at least I only deal with one item at a time; I don't have a shopping list.'

She glanced round, we were alone. Charlie had already darted off to see what the others had discovered. 'So which is it to be; who's at the top of your list? Is it Lady Rowe senior, Lady Rowe junior, or the Randy Restaurateur?'

'There is no list, and therefore there's no one on it, either at the top, the middle, or the bottom,' I denied.

'So if you're not Charlotte's gigolo, Harriet's old flame, or the Sexy Chef's dish of the day, why are you here?'

'I'm supposed to be investigating the Rowe family curse and those mysterious disappearances from hundreds of years ago.'

'And now we've got one that's just a few hours old.'

None of the others had returned to the sitting room when we reached it, but they entered in a large chattering bunch shortly after our arrival. Nobody had discovered anything of the slightest significance. It was, as Polly remarked, 'as if he vanished into thin air.'

If Eve had been mildly sceptical about my theory regarding Beaumont's disappearance, the rest of the gathering were frankly either incredulous or dismissive; in most cases both.

Polly Jardine was the most critical of the idea. 'You can't honestly expect anyone to believe Beaumont would have ventured out into a snowstorm on a night like last night. What possible reason could he have?'

Harriet was scarcely more supportive. 'Polly's right, Adam. Apart from Beaumont having no reason to go out, nobody uses that entrance except in summer. The rest of the time it's kept locked and bolted. Even if Beaumont had wanted to go outside he would have found it far easier to use the kitchen entrance.'

'In any case what possible motive could the man have for venturing out in the middle of a blizzard?' It was

Tony's cousin Russell Rowe who was next to ridicule my ideas, 'I'm afraid you're barking up the wrong tree there, old chap.'

'Perhaps he wanted to meet someone and wanted to keep that meeting secret,' was all I could suggest.

'He wouldn't have to go outside to do that,' Russell pointed out. 'There are more than enough secret meeting places within the castle walls without going outside. No, I'm afraid you've been reading too many of your own thrillers, old man.'

Russell was beginning to irritate me and the smug expressions on the faces of some of the others at my discomfort didn't help. I decided I'd had enough and switched from defence to attack. 'Very well, then,' my voice was tinged with sarcasm from the start, by the finish it was deeply coloured, 'as you've all returned with your hands as empty as your brains from searching inside the castle, perhaps one of you brilliant detectives would favour us with your own, more convincing explanation of Edgar Beaumont's disappearance. In the unlikely event that you can do so, I'll be more than happy to hear it, because all you've done so far is to pick holes in my theory, the only theory we have, may I remind you, without offering up an alternative,' I sat back and waited, 'Go ahead, I'm listening. Just don't all talk at once.'

It was another great Adam Bailey conversation stopper. The angry silence was broken only by Tony who gave an embarrassed cough. No other explanation was forthcoming but I could tell by the expression of deep disapproval on most of the congregation's faces that my stock was at zero; if not below. Not that I was particularly upset by that. I expected no support. Even though, as I'd pointed out, it was our only theory and was a pretty wild one. I was as surprised as the rest of the gathering therefore when I found I had two allies.

'I don't give a toss what the rest of you think, I reckon

Adam has a point and I think we should at least make *some* effort to investigate his idea,' Eve told them.

If I'd silenced the audience a few seconds earlier, Eve's outburst stunned them. They were still recovering from this unexpected shock when my second supporter added his voice. 'I agree with Aunt Evie,' Charlie piped up. 'I think you're all being a bit mean to Adam. At least he has got an idea, which is more than can be said for the rest of you. I think we should go have a look outside.'

His final remark had everyone glancing out of the window, including me. My heart sank. Any prospect of raising a worthwhile search party was remote. The snow was beginning to fall heavily once more. Anyone not totally committed to the idea would see that as sufficient excuse. That meant virtually everyone.

Charlie was as successful at creating silence as Eve and I had been. He waited then said, 'Come on, Adam, you and I will go look. Leave the rest of them by their cosy fireplace.'

The stinging rebuke implicit in this remark uttered by a twelve-year-old was a bit strong for a few of the party and I could see one or two about to respond when Eve entered the fray once more. 'Good for you, Charlie, I'll come with you as well.'

'You'll risk missing your Christmas dinner, we plan to serve it in an hour,' Polly's tone was just a little catty.

'Yes, and Cathy's taken great pains to inform us we should be ready on the dot,' Harriet backed her friend up.

I could see Tony was becoming more and more uncomfortable by the signs of an impending rift. I was about to make some soothing remark but I was beaten to it by Eve. 'If you lot are more concerned with feeding your face than looking for a missing guest, then all I can say is you're a miserable shower that I wouldn't want to sit down to Christmas dinner alongside,' she told them roundly.

If there had been the remotest chance of us getting any

support in our search that remark ended it effectively enough. 'Go ahead and make martyrs of yourselves, but don't blame me if there's nothing left for you,' Polly added her pennyweight.

Eve was in fine blazing form by now. 'I'm sorry,' the sweetness of her opening belied the sting in the tail, 'I didn't realize Mulgrave Castle had been added to your chain of restaurants and that you were now managing the place,' she told Polly.

We walked out of the room; the only sound that of our footsteps.

Chapter Six

Five minutes later we were selecting suitable footwear from the collection of wellington boots lined up against the wall of the passage next to the kitchen entrance. From inside we could hear the clatter of pots and pans. Polly had rejoined Cathy Marsh in the kitchen and there seemed an angry tone to the way the utensils were being handled. As we put on weather-resistant coats I admitted to Charlie that I was puzzled none of the other children had joined us. 'It's snowing hard, there's a game of hide-and-seek and the outside possibility of a gruesome discovery,' I suggested, 'I can't see that failing to attract kids.'

He acknowledged the truth of it with a grin. 'Normally they would. As for the twins, Sammy would certainly have been along but for the fact she's got a sore throat and Ma's banned it. Becky, well, you wouldn't get her outside unless it was one of her precious books that was missing. As for my dear cousins,' there was as much sarcasm in his voice as I'd managed earlier, 'they're all dominated by their doting parents.'

Eve was having difficulty with a recalcitrant wellington. She put her hand on my shoulder to steady herself. I didn't think it worth pointing out that she could have used the wall to equally good effect. When she had mastered the misbehaving boot she straightened and looked at her nephew. 'You don't think much of Russell or Colin, do you, Charlie?'

His tone was as dismissive as a twelve-year-old could

muster, 'They're a pair of creeps and spongers,' he told us.

Eventually, we were suitably attired. I inspected my companions and made one minor alteration. Eve had opted for a red bobble cap. I removed this and replaced it with a smartly checked deerstalker. 'It's better for keeping your ears warm and it won't clash as violently with your hair colouring,' I told her.

We encountered our first difficulty with Rathbone, the butler, when we attempted to obtain the keys to aid our expedition. He told Charlie that he could not release them 'without Sir Anthony's permission'.

I'm not sure if Charlie inherited his temper from his aunt or whether it came from elsewhere. 'Don't be a prat, Ollie,' he told the butler, 'otherwise I'll have to tell Pa I've seen you watering the port down.'

We got the keys without further objection. Rathbone opened up a small cupboard in his pantry and there was an impressive array of keys hanging from nails inside. Each key was neatly labelled.

'Which ones do we want, Adam?' Charlie asked.

'All the outbuildings plus the garden door, where we found the puddle.'

Charlie passed the keys to Eve and me, with Rathbone looking on in smouldering disapproval. He paused after selecting keys to the stables, the greenhouses, and the family chapel. 'Ollie, where's the key to the garden door?'

'It should be there,' the butler muttered sourly. 'That door hasn't been opened since October.'

'Well it isn't, look for yourself,' Charlie insisted.

After a long, close scrutiny Rathbone reluctantly admitted that the key was indeed missing. It was at that point that my belief in my theory strengthened. My fear for Beaumont's safety increased in proportion.

'Don't forget that dinner will be served in three-quarters of an hour's time,' Rathbone still had one shot in his locker.

'That's all right, you have my permission to start without us,' Charlie told him.

'Don't worry, we will,' the butler promised.

'Sour-faced old dork,' Charlie muttered as we walked away.

'Charlie,' Eve protested, 'you shouldn't use words like that, it's not nice.'

'You use it all the time,' Charlie pointed out.

'That's different,' she said weakly.

'Actually, that's pretty mild for your aunt,' I told Charlie, 'you should have heard some of the things she called me last night.'

'Oi! I thought we were supposed to be calling it quits?'

I smiled sweetly. 'That was just to let you know I hadn't forgotten.'

We walked back through the kitchen watched in disapproving silence by Polly Jardine and Cathy Marsh. I was the recipient of a particularly hostile glare from Polly. The look wasn't lost on Eve. When we reached the passage to the outside door she said, 'The queen of quiches is certainly not amused. That's because you're with me, not dancing attendance on her; she doesn't like competition.'

'Competition for what?' It was a dangerous, leading question.

'Competition for any man's company and attention,' she told me. 'She has a bit of a reputation.'

'Whereas you're as pure as the driven snow, I suppose?' I'd have got a tirade of abuse for that remark the previous day, but twenty-four hours seemed to have wrought a remarkable change in Eve.

'I can be wicked if I want. I'm just a little more selective.' Eve turned to Charlie and asked, 'Have you really seen old Rathbone watering the port down?'

'No, of course not. But I know he drinks it, so it seemed natural he would,' Charlie grinned.

Eve hugged him. 'You're great, Charlie,' she told him. 'That was very clever.'

'OK,' I said when we reached the outside door, 'which way do we play it. Charlie, you're the local expert.'

'Stables first I reckon, then the greenhouse, and finally the chapel.'

'Right,' – I'd had chance to think things over – 'remember we're not just looking for Beaumont. We're also looking for signs that he met someone in one of those places.'

Both of them looked at me in surprise. 'If Beaumont went out and didn't come back then he definitely met someone. Otherwise, how could the garden door be locked and bolted from the inside? That explains the puddle on the floor. That must have been done when someone came back inside the castle. Beaumont isn't inside, therefore the puddle must have been made by someone else. Despite what the cynics back there think, I'm very much afraid for Beaumont's safety.'

'Do you think it might be the Rowe family curse?' Charlie asked, half hopefully. 'Do you think he's disappeared, never to be seen again?'

'Maybe, although I'm not a great believer in the supernatural. I think it might be something more sinister than a legend.'

I opened the door and allowed Eve to step outside first. 'Brace yourselves, men,' she called over her shoulder and was immediately enveloped in a thick cloud of whirling snowflakes.

'Come on, Charlie; don't let your auntie show us up.'

We followed Eve outside. I closed the door behind us and we were at once in that magical silent world a heavy snowstorm brings. As with the previous day, now there was little or no wind. This was a minor blessing in that it reduced the wind chill factor and stopped the snow driving into our faces. Set against that was the major disadvantage that it failed to take the snow clouds away.

Eve had the stables' keys and unlocked the door for us. There were no longer horses kept at the castle; none of the family had much interest in riding, Charlie informed me. The buildings had long since been converted into workshops and storage rooms. It took only a few minutes inspection to realize that wherever Beaumont had been headed it certainly wasn't the stables. 'Let's try the garages whilst we're close by,' Charlie suggested.

Again there was no sign that there had been any entry to the garages since the snow had begun. 'OK, where now, Charlie?' I asked.

'The kitchen garden greenhouses are on the way to the chapel, why not go there first?'

'You're the boss.'

We were already almost at the point where we would be risking the first course of our Christmas meal by the time we reached the greenhouses. They stood forlornly like three giant igloos covered in several inches of snow. The heat inside, whilst it was obviously kept low at this time of year, had been sufficient to melt some of the snow that had fallen on the glass, but obviously the effort had been too much, so there was a thick layer of ice. I wondered if the weight might eventually cause the frame to collapse. The effect would be spectacularly expensive, dangerous too, for anyone unlucky enough to be inside at the time.

That had not been Beaumont's fate and when I thought about it the greenhouses were an unlikely venue for a secret rendezvous. They were far too visible, particularly if the meeting had been planned in advance of the snow. Eve seemed to have taken responsibility for securing the buildings, so Charlie and I waited whilst she fiddled with the padlock on the final glasshouse. 'There's only the chapel left,' Charlie told me, 'and that means a half-mile walk.'

'Don't you think that's a bit of a trek?' Eve asked as we set off. 'For Beaumont I mean, not us. Do you really think he'd have gone that far just to meet someone, when there were the stables and garages closer at hand and quite secret?'

'True enough,' I agreed. Even I was beginning to wonder if my theory had been just a wild fantasy based on the slimmest of evidence. I remembered the puddle, I remembered Beaumont's missing clothes, and my resolve stiffened. 'We must check it out, no matter how unlikely it might seem,' I maintained.

Eve gave a sigh of mock reluctance. 'Never mind,' she consoled me, 'I was never that keen on turkey anyway.'

The snow was almost to the tops of our wellingtons in places, making our progress slow. Eventually, through the blurring curtain of snow, I saw the outline of a building ahead. Indistinct though it was I recognized it as our objective immediately. As we struggled through a particularly deep stretch, Eve remarked suddenly, 'I suppose you must be used to this sort of thing?'

'How do you mean?' I asked.

She turned to reply, which was her undoing. Her foot slipped in the snow and before I could put out a hand to steady her she had gone full length and was lying face down in the snow. I lifted her to her feet, thankful that Charlie was far enough ahead not to hear the rich and varied assortment of expletives his aunt was capable of producing. I began helping her to dust the snow that had attached itself in liberal proportions to almost every item of her outer clothing. 'Are you all right?' I asked.

'My leg hurts,' she said and winced. She leaned against me. I brushed vigorously at her coat. As I started to knock the snow from the chest of the garment I saw her eyes sparkle dangerously and shifted my target immediately.

'Sorry,' I said, 'I didn't think.' I turned her and began attacking the rear of the coat. It fitted her snugly and I thought suddenly that Eve had a really attractive figure. As I removed the last of the snow she leaned against me. 'Where does it hurt?' I asked.

'My ankle,' she said, 'it's really painful.'

'Are you OK, Auntie?' Charlie had returned to see what was holding us up.

'She's taken a bit of a tumble and hurt her leg,' I told him. 'Do you think you'll be able to walk the rest of the way?' I asked her.

'I'll do my best,' she said through gritted teeth. 'If you'll support me.'

'No problem, just lean as much of your weight on my arm as you want.'

Our progress was even slower after Eve's fall. 'Bang goes the Christmas pudding,' I said flippantly.

'I'll not miss that,' Eve said. 'You never answered my question.'

'What was that?' I struggled to remember what we'd been talking about.

'Snow. I said you must be used to snow, from the time you spent in the mountains.'

'How did you know about that, did Harriet tell you?'

'Harriet hasn't told me a thing about you. I reckon she wants to keep you to herself. She and you were an item at one time, weren't you?'

'You mean you didn't know about us? When we were at university together?'

'Not until years afterwards. No, I read *War in the Hills*, that's how I know about your escapades.'

'When did you read that?'

'Last night. I went into the library looking for something to read and found a copy on the table. I took it to my room; started to read it, and I couldn't put it down. The only thing to disturb my reading was the succession of females visiting your room.'

'How did you know about them?'

'My room's opposite yours. Anybody going to your room has to pass my door. When you hear tiptoeing footsteps in the middle of the night in a castle with a dodgy reputation it makes you curious. So I looked out and saw your harem coming and going.'

'My harem! That's a bit strong, isn't it?'

'Well, what else would you call it? First there was Charlotte, she's a bit long in the tooth for you though, don't you think? Then my dear sister Harriet turned up, trying to rekindle the past, just in case her husband has inherited the family lunacy. Finally the Sexy Chef came along with the aphrodisiac whisky. Once that was over I was able to concentrate on the book. I'm not sure which was more exciting.'

Eve had been leaning against me with every step. I could feel her body against mine as I helped her towards our destination. It was a strange sensation, mildly sensual through the layers of our various garments. I had watched her face as she was speaking and she seemed to be in much less pain than previously. Eventually, we stood outside the chapel. It was an ancient building; small and sturdy, but a perfect cruciform church in miniature. I tried to estimate its age but I'm no expert on architecture. 'How old is this building, Charlie, do you know?'

'I'm not certain, about four or five hundred years, I think.'

That would place it at about 1500. I tried to remember my history. As far as I could recall that was slap in the middle of the Tudor dynasty. One of the last two Henrys would have been on the throne at the time if Charlie's information was accurate. I looked at the building again. 'Is there power to the chapel? Is there light inside?' I asked him.

'Oh yes,' he told me. 'Well, there's some electricity. We hold four services a year in the chapel. One of them should be tomorrow ...' He smiled. 'But I don't think the priest will make it somehow.'

'Right, so if you unlock the door,' I handed him the key, 'can you switch the light on without actually going inside?'

'Easy, the switch is on the wall just to the left of the door.'

'OK, do that and we'll see if anyone's been inside, shall we?'

I helped Eve over the step into the porch whilst Charlie fiddled with the large iron key. 'If anyone has been in here we'll be able to tell easily enough. The building will be cold enough for the snow not to have melted.'

As soon as Charlie switched the light on we could tell there had indeed been at least one visitor to the chapel. As I'd guessed, the snow they'd got rid of from their footwear hadn't melted. It glistened in the dim reflection of the single bulb above the entrance. 'Well that answers one question,' I told my companions, 'but at the same time it raises a few more.'

'So you were right all along, Adam. Beaumont did come here,' Eve said.

'Someone did, for sure. But we can't be certain it was Beaumont.'

'Who else could it have been?'

'It might have been the person he'd arranged to meet.'

'So what are the other questions it raises?'

'First of all, the obvious one; why did they come all this way to meet up? It doesn't make sense. Second, if Beaumont didn't return to the castle, where is he? If we don't find him in here that's another unsolved mystery. The other thing that's niggling me is the keys. Why was the chapel key in Rathbone's pantry when the garden door key is still missing? At first I thought the person who had used the garden door had been unable to return the key to its hook; but the fact that the chapel key was in place knocks that theory for six.'

'No it doesn't, Adam,' Charlie said quietly. 'There are two keys to the chapel door. I've only just realized it but when we collected them from Rathbone there was only one in place. Someone has the other key.'

'Which means they either haven't had chance to return the keys unnoticed or they intend to use them again.'

'I can live with that theory. Don't you think we should go inside and see if we can get the answers to your other questions?' Eve said. 'Apart from anything else I want to take the weight off my leg. I know church pews aren't the most comfortable seats going, but I'd prefer one to standing up much longer.'

'I'm sorry, Evie; that was thoughtless of me.' I'd intended to say Eve but the word Evie slipped out. She didn't seem to mind.

The chapel was small, as befitted a private family place of worship. There were only six pews on each side of the aisle, but although the building was in miniature it was complete in every detail: altar, pulpit, font, vestry, choir stalls, and a lectern on which stood a large and ancient-looking Bible. As we reached the aisle I saw Charlie cross himself. I glanced round the church again and saw a confessional. I stopped suddenly.

'Charlie,' I said, 'I didn't realize the Rowe family are Catholics?'

'Sort of,' he admitted, 'there was a bit of trouble about it a few hundred years ago.'

'Yes, I had heard something about that, I just didn't realize it. I suppose because I knew your mother to be an Anglican.'

I glanced at Eve who nodded a confirmation. 'It's all a lot more relaxed nowadays,' Charlie said, 'none of the old renunciation business. Pa's more or less lapsed anyway, he just continues with the traditions for Grandma's sake.'

'Right, we'd better get on with what we came here for. Time's getting on and the weather doesn't look like relenting. It'll be dark before we get to the castle, especially as we'll have to take it slowly.' I smiled at Eve. 'Charlie and I will search the chapel, you rest your leg a bit longer, Evie.' There – I'd said it again, but again Eve didn't seem upset by the familiarity. Perhaps the snow was forming a small bond of friendship …

Aside from the main body of the chapel there was a small transept on either side. In each of these was an impressive tomb. 'Who lies in those?' I asked Charlie.

He grinned. 'Two of the bad lads of the family. They're the reason this place was built. It's one of the few family legends my father enjoys telling. Roland and William Rowe were twins. They were notorious for almost anything wicked: rape, kidnapping, murder. You name it, they did it. The only reason they got away with it was because they were rich and powerful. They were so evil the Church told them they would never allow them to be buried in consecrated ground so they had this place built to thumb their nose at the authorities. In the end they fell out over some female. Apparently, Roland had carried her off and was keeping her to himself. William wanted a bit of the action so he snatched her one night when Roland was drunk and took her off so he could enjoy her. They fought over her and killed each other.'

'They sound like a nice pair of lads,' I remarked gently. 'So what happened to the title after they came to a sticky end?'

'There was no problem with that, they had plenty of children between them; both legitimate and otherwise. Legend has it they fertilized most of the female population for miles around, but they were both married. William was married twice. He was the elder twin and he had eleven legitimate children; although only two of them survived infancy. It was from Roland and William that the stories about the family madness originated.'

'Who wants boring ancestors anyway?' I suggested.

'I'm not sure the local inhabitants at the time would have agreed with you.'

We searched the vestry, a tiny room with barely room for both of us, the choir stalls and the nave before examining the transepts. I took the one containing William; leaving Roland for Charlie to examine. The tomb was a large oblong marble construction, topped by a sleeping effigy of a knight. His expression was of a soul at peace and I wondered if the stonemason had been instructed to sculpt the features like that or whether his sense of humour had taken control. I turned away. There was nothing to indicate Beaumont had been there; or anyone else I thought. As I did so, I noticed out of my eye corner a small speck of colour against the grey marble of the shield and sword of the sleeping knight. I turned back and looked again. I peered closely and saw that it was a spot of reddish-brown. I reached out and touched it with the index finger of my right hand. I looked at my finger. Whatever the spot was it was still damp. 'Charlie,' I called out, 'come here a moment.'

He hurried over and Eve hobbled after him. I showed them the tiny stain on the tomb and they looked at me; their thoughts the same as mine. 'Is that blood?' Charlie asked in awe.

'I think so, but there's only one way to be sure.' I licked my finger, bringing a look of distaste to both their faces. There is no mistaking the taste of blood. 'Yes,' I told them, 'I'm sorry I had to do that; and I'm sorry to say it is blood.'

We walked slowly from the tomb back along the transept towards the rear of the chapel. Now that we had found one bloodstain others became easier to see. I counted six in an irregular line before we reached the entrance to the building. 'Someone has walked along here with blood dripping from some sort of wound,' I told them, 'and what's more, the wound was beginning to bleed

70

more profusely as he walked. Look, these bloodstains are much larger than the ones nearer William's tomb.'

We searched again, concentrating on the rear of the building but were unable to find any further sign of either Beaumont or whoever he had come there to meet. Eventually, we had to give up on the chapel. We left the building and as Charlie relocked the door I looked at the scene outside. The snow had lessened whilst we were inside; but darkness was approaching rapidly, delayed by the lying snow. 'Time we were heading back anyway,' I said, 'there still looks to be a lot more snow in that sky.'

I looked at Eve, 'Will you be able to manage the walk?' I asked.

'Yes, if you give me a hand I'll get there,' she said with a brave smile.

There is something about children, boys in particular, and snow. Boys are rarely able to resist a decent-sized snowdrift. Whereas adults avoid them, boys like to plough through them. We had only gone about a quarter of the way back to the castle when Charlie, who was ranging on ahead, saw a good looking mound of snow off to his right near a small retaining wall.

He went to churn up the snow, which was about two-feet deep. I was smiling a little at the boyishness of his antics when I saw him stumble against some unseen obstacle and went sprawling full length. 'Not another injury,' I groaned as he stayed down. 'Come on, Evie; let's see if he's all right.'

We were attempting to reach him as fast as we could, given Eve's injury, when he sat up. 'Adam,' he called and it was obvious he was in some distress. 'Adam,' his voice was high with incipient hysteria, 'Come here please, Adam, now.'

We reached him. Charlie was staring fixedly at the snowdrift; his face a mask of horror. Eve hugged him tightly. 'Charlie, are you hurt?' she asked.

He shook his head and pointed to the snowdrift, his finger trembling. Only it wasn't a snowdrift at all. It was the body of a man, the corpse of what I could only assume had recently been Edgar Beaumont.

Chapter Seven

There was nothing in the least triumphant about our return to the castle. Every aspect of my theory had been proved correct. Eve and her nephew had been fully justified in championing me. Nevertheless, our mood was sombre. Shock was fast overcoming young Charlie; he held tight to his Auntie Eve for comfort. For so much of the day I had forgotten his age; for he had talked and acted far in advance of twelve. Now he was just another young boy, witness to a dreadful sight and in need of comfort.

Eve was also in great distress, partly from shock and partly from the pain of her ankle injury. She clung to me as tightly as Charlie clung to her. I held her tightly, partly to comfort her and partly for the solace I got from it. I don't care how much experience of war or the dreadful acts of man against man you experience; there is never a point when you become inured to the sight of violence.

In this case it was the unexpected encounter with what seemed at first sight a brutal assault that enhanced the shock. We reached the kitchen entrance and walked through, careless of our appearance. The kitchen was now an oasis of calm compared to the frenzied hive of activity we had left. Only Cathy Marsh was there, superintending the steady dripping of coffee into the filter jug. 'You've missed your dinner,' she told us curtly. 'There's nothing left for you, I'm afraid.'

She should have said, 'I'm glad,' for it was what she meant.

I was quick enough to beat both Charlie and Eve to a reply. 'If you'll take my advice I'd stick a bottle of brandy in that coffee and dish out some indigestion tablets instead of the After Eights. That lot in there will need them by the time I've finished.'

I turned to help Eve and Charlie into the dining hall and turned back. 'You can also have your husband and Rathbone here in the kitchen in half an hour to await my orders.' I saw a look of astonishment on her face as I left the room.

If the dining hall at Mulgrave Castle had a Shakespearian feel to it, our entrance would have done justice to any Stratford production of the Bard's works. From Charlie's white, tear-stained, and woebegone face to Eve, distressed, limping, and obviously in pain the replete diners gaze transferred to me. In hindsight I suppose my appearance would have been admired by the make-up artists in charge of any performance of the Scottish Play. There was blood on my hands from where I had examined Beaumont's sickening wounds. This seemed to have transferred to my coat and trousers in great quantities.

Polly Jardine was in the middle of a sarcastic, 'The wanderers return,' when she saw the state of us and fell silent. The rest of the party fell silent as well. Bailey, I thought irreverently, you've done it again.

'Harriet, would you help Eve take Charlie upstairs and look after him, he's had a pretty nasty experience, I'm afraid. When you can spare some time, take care of Eve's ankle too. I'm afraid it's badly sprained.'

Lady Charlotte stood up. 'I'll go with Harriet. I was a nursing sister during the war,' she said by way of explanation. Harriet sat there a second too long. 'Harriet, now!' Charlotte said.

I turned to Eve. 'Will you be OK? I must start sorting things out.'

She laid her hand on my arm. 'Come up to my room

when you get chance, don't leave me out of things.'

'Don't worry, I won't.'

Harriet appeared at her son's side. 'No Harriet, this side,' I told her curtly. 'Eve needs help as well.'

I looked up. Tony was on his feet, concern on his face. I waited until Harriet and Charlotte had taken Charlie and Eve out of the room then turned to the now downcast looking gathering. 'Tony, we need to talk in private. Your study, I think.'

I addressed the gathering and I couldn't resist the dig, 'You might as well know that whilst you lot were feeding your faces and no doubt laughing at our stupidity for venturing out in a snowstorm on a wild goose chase, we found your missing guest. He was lying in the snow as he must have been since last night. He was lying there because somebody beat his brains to a pulp. Somebody from within this house, because it wouldn't have been possible for anyone from outside to reach the castle. So if you start to feel just a tad complacent, remember the person next to you could be a murderer.'

I'd done it again. If anyone wanted the ideal person to introduce a mime artist I'd be the one. Tony and I exited the dining hall to the sound of our own footsteps.

When we reached the privacy of his study Tony sank into the chair and said pleadingly, 'Adam, can you go through it for me, slowly. Just what happened out there? What did you discover and what are the implications?'

By the time I'd finished Tony was ready to pick the phone up. 'Listen, Adam, I'm sorry I misjudged you. There's so much going on around me that I don't understand. I'm good with money but I don't understand people like you do. You seem to attract women and they respect you. You also think through situations like I can't do.'

My heart warmed to Tony. He was a baronet, wealthy beyond anything I could achieve, with a mansion that just missed being a palace and countless acres of land. He had a loving wife (I hoped), and a trio of delightful children, yet in that moment I realized he was as confused and lost about life as the rest of us were as we blundered along, trying to find our way. 'Tony,' I told him directly, 'I think before you phone the police we should have a straight talk. One thing I am not is a ladies' man. Neither am I a magnet for them. Quite the opposite. My track record speaks for itself. Let me tell you something. Your wife, as you well know, had an affair with me when we were at university. That has nothing to do with what is going on today. It happened years ago; before you met Harriet. Last night she came to my room,' – I held up my hand to still his protest – 'and why do you think she came to my room? Because she was dreadfully worried about you, that's why. She loves you and knows you are frightened stiff about this inherited family madness nonsense. Can I ask you a serious question, Tony? What on earth makes you worried about the madness thing? Because you seem to me to be one of the sanest men I ever met.'

Tony smiled. 'Adam, I had my doubts about you, I admit. Then I met you. I like you. You don't weasel about like some of my so-called friends and relatives. I just hope you can help us with this fix we're in.' He dialled 999.

He was still trying to get through to a police officer of some rank when to our surprise Eve hobbled in, followed by Rathbone, bearing a tray with three glasses and a whisky decanter. 'Tony,' she told her brother-in-law, 'kindly order this cretin back to work. Adam hasn't eaten since breakfast, neither has Charlie, and neither have I. We all need something to eat and he's whinging that you said the staff could have the rest of the day off. He doesn't seem to realize what the situation is.'

Tony held up one hand and spoke into the receiver, 'Hold on a moment.' He turned to the butler who was dithering about arranging the contents of the tray.

'Rathbone,' he told him, 'All bets are off. I want you and Marsh in the kitchen, that's both Cathy and Frank. First of all I want a round of sandwiches and a cup of hot chocolate sent to Charlie's room, then another salver of sandwiches in here at the double. I want them delivered within the next five minutes.'

Rathbone trudged disconsolately from the room and I pulled a chair out for Eve. 'You shouldn't be here, you ought to be resting your leg,' I told her.

'I didn't want to miss out on anything and I thought you might need some help,' she told me.

'Devotion beyond the call of duty. Sit down and I'll pour you a drink.'

After several minutes of frustration, Tony eventually extracted a promise that a detective would ring him back. We waited, sipping the excellent whisky. Within the allotted time span Rathbone appeared with a salver. I was gnawing contentedly on a ham sandwich when the phone rang. Tony told the caller briefly what had happened then mentioned that most of what he knew was second hand. 'To be honest, it was a friend of mine who discovered most of this, he's the one you should be talking to. Yes, his name's Adam Bailey. Yes, that's the one. I'll put him on now if you like.'

Tony held out the receiver. 'It's Detective Constable Pratt. He's the only one on duty, apparently. Sounds like a decent sort of chap and he recognized your name, which is a help.'

I took the handset. 'Adam Bailey,' I said.

'DC Tom Pratt,' the caller told me. 'Sir Anthony's given me a rundown about what's happened. The problem is all the roads are blocked. We need somebody on the spot to act *in loco parentis*, so to speak. Would you be prepared to do that?'

'Yes, I suppose so, but you have to remember I'm no detective. I don't know what to look for; what questions to ask, or much about police procedure.'

'You're the closest we've got. You've done some crime reporting as I remember, and your factual reports seem to be accurate. I read *War in the Hills* and that seemed a good piece of reporting.'

'OK, I'll do what I can. First things first; what do you want us to do about the body? It's dark now but I suppose we ought to get it shifted soon to avoid possible predation.'

Out of the corner of my eye I noticed Eve shudder. I grinned at her, hoping that I hadn't repulsed her too much.

'Normally I'd disagree, but in this case I suppose you're right. Is there any chance you could take some photos of the body before you move it?'

'I can do that. We'll have it indoors within the next hour. I'll pass you back to Sir Anthony now whilst I make a start on finding my camera and organizing a stretcher party. Will you tell him what you need regarding witness statements and so forth? I suppose you want me to do some sort of brief examination to try and establish a time of death? Can you give me any guidance as to what to look out for?'

I listened to Pratt's instructions before passing the phone back to Tony. I'd only had chance to eat one sandwich. In view of the task ahead of me my stomach rebelled at anything further at this stage. 'I'm off to sort out a camera and get some pallbearers,' I told Eve. 'When Tony comes off the phone will you tell him where I've gone? I don't suppose you do shorthand, do you?'

Eve smiled. 'Naturally, doesn't everyone?'

'That's great news. You can stay here, rest your leg, and act as liaison with the police. When we get back we'll have to interview everyone and you can take notes; then we can type up their statements.

The dining hall had emptied by the time I walked through; although no attempt had been made to clear the debris of the Christmas dinner. Rathbone was waiting in the kitchen; alongside him was a tall, strongly built man I was told was Cathy Marsh's husband, Frank.

'Do you know of anything we can use as a makeshift stretcher to carry the body on?' I asked. 'I know it's an unpleasant task but we have to get it indoors as soon as possible.'

'Yes, sir,' Marsh answered, 'we do have a stretcher. It's in the gun room. I can go fetch it.'

'Good, I'm going to need some powerful torches if you have them as well. I'm afraid I have to take some photos of the corpse in situ. I'll go get my camera and meet you back here in five minutes.'

Tony had not joined the waiting members of staff when I returned to the kitchen. I took the torches from Marsh. 'Tell Sir Anthony I've gone to take photographs of the body as the police requested. We need a place to move Beaumont to; the stables will be the best place so don't forget the key. One of you must get it from Ms Samuels. She's with Sir Anthony in the study at the moment. And don't waste time. I want this job over and done with as soon as possible.'

I left without giving them chance to question the orders I'd barked at them. I wasn't about to enter an argument with them. I was tired and not a little angry at the seeming lack of co-operation I had received from the moment we had discovered Beaumont was missing.

I set the four torches in the snow around the head of the corpse to give some additional light and attached the flash to the camera. I took photographs of the corpse from every angle and at every distance I thought would be helpful. Fortunately, the camera was a sophisticated one so I hoped the results would be good enough when the film was developed. It took over twenty minutes, by which time Tony had joined me, together with Marsh and Rathbone. All three of them looked mournful enough to get work as pallbearers. Marsh and Rathbone opened out the stretcher; a venerable and stout one with sturdy carrying handles and a canvas litter.

'If you two take a leg apiece and lift his lower limbs onto the stretcher first, then Tony, if you grab his arms and lift the chest region, I'll put my hands under his shoulders and lift there,' I instructed them.

They all looked marginally relieved they hadn't been allocated the messy end to deal with. We got him onto the stretcher easily enough; although when I lifted the body by the shoulders the head was resting against me and I finished up in a fairly gory mess. I could tell by what little I had chance to see of the injury that the back of Beaumont's head had taken the brunt of the attack. The skull appeared to have been crushed. We got the body to the stables but I insisted on taking several close-up shots of the crushed skull before we left the makeshift mortuary. Even though I had remained calm throughout I was more than happy when Tony locked the stables door; leaving Beaumont lying in state in a room that, I discovered later, had once been home to a Grand National winner.

I followed the other three back inside the castle. I was shocked to see how bloody my clothing and hands had become; so too were the others, to judge from the way they avoided looking at me. 'Is there another way upstairs?' I asked Tony. 'I'd rather avoid everyone until I've had chance to get cleaned up.'

He showed me a servants' staircase I hadn't noticed earlier that ran from a door at the end of Rathbone's pantry. I wondered how we'd come to miss it during our earlier search. I was in my room about to start washing my hands when the door opened. I glanced over my shoulder to see Eve hobble in. 'You shouldn't be walking around, you ought to be resting that leg,' I told her.

She sat on the bed. 'I came to see if you're OK,' she said quietly.

'I will be when I get cleaned up. At the moment I feel like Lady Macbeth. How are things downstairs?'

'All the others are in the sitting room at Tony's order. They're staring at each other as if the person next to them is Jack the Ripper.'

'Hardly surprising, I suppose. I can't say I feel too much sympathy for them.'

I turned to the washbasin and took the soap from the dish and began washing the blood from my hands. I went to replace the soap on its shell-shaped receptacle and stopped. I peered at it closely. 'That's odd,' I said, half to myself.

'What's odd?' Eve asked.

'Here, on the soap, what do you think that is?'

Eve hobbled across and stood looking over my shoulder. She was wearing a gently musky scent that I found mildly disturbing. She looked at the bar of soap I was holding, 'Those bits, you mean? What do you think they are?'

'They feel like grit to me,' I said, having rubbed one of them between my fingers. 'That's strange; I wonder how they got there?'

'Have you been handling stone at all?'

'No, you were with me until we went out to photograph and move the body. That's just what we did; which to my mind seems to indicate that the grit was mixed with the blood. That's the only way I can think that it could have got onto my hands.'

'What you're saying is that whoever murdered Beaumont hit him over the head with a stone?'

Eve was still standing close to me. I picked up the towel and began drying my hands. 'You've got blood all the way up the sleeve of your sweater.' She took my hand and was pointing to it when the door opened. I suppose to anyone looking from a few yards away it must indeed have looked as if we were holding hands.

81

'I came to see if you were all right,' Polly said. 'But I see you have company,' – her lip curled – 'of a sort. I didn't realize your preference was for jailbirds.'

I winced as the door slammed into the frame. Fortunately, both were of solid oak otherwise I reckon they'd have splintered into matchwood under the force of Polly's ill-tempered departure.

'Oh dear, I think I've spoiled her little scheme,' Eve said.

I looked at her in mild surprise. The Eve I'd met yesterday would have been raging with fury by now. 'Does that upset you?' I asked.

'Not in the slightest,' she replied. 'More to the point, has it upset your plans?'

'Certainly not, contrary to popular belief round here.' Eve grinned as I continued, 'I have absolutely no plans. Not for Polly or anyone else. What was the jailbird crack about?'

We were suddenly both aware that we were, to all intents and purposes, still holding hands. Eve didn't seem in any hurry to let go and I wasn't either. 'That woman should have a Government Health Warning tattooed on her forehead,' Eve said, 'that or a skull and crossbones.'

'What is it between you two?' I asked. 'She hasn't a good word to say about you and she certainly isn't at the top of your popularity poll.'

'I think she detests me because I've been moderately successful in life,' Eve said thoughtfully. 'I think she believes I did it on the back of father's money but that isn't true. Everything I have is down to what I've earned. I resent her influence over Harriet. I don't think it's a healthy one and I dislike the way she uses people, men in particular; then casts them aside when she's had what she wants from them.'

I released her hand and turned to take my bloodstained sweater off. 'There, and I thought you were fighting over me,' I joked.

Eve's reply was so quiet I didn't hear it, but I was looking into the mirror and I've always been a fairly good lip reader. Maybe I got it wrong. The mirror was a little distorted but as far as I could tell Eve had said, 'Maybe that's true also.' Or perhaps that was just wishful thinking on my part. It was only later that I realized Eve hadn't answered my question about Polly's jailbird statement.

Tony was waiting for us at the foot of the staircase when we reached the ground floor. To all intents and purposes we must have looked like an old married couple as we came down the flight of shallow steps. The handrail was on the wrong side to be of any use to Eve, so I offered her my arm for support; which she was glad to accept.

'Adam, I want a word in my study; Eve can wait in the sitting room with the others,' Tony said tersely even before we'd finished our descent.

I let him go a couple of paces before I spoke. 'You'll have to wait a while,' I told him.

Whether it was my tone or the fact that I'd contradicted him that pulled him up I wasn't sure. He turned and for the first time I saw a tinge of anger in his cheeks. 'We need to start work as the police have asked,' he told me shortly.

'Yes, I accept that; but Beaumont's dead. A few minutes here and there isn't going to make any difference to him. In the meantime if you want me to try and find out what happened to him and if you're serious about me investigating this curse business; we'll do it my way, thank you. The first thing I'm going to do is find a suitable walking stick for Eve to use. She insists on walking about when she should be resting, so at least we can get her a bit of help. Secondly, I want to know how young Charlie is after his ordeal. Then, when we do start taking statements, I want Eve in the study taking notes. She and I are the only ones who do shorthand.'

I'm not sure if anyone had ever spoken to Tony that

way before. I wanted to get the ground rules straight before we started. I also wanted to see if his annoyance would flare into anger.

Tony smiled. 'Sorry,' he said mildly. 'I was getting above myself. The whole mess has got to me a bit, I'm afraid. You see to Eve, then come along and we'll make a start, shall we? Doing it your way,' he added.

I was pleased that my opinion of Tony had been so rapidly endorsed.

'You were a bit hard on him, weren't you?' Eve asked as I helped her choose a walking stick of the right length.

'I want to run this my way; that was one reason. I also wanted to test a theory.'

'What, another theory?' Eve arched her eyebrows in ironic mock surprise.

'Yes, believe it or not I have more than one. I just wanted to see how Tony reacted to having his orders countermanded so abruptly.'

'And the theory?'

'If there is truth in the Rowe family madness legend, then Tony isn't affected by it; he's as sane as you or I.'

Having been put to rights over procedure, Tony was keen to show his compliance. When Eve and I returned to his study he had drawn three more chairs up around his desk. Two of them placed alongside his own and the third on the opposite side facing the others. Tony indicated his own seat. 'You sit there, Eve, it will be more comfortable for you to take notes there. Adam and I can sit on either side of you and ask the questions.'

'That sounds fine by me,' I agreed, noting that Tony had even supplied Eve with a shorthand notebook and pencil during our brief absence.

We interviewed each guest in turn; then all the household staff. I was forced to point out to three of the witnesses that their statements would be handed to the police and asked them to reconsider the omissions in their account of their activities. The witnesses were the only ones to be embarrassed by this as Tony, Eve, and I already knew the information they had left out. Neither Lady Charlotte, Harriet, nor Polly Jardine had thought it prudent to mention visiting my room the previous night.

By the time Rathbone, the last to account for his movements, had departed, we were no nearer discovering the identity of Beaumont's killer than we had been when we started. Tony commented on this fact as he watched his butler leave the study, 'Well I don't see that's done us any good at all,' he said.

'Not directly, I agree. However, if we come across any inconsistencies later, these statements will prove a valuable reference point.'

'What's next, Adam?' Eve asked.

'First of all Tony ought to ring DC Pratt and tell him what we've achieved. Then I think we ought to have another look at Beaumont's room. It just might give us some clue as to what he was up to going out in that blizzard last night. I'm still puzzled as to why he went all the way to the chapel to meet someone when they could have met just as secretly nearer to hand; unless there was a particular reason for the meeting place being at the chapel.'

'What reason could there be for that?' Tony asked.

I was aware that Eve was looking at me as I replied that I had no idea. I was also aware that she thought I was telling less than the truth.

Chapter Eight

Our inspection of the dead man's room and personal effects had an oddly disturbing effect. 'I feel rather like a grave robber,' Eve confessed as she was checking the drawers in Beaumont's bedside cabinet.

'I know what you mean,' – Tony turned from the wardrobe where he had been going through Beaumont's clothing – 'it's all a bit distasteful.'

I looked up from the papers I was studying; documents I'd taken from the dead man's briefcase, 'Think of yourselves as detectives,' I advised them. 'This is a job they have to do on a regular basis.'

I returned to my perusal of the paperwork. For the most part the documents referred to business meetings, contracts, and tenders which seemed to have no relevance to Beaumont's murder. In the last pocket of the briefcase however, I came across one document that had me staring at the intricate wording with a mixture of alarm and uncertainty. I placed this carefully back where I had got it from; then shovelled all the other papers into the main body of the case. I closed the lid and snapped the locks. 'I think we've done about all we can for tonight,' I told the others. 'I'm worn out. I think what I should do is take Beaumont's briefcase to my room and look at the contents in the morning when I feel fresher. Tony, will you ring Pratt and update him with the current situation, please?'

Tony looked more than a little relieved at the thought of getting out of the room. 'No problem, Adam. I don't wonder you're tired, I'm only sorry it's been such a lousy Christmas Day for you. That wasn't the intention when we asked you here. As for that,' – he pointed to the briefcase – 'like you said earlier, there's nothing we can do for Beaumont tonight that won't wait until tomorrow.'

'I agree, Tony,' Eve said with a suspiciously innocent expression. 'We ought to let Adam catch up on his sleep if he can. After all, he didn't get much last night. Let him take these to his room and hope he doesn't get interrupted.'

I looked at her closely then said, 'OK, I'm off. Don't forget to lock up, Tony.'

After reaching my room I placed the briefcase on the dressing table, walked across to the window, and sat in one of the armchairs to wait for my visitor to arrive. Five minutes passed before the door opened. 'Don't you ever knock?' I complained.

'I would have done, but I knew you were expecting me,' Eve replied.

'How did you work that out?'

'You might have fooled my brother-in-law with your tiredness act, but you didn't fool me for a second. You knew that; and knew I'd be coming to ask you about your theory as to why Beaumont went to the chapel,' she paused, 'and to have a look at whatever it was you found so interesting in his briefcase.'

'It appears I didn't fool you,' I agreed. 'I don't suppose you brought a corkscrew with you?'

'A corkscrew? Why would you want a corkscrew?' she enquired, innocently.

'I thought we could open that red wine you gave me – no doubt filched from Tony's wine cellar. After that we could experiment with the mistletoe if you like.'

Eve went pink in the face. 'What makes you think it was me?' she asked weakly.

'Given the events of yesterday evening, I opted for the

least likely candidate. Also, remembering one part of what passed between us, I thought the mistletoe might mean you were keen to repeat the experiment.'

'That was a joke.' Her colour deepened even more.

'That's a shame. In that case, will you settle for a glass of wine?'

'You said you needed a corkscrew.'

'I've just remembered I've got a Swiss army knife with a corkscrew on it.' I produced the tool and removed the cork. There were two tumblers on the dressing table I filled each and passed one to Eve.

She looked at it, her eyebrows raised. 'That's a hefty measure.'

'I thought it would get you in the mood for the mistletoe. Now what was it you wanted to ask me?'

She eyed me suspiciously, and I guessed she wasn't certain whether I was joking or not. 'You know why Beaumont went to the chapel, don't you?'

I smiled at the neat way she side-stepped the mistletoe issue. 'Not for certain, it's just an idea that came to me when we were talking it over.'

'Go on then, share it with me,' she demanded.

I began with, 'If you leave out the thought that Beaumont was deeply religious,' which caused Eve to laugh, 'the only reason I can think of for choosing such an inconvenient meeting place was because of either the chapel itself, or something inside it.'

Eve thought this over for a moment. 'You mean somebody had put something in the chapel for Beaumont?'

'That's one possibility,' I conceded. 'Alternatively, it might have been there all along; I don't know. One way or the other, I think we should have another look round the chapel.'

'OK, I see the logic in that. I certainly can't think of another reason for traipsing all that way in a snowstorm. So what was it you found so interesting in Beaumont's briefcase; something you didn't want to talk about?'

'I don't mind talking to you about it, but I have to admit I found it more than a bit worrying.'

I walked over to the dressing table and took the document from the briefcase. I handed it to Eve and sat down to watch her read it. She scanned the paperwork twice before looking up. 'You realize what this implies?'

I nodded. 'Yes, I believe it's quite a common practice amongst business partners nowadays to take out life insurance on each other. However, when one of those partners has been murdered, the implication of a mutual policy that benefits the surviving partner to the tune of five million pounds from their death could be extremely sinister.'

'You don't honestly think Tony murdered Beaumont for the insurance money?'

'I don't think Tony's capable of murdering anyone. But on the face of it, five million pounds is a hell of a good motive,' I paused. 'I'm just saying what a policeman might think; someone who doesn't know Tony. I reckon you're more capable of murdering someone than Tony is.'

'Oh, so now you think I'm a murderer, do you?'

'Not the way Beaumont was killed. I reckon you could kill a man, given strong enough provocation, but I think you'd want to look him in the eye when you did it.'

I said more than I intended, which might have been because of the red wine or maybe I was growing to like Eve.

Strangely she took my unguarded remark as a compliment, 'Maybe you're right, and maybe you see more that you let on.'

I was still grappling with this cryptic remark when Eve suggested we look at the other documents. I took the briefcase from the dressing table and carried it across to the bed, upending it to tip all the contents onto the duvet. I sat on the edge of the bed and patted the quilt alongside me. After a moment, Eve hobbled across and sat down, and we commenced examining the papers. She stared intently at the wording of every page whilst I watched her reflection in the mirror of the dressing table. She was undoubtedly beautiful, very like Harriet but with that glorious mop of red-gold hair to enhance her lovely features. She looked up and saw me watching her. 'Have you found anything?' I asked to cover my confusion.

'Nothing that I know of; but a lot of it is beyond me. I think we need an expert.'

'Well that counts me out.'

'So what do you suggest we do now?'

'Have another glass of wine, then go to bed,' I said it without thinking. I felt myself going red and hoped Eve hadn't noticed the unintentional double meaning. I should have known better.

'It takes more than a couple of glasses of wine, buster. If you want an easy lay try the caterer.'

'I'm sorry, you got me all wrong, I didn't mean we should go to bed together …' I stopped, because Eve was laughing at me.

'Gotcha,' she said, triumphantly.

'Oh very well, have your joke,' I told her, crossly.

'I'd rather have my wine,' she smiled and held out her glass.

After we'd finished the wine I stood up and held my hand out to help her. After a moment's hesitation she took it and allowed me to lift her to her feet. She stood facing me, allowing her weight to rest on my arm as I helped her towards the door. I caught that musky perfume again. 'How's the leg?' I asked.

'Still a bit sore, but better than it was.'

She held on to me longer than I thought was absolutely necessary, then, almost as if she had made a decision, reached across and kissed me. 'Who needs mistletoe?' she said; then closed the door behind her. A second later she opened it again. 'I should lock this if I was you.'

I slept badly, and I suppose that was only to be expected after everything that had happened following my arrival at Mulgrave Castle. Such fitful sleep as I was able to manage was punctuated by a variety of strange dreams. Of these; one concerned the ancestors of the Rowe family whose tombs I'd seen in the chapel. The second concerned Eve and this was possibly the most horribly realistic of all. In it I was searching Mulgrave Castle for her but although I walked from floor to floor up seemingly endless staircases and along never-ending corridors calling her name, I was aware that my search was a vain one; that Eve was dead.

I knew Eve was there somewhere, I knew the others who had disappeared were there but I could not see them; could not hear them; could not touch them. I knew they were dead and with a shock I realized why I knew all this; why I was unable to contact them; for I was also dead.

I awoke suddenly and sat up. So real had been the dream that I was momentarily disoriented. Although the night had been cold and although at some point in my nightmare I had thrown the duvet from me I was sweating profusely. The terror the nightmare had inspired crept into my waking state and I was suddenly afraid that whatever happened, whatever the truth or not of the Rowe family curse; I might not leave Mulgrave Castle alive.

I glanced at my watch on the bedside table. It was only 6.30. I thought briefly about trying to go back to sleep but rejected the idea. Sleep had brought such dreadful visions that I was unwilling to risk a repetition of the ordeal. I opted to get up and see if a shower would help me. I crossed to the window and drew the curtains. I stared into the darkness at the stars and was pleased to find that overnight the snow had stopped.

I had just emerged from the shower room and was feeling decidedly better when I heard a knock at the door. I opened it. Eve was standing there. 'Can I come in?' It was a bit late to refuse as she was past me before I had chance to reply. I turned round. Eve looked at me. 'Oh,' she exclaimed, 'I'm sorry, I didn't realize you weren't dressed.'

She didn't sound particularly sorry; she didn't stop looking either.

'Eve!' I protested. 'I was taking a shower,' I told her, clutching the bath sheet round my waist.

'I'll wait until you're dressed, then.' She sat on the end of the bed.

I snatched the clothes I'd laid out from the chair and hurried through to the shower room to dress. 'What was it you wanted?' I called through the open door.

'I've had an idea about that paperwork.'

'What is it?'

'I have a friend who works in the City. He'd know if those papers were significant. I could read them to him over the phone. It might take a day or two before we can get hold of him as it's the holidays but it could be worth a try.'

'I agree, why not give it a shot?'

I finished dressing and came back into the room. I sat next to Eve on the bed. 'There, decent again,' I said with a measure of relief.

She had a mischievous smile on her face that unnerved me slightly. 'Yes, Adam,' she agreed, 'there's just one thing,' she pointed towards the open door of the shower room.

I followed the line of her finger. To my horror the full-length mirror on the wall that had been steamed up earlier was now clear. It reflected the spot where I had stood to dress. 'You're not supposed to look,' I told her severely. 'It isn't ladylike.'

'You're confused, Adam. It's my sister who's a Lady, not me.'

'Oh, very droll,' I said grumpily.

She looked at me. 'What's matter with you, didn't you sleep well? No lady of the manor to tuck you in, no chef to bring you a nightcap at the witching hour? An appropriate time for her to be abroad I reckon. Perhaps she couldn't find a parking space for her broomstick.'

'Evie, behave.'

'You really are an old grouch today, what's wrong?'

'If you must know, I had a dreadful night. I didn't get much sleep and I had some awful dreams.' I told her about them. She patted my hand consolingly. 'Well, they were only dreams, Adam. I'm alive, you're alive, and it's a lovely morning.' She pointed out of the window to where the sun was peeping over the horizon.

There was no doubt her presence cheered me. I looked at her and smiled. 'Yes, thank goodness. And let's hope we can get through all this without anyone else getting hurt.'

I certainly wasn't going to tell her of the other dream I'd had during the night. It had been only a fleeting one and was the only pleasant one of the lot. It concerned Eve and me. No, I certainly wasn't going to mention that dream; not to Eve or anyone else.

'What are your plans for this morning?' Eve asked. 'I thought I would type up those statements on Tony's typewriter. That is unless you want me,' she paused before adding, 'for anything else.'

She was teasing me unmercifully and enjoying every minute of it. I knew it and she was aware that I knew it. That seemed to add to her enjoyment.

'If I told you what I really want you for you'd probably slap my face again, so, no I don't think so. I'm planning to have a talk with Lady Charlotte this morning. I really need to get to grips with this family curse business.'

Eve wasn't sure if I was joking or serious, which was perhaps as well. 'Do you honestly think Beaumont's murder might be connected to that old fairy tale?'

'It seems unlikely, I agree. On the other hand it's a bit of a coincidence, don't you think?'

'Coincidences do happen; they happen all the time.'

'How much do you know about the so-called curse?'

'Probably no more than you do.'

'Well if we're talking coincidences don't you think that it's a bit too much of one for the same thing to happen twice? I mean the wife gallivanting conveniently off to the Continent with her lover; never to be seen or heard from again. And you can't deny it was a particularly opportune time for the young baronet to drown when his brother was up to his eyes in debt and needed the revenue from the estate.'

'What you're implying is they never left Mulgrave Castle? They were all murdered here?'

'I reckon you could have dragged that lake time after time and you'd never have found a trace of Sir Richard. I reckon you could have travelled the continent and not discovered a trace of Lady Elizabeth, Lady Amelia, or their lovers.'

'That would lend credence to the other legend, the inherited insanity theory.'

'It would, and I'm sure Tony and Harriet believe it, as does Lady Charlotte. I'm certain that's why they're so worried. Worried that Tony might have inherited the curse. Or even that young Charlie might have it.'

Eve looked appalled. She rejected the idea violently. 'That's impossible. Charlie's a lovely lad. He's a caring, gentle boy. Not only that, but could you see Tony as a deranged killer?'

'No, I couldn't,' I agreed. 'But that's because we know them – you certainly know them well. Others might see it differently should something happen. That's why I must try and find out more about the curse and the family history before something does happen.'

'I think talking to Charlotte's a good idea,' Eve said after some thought. 'She doesn't say a lot but she doesn't miss much either, and what she doesn't know about Rowe family history isn't worth knowing. I'm off now,' – she got to her feet – 'I want to get some breakfast then get on with those statements.'

'I'll come down in a few minutes,' I said.

She limped across to the door. 'How's the leg this morning?' I asked.

'Tons better,' she told me. She turned by the door. 'Nice body,' – she grinned. She was getting to be an expert at delivering unanswerable exit lines.

There was a large screen at one end of the dining hall which was opened out to conceal the breakfast buffet table. Quite why this had to be hidden from the gaze of those eating the meal I never fathomed out. There was nobody seated at the dining table when I walked into the room. This wasn't altogether surprising as it was only 7.15. I could hear voices from behind the screen, one of which I recognized as Eve's. I was about to join her when I heard my name mentioned. I paused. Then I recognized the other voice as Harriet's. 'You were seen going into Adam's room last night and coming out again this morning. What more proof does anyone need?'

'How come you're watching Adam's room so closely, sister dear? Waiting your chance, were you? Wanting to relive the past a little perhaps? Trying to get in there before the Black Widow gets to him? I wouldn't blame you for that; there wouldn't be much left after she'd finished with him. He'd be like all her other victims.'

'Do you deny you slept with Adam last night?' Harriet sounded almost hysterical.

'I deny nothing. I admit nothing. Why should I? Neither Adam nor I are married; unlike some people round here, in case you'd forgotten that little fact. If we want to sleep together that's our business and nobody else's.'

I thought it was high time I made my presence known. I ambled round the end of the screen. 'Good morning, Harriet, hello again, Evie darling,' I greeted them, 'did I hear my name being mentioned just now?'

'Have you been there long?' Harriet demanded angrily. There were two spots of high colour on her cheeks.

'A few minutes,' I admitted shamelessly. 'I stopped to re-tie my shoelaces on the other side of the screen.'

Harriet turned on her heel and departed with her breakfast plate. I'd never quite understood exactly what the word 'flounced' meant until that moment. It suited her action perfectly.

I turned to look at Eve. She was also a little pinker in the face than nature had intended. 'Hello, lover,' I said quietly.

'Hah,' she laughed scornfully. 'If you're going to tell lies at least make them marginally credible.'

'Lies, what lies? I've no idea what you mean, sugar plum?'

'Re-tying your shoelaces,' – she pointed to my shoes – 'what laces?'

I'd forgotten I was wearing slip-ons. 'Oh, yes. I was so interested in what you were saying to Harriet it slipped my mind. Whilst we're on the subject of lying, what was it again?'

'Ah, well, that was different,' Eve said, uncomfortably.

'Yes of course it was, dear heart,' I agreed, straight faced.

'One more snide endearment and you'll be wearing that porridge instead of eating it.'

'That,' I told her sternly, 'is no way to speak to your lover, the man whose bed you have only just left.' I had moved the porridge bowl out of her reach; a wise precaution. I was still far from comfortable though, as Eve had picked up the long handled fork used for spearing sausages and was eyeing me with a slightly manic expression. 'I think I'll go sit down now,' I said.

I turned to leave, only to find Eve blocking my path, the fork held dangerously close to my throat. 'Don't let me down,' she whispered fiercely.

The fork hovered close to my tonsils. 'Of course I won't,' I reassured her, adding as I moved the fork to one side, 'Honey-bunch.'

Fortunately, the wound to my backside was only a superficial one, but the tines on that fork were pretty sharp. I reached the table. Harriet was seated at the far end. I set my bowl down next to Eve's place and smiled sweetly at Harriet. 'Evie, darling,' I called out, 'don't struggle with your coffee, sweetheart, I'll get it for you when I bring mine.'

Eve appeared from behind the screen. 'Thank you, Adam dearest,' she smiled at me and sat down alongside me.

As silences go what followed was one of the longest and most awkward I'd experienced in some while. At times I had to keep fierce control to avoid giving the game away by laughing. I was determined not to break my promise to Eve though. I was also more than a little annoyed. Eventually, I could stand it no longer. 'How's Charlie this morning?' I asked Harriet.

'Much better, thanks,' she replied. 'Boys of that age are pretty resilient, don't you think?'

'I wouldn't know,' I reminded her. 'I'm not a family man.'

'No, of course not, I'm sorry, I hope I didn't, I mean you weren't thinking I said that, er ...' the sentence tailed off.

I let her stew over that one.

'Did you sleep all right,' Harriet tried again. 'Was the bed comfortable enough?'

The concerned hostess routine had me checking a thousand unsuitable replies. 'Well enough thank you;

when I eventually got to sleep. I was a lot later than I normally am but,' – I turned to Eve and gave her a sickly smile – 'that was Evie's doing.'

'That's right, go ahead and put all the blame on me,' Eve said with mock anger. 'You weren't involved I suppose? The next thing is you'll claim you weren't even on the bed with me.'

That was my worst moment. The sheer audacity of the remark, and the fact that it was true in a way, had me gripping my lip between my teeth to avoid laughing aloud.

'I'm not sure I want to hear another word,' Harriet said in disgust. 'Particularly during breakfast.'

I finished my porridge and put my spoon down. In an instant, Eve was hovering at my side, her injury apparently forgotten. She reached and took the bowl. 'Now how about a nice plate of bacon and eggs, darling,' she asked solicitously, 'after all you had such a tiring time yesterday and you must keep your strength up.'

That did it; Harriet rose to her feet and stalked from the room leaving her breakfast half-finished. The earlier flounce had been replaced by a strut.

I looked at Eve. Now the curtain had come down on our little piece of play-acting reaction had set in. 'Are you OK, Evie?' I asked her.

She shook her head, fighting back tears, of anger I guessed. 'What right has she to interfere? Why should she assume that I would sleep with a man I've only known twenty-four hours? What sort of a slut does my own sister take me for?'

'Perhaps she's concerned for you. It's natural for an older sister to worry.'

'Adam, she isn't concerned about me. I'm not a child anymore. I don't sleep around. It's not Harriet and you know it. It's that blasted Jardine harpy that's behind this. She saw you and wanted you to add to her collection. She's jealous because I, er, I mean we spent so much time together and she's put Harriet up to all this. Harriet's never the same when that slapper's about.'

'Evie,' I said, 'forget about it. I'll make damned sure it won't happen again. Nobody's going to upset you like this, I won't allow it.'

She looked at me in surprise. 'I mean it,' I said. 'Leave it to me. The subject won't come up again, I promise you.'

She smiled, a little complacently I thought. It puzzled me slightly, but then again, like I said in the first place, I'm no ladies' man.

'How about that bacon and eggs?' I suggested. 'Neither of us had much to eat yesterday.'

'That would be nice,' Eve agreed.

'You did say I had to keep my strength up,' I reminded her.

Tony and Charlie walked in at that point, pre-empting a response from Eve that I'm reasonably certain would have been in Anglo-Saxon.

Tony briefed me on the gist of his conversation with DC Pratt whilst I was eating my breakfast. Immediately I had finished I left the dining hall in search of Harriet. On my way upstairs I paused to have a word with Sammy and Becky, who were accompanying their grandmother towards the dining hall.

I ran Harriet to earth as she was leaving the twins' room. 'Harriet,' I told her, 'I want a word with you in private.'

I think she knew by my tone of voice that I was angry. I made her sit down in one of the armchairs next to my bedroom window. 'I hope you realize how upsetting all this bickering and back-biting is to both Eve and me? I don't know what's behind it but it must stop, and stop now. I want to help you and Tony sort this mess out but I can't and won't unless the atmosphere round here changes.'

She looked at me for a long time. 'Adam, just answer

me one question, will you?'

'If I can, of course I will.'

'Did you sleep with my sister last night?'

'No, of course I bloody well didn't.' I was suddenly angry, as angry as Eve had been earlier, 'What on earth are you thinking about, Harriet? Eve and I have only known each other a day and a half. What sort of a tart do you think she is?'

'Yes, but I know you. I know how you can charm women.'

'Harriet, you're talking absolute garbage. I've been on my own since Georgina died. And that means exactly that. I haven't slept with a woman since Georgina died, nor was I unfaithful to her when she was alive. I once shared a bed with a goat in Ethiopia but we both behaved ourselves. So where the notion about me and women comes from I've no idea.'

'That's not what I've heard. According to rumour you were one of the hottest catches on the New York scene when you lived there.'

I stared at her in astonishment. 'Where the hell did you get that from? I only went to a few parties during all the time I worked in New York and that was for Georgina's benefit. Come on, Harriet, out with it, who's been spreading malicious gossip?'

'I don't believe it,' Harriet said slowly. 'What reason would Polly have to lie?'

'Oh, so it was Polly Jardine who was behind this, was it? Harriet, pardon me for saying so but you're an idiot, a bloody stupid naïve idiot.'

'Adam, I don't care what you say, Eve's my sister and a guest in my house. I have to protect her.'

'Eve is very capable of protecting herself.'

'But that's just it, she isn't. Let me explain. Eve's not good with men. I've tried to introduce her to lots of nice men, but they turned her off or she turned them off. The only time she did fall in love the man was a complete bastard. Eve got beaten black and blue by him. In the end,' – Harriet gulped – 'she almost killed him. She was tried for attempted murder and spent over a year in jail before her appeal reversed the conviction. She was lucky they believed her account of the incident, that he was attacking her and ruled that it was self-defence. Now do you understand why Eve is as she is; why I feel I must protect her?'

'Yes,' I conceded, 'I understand that, but you must also understand something, Harriet. Eve is a decent young woman. I am not some sex-starved stud. To suggest we leapt into the sack after twenty-four hours; do you realize how insulting that is to both of us?'

'But she was seen going into your room last night and leaving it this morning. Then at breakfast, neither of you denied it.'

'That's right, she did come into my room last night. If you or whoever's been spying on us had hung around they'd have seen her leave again. And if your sentinel had been more awake this morning, they'd have seen Eve come into my room ten minutes before she left. As for breakfast, of course we didn't deny it. Neither, if you think about it did we admit it. That was because we both thought it so absurd and insulting we decided to take the piss out of you. And you richly deserved it.' I looked at Harriet, I could see she was still torn with doubt. 'Now, I suggest you get your act together and do a bit of apologizing otherwise I'm out of here the minute the roads are clear. Either that or I go to Tony with the whole story.'

I saw the look of dawning horror on her face and pressed home my advantage. 'Your course of action is quite clear. First I want an apology. Second, your sister needs an apology. After that, you'd better seek out Polly Jardine and warn her to keep out of my way. And if I hear of one more malicious rumour that's originated from her,

I'll slap her with a writ for slander. If you don't do that, *I'll* speak to her and by God she won't enjoy that.'

Harriet was crying by the time I'd finished. 'I'm sorry, Adam; I've fouled everything up, haven't I?'

'Perhaps you were led on, Harry,' I consoled her. 'Now come on, give me an apology and we can be friends again.'

She managed a watery smile. 'Nobody but you ever called me Harry,' she said. 'Oh, Adam, I am sorry, it was everything at once, you see. I've been so worried about Tony and this madness that infects their family; then with Beaumont's murder on top. But to think that about you and Eve was inexcusable. Is she very upset?'

'Harry,' – I put my arm round her – 'you're a lovely girl but sometimes you're as daft as a brush. Your husband is one of the gentlest, nicest, sanest people I've ever met. I know the Beaumont thing's a worry, but we'll sort that out. As for Eve, I'd go in waving a white flag if I was you, her language could be a bit salty otherwise. Now hop it or you'll be getting a bad reputation; that's what happens to women when they hang around my bedroom.'

Chapter Nine

Lady Charlotte occupied what was in effect her own apartment on the first floor of the east wing of the castle. There was a calmness about Charlotte Rowe that I found relaxing. 'I feel rather strange about this,' I told her when we were seated in her drawing room. 'I came here to help with the problem Tony and Harriet wanted solving but this business of Beaumont's murder has thrown me completely off track.'

'Do you think the two are in any way connected?'

'That's a lot harder question to answer than it sounds. I can't honestly say one way or the other. To be honest I don't know enough about either to form a judgement yet. If you were to pin me down to some sort of decision, I'd probably say there was a link, but I've no idea what it might be.

'When and where do you intend to start looking?'

I smiled. 'I've already started, that's why I wanted to talk to you. I can't do much regarding Beaumont's murder at present. I've done all I'm really qualified to do in that respect. The investigative side of it is down to the police. They're the professionals. I'm only a reporter, and a retired one at that. I'm certainly not a detective.'

'Don't you think reporters and detectives are similar? They both call for someone with an enquiring mind, surely?'

'Possibly so, but I'm not really sure where to start looking for Beaumont's murderer. I'm a little hesitant to go ahead in case I mess things up for the police.'

'What information do you want to grill me for?'

'I hardly think grilling is going to be involved. I'm told you know more about Rowe family history than anyone else.'

'That may be true but it's not saying a lot.'

I raised my eyebrows questioningly.

'The Rowe family,' Charlotte told me, 'have made secrecy into a fine art. I'm not talking about just one or two of them; I'm talking about generation upon generation. There must be centuries of unknown, unrecorded events. It's almost as if they had a pact whereby they would live out their lives in some sort of self-created Dark Ages. Things have been different recently of course. Both my husband George and his father were extremely open, as is Tony, but before them,' – she cast her eyes heavenwards – 'anyone would think they'd all signed the Official Secrets Act.'

'When you talk of them being secretive, do you mean there are no diaries or personal journals or anything of that nature?'

There was a fractional hesitation before Charlotte replied. 'If there was I've certainly never seen one, and I've lived here over forty years.'

'Doesn't that strike you as extremely odd?'

'Yes and no,' she smiled. 'I realize that's no sort of a reply but there are certain facts you need to understand. Yes, I agree on the face of things it must seem obsessive, which is what I assume you mean by odd, but that obsession has its roots in the persecution the family undoubtedly underwent because of their Catholic faith.'

'Did they suffer much?'

'Most certainly they did. Their lands were threatened with confiscation and they were stripped of some of their titles. Only the baronetcy survived.'

I stared at her in surprise. 'I didn't realize that. I wasn't aware that sort of thing went on.'

Charlotte smiled. 'Yes, it is a little difficult for us to grasp, isn't it? That's probably because we have been brought up in a parliamentary democracy. However, at the time we're talking about the rule was that of autocratic monarchs, and what they could give with one hand they could just as easily take away with the other. Sometimes they did it to the same people within the space of a few years. Henry VIII was probably the prime example but there were plenty of others.'

'In effect, what you're saying is there is nothing by way of a family history in existence?'

Charlotte paused and looked at me for a moment. 'I'm not really sure how to answer that. If you mean have I ever seen such a volume, as I said earlier I would have to say no. As to whether one exists that I haven't seen, all I can say is I have heard rumours about a book, nothing more.'

'I think you're going to have to explain that.'

'All I know is what my father-in-law told George when George was a boy. Apparently, George's grandfather used to read extracts from a book to George's father, but George seemed to think it was as much a history of the castle as of the family. That's about all I know.'

'Hang on, Charlotte; I'm getting a bit confused. Can you give me a quick rundown on recent family history so I'll know who's who?'

'Right, let's start with Sir Frederick and Lady Amelia. If you remember, she was the one who disappeared with her lover. Sir Frederick and Lady Amelia had two sons before she skedaddled. Henry, the elder son, was my father-in-law. In other words, Henry was Anthony's grandfather and Albert, Henry's younger brother, was Russell Rowe's grandfather.'

'I thought Tony and Russell were first cousins?'

'No, Colin Drake is Tony's first cousin. His mother Edith was George's elder sister.

'Right, I'm with you now.'

'When Sir Frederick died, the title and estate passed to Henry. The two go together, always to the eldest male. So from Henry it passed to George – and when George died Tony inherited both the baronetcy and Mulgrave Castle and all the estate that goes with it.'

'Do you believe a journal exists; or if it ever existed?'

'I have grave doubts. If it does it has been very well hidden. So much so, I doubt whether you would find it.'

'Did your husband ever say anything about it?'

'If I remember correctly, all George said was that his father was a "secretive and cantankerous old bastard". And I didn't know George's father very well at all, as he died not long after we got married, which I don't think helps you much.'

'No, not a lot,' I agreed. 'But my thought is that if we are to get to the bottom of those disappearances we might find some clues in that journal.'

Charlotte smiled. 'That's quite possible, if you could locate it.'

'One possibility occurs to me: that the journal may have been hidden precisely because it does contain information that would give a clue to the truth, and that someone was desperate the truth should remain hidden.'

When I wandered into Tony's study shortly before lunchtime, Eve had finished typing the statements and was removing the carbon paper from between the pages. She greeted me with a wide, welcoming smile that did my pulse rate no good. 'I've got these ready for the police. I don't think there's anything more I can do.'

'You've had a busy morning,' I said mildly.

'Not half,' she replied, 'and that's not all. I don't know exactly what you said to Harriet but she came to see me about half an hour ago. She was very apologetic. So much so, she finished up in tears. That shocked me, I have to say. I've never seen Harriet so upset. You must have really gone to town on her. What exactly did you say?'

'I told her she had grossly insulted you. I said she had implied you were a tart, and that in passing, she had been rather less than complimentary to me. I told her that unless her attitude improved immediately I was going to leave here as soon as road conditions allowed. After that I told her I was disgusted by her behaviour and that I expected better from her.'

'I think I'm beginning to see why she was so upset,' Eve said dryly. 'Did Harriet offer any explanation for the way she behaved?'

'Yes she did and that's when I guessed it wasn't all her fault. I didn't go into the finer details but I think she's been fed some scurrilous propaganda. She certainly had some gossip about me that I found highly offensive, and it made me wonder if you'd been the subject of similar disinformation.'

'What was the offensive gossip or would you rather not say?'

I thought about this for a few seconds. I've never been one for letting the world know about my most private and personal business but I felt it important not to keep anything back from Eve. 'I wouldn't tell anyone,' I said eventually, 'but I don't mind you knowing. The gist of it was that when I was living and working in New York I was unfaithful to my wife Georgina, on a regular basis. That I was a serial adulterer in fact.'

Eve stared at me in astonishment. 'You don't mean to tell me Harriet was naïve enough to believe such a load of claptrap?'

I nodded. 'Apparently so, it must have been quite convincing.'

'What a load of bollocks. I gave my sister credit for more sense than that. After all the time she's known you, she still believes a bullshit tale like that. I only met you a couple of days ago and you couldn't convince me to believe it.'

'Thank you for the testimonial.' I bowed slightly. 'It must have been very persuasive; either that or Harriet's not thinking straight at present.'

'Was it very hurtful, Adam? I don't know enough about your wife, except that she died, and I can imagine that was a very nasty reminder of things you might be trying to forget.'

If Harriet's behaviour had been out of character mine was scarcely less so. For the first time I found myself able to relate my story. 'Georgina was an actress; a very good actress at that. Unfortunately, after we married she got less and less work. Then I got shipped off to Ethiopia. I was wounded covering the war and finished up in hospital. Whilst I was recuperating I got a visit from a British Embassy official. He told me Georgina had thrown herself off the balcony of our apartment. Loneliness and depression they called it; the two things Georgina wasn't able to cope with.'

'And you've been blaming yourself ever since?'

'Of course I have. I know it isn't logical but I can't help it.'

'I'm not sure logic enters into a situation such as that.'

I realized as she said it that Eve was thinking of her own situation as much as mine. 'I think Harriet may have been fed the same sort of rubbish about you as she was about me,' I suggested gently. 'She hinted that there were reasons you might be vulnerable.'

'Did she suggest that I'm an emotional cripple perhaps? That I'm hopeless with men? That I'm no stranger to a police cell? That I'm a dab hand with a carving knife?'

'Something of that nature,' I agreed. 'But then, I already knew you to be a woman capable of extreme violence. After all, I have such a wide experience of women, and you're the first to regard a punch in the face as an essential part of foreplay.'

I was lucky; my absurd remark stemmed the rising tide of anger I could sense growing within Eve. She giggled. 'Did it hurt a lot?' she asked.

'Just a bit,' I smiled, 'but I forgive you, we're friends now, aren't we? Do you want to talk about what happened to you or is it a forbidden subject?'

'I don't go around bragging about it but neither do I run away from it. It's still painful and I guess it always will be. It happened a long time ago but I've never been able to forget for long. I met John when I was doing an MBA in London. He was one of those golden boys, bright, talented, and handsome. He was also, as I found out far too late, a serial womaniser with a drink problem and a propensity for violence. He put me in hospital three times in the year we were together. I left him twice and went back home to my parents but he turned up and made a scene,' she paused and I could see there were unshed tears in her eyes; but whether they were tears of regret or anger, I couldn't tell.

'My father was very ill,' Eve continued. 'In fact he was dying from cancer. So I had no choice but to go back with John. It wouldn't have been fair to Mum or Dad otherwise. Mum was nursing Dad at home, you see.'

'So you chose to go back in spite of the danger; that was brave of you.'

'Brave or foolish, I'm not sure which. Anyway, I'd only been out of hospital just over a week and still had my arm in plaster. He'd broken it when he came home pissed and angry one night.'

Eve rolled up her sleeves and displayed large areas of mottled, discoloured skin. 'He'd found a new game he really enjoyed. The rules were quite simple. You play it by boiling a kettle full of water. After that you hold Eve's arm over the sink and scald her with the water from the kettle until she screams or passes out. He was good at it too; a real expert. Only this time I cheated. I didn't scream and I didn't faint. I picked up the carving knife and stabbed him with it.'

She smiled grimly. 'Of course I was arrested. I was convicted of attempted murder because he gave evidence that the attack was unprovoked. He could be very convincing when he wanted to. My injuries weren't mentioned. It was only at the appeal when the doctor and nurses who treated me gave evidence that the conviction was overturned.' She looked at me challengingly; as if my reaction was important to her.

'I don't see you need feel the slightest degree of guilt. As far as I can see the bastard deserved all that was coming to him and more besides; but as you say logic doesn't come into it.'

Eve was still watching me closely. 'You're not scared or repelled by what I've told you then? Most people are; but then they seldom get to hear my version. They only hear the gossip together with the embellishments.'

'More fool them. The only thing that I find repulsive is what that brute did to you, and you certainly don't scare me; not with the lights on anyway.'

Eve grinned; suddenly she seemed more relaxed than at any time since we'd met. I put that down to the improved relations between her and Harriet, but then I'm no expert where women are concerned.

'So tell me about your chat with Lady Charlotte, did you find out anything useful?'

'Yes I did. Or at least Charlotte told me something that might prove very interesting. However, there is a major snag.' I went on to tell her about the rumoured existence of the family journal. 'The problem's going to be in locating it. Charlotte says it hasn't been seen in at least forty years. She reckons there's considerable doubt as to whether it is any more real than the other family legends.'

To my surprise, Eve was more inclined to believe in the existence than I'd imagined. 'I wouldn't set much store by the fact that none of the family has seen it,' she told me.

'None of them are what you'd call voracious readers, with the exception of Becky. Tony restricts himself to the *Shooting Times*, *Field and Stream*, and *Cricket Monthly*. Charlie reads football fanzines, Sammy reads sloppy teen romances, and Harriet reads sloppy adult romances. As for Charlotte, I don't think I've ever seen her with a book in her hand, and to the best of my knowledge Tony's father had the same reading habits as Tony.'

'So the library doesn't get used much?'

'Hardly.' Eve's tone was amused. 'In fact, Tony wanted to have it converted to a rumpus room for the kids a few years back but Harriet put her foot down. Not because of the priceless books in there; although there are quite a few of those. Harriet was more concerned about the exquisite bookshelves and furniture that Tony wanted to get rid of. She said it would spoil the ambience; whatever that means.'

'In that case I reckon we ought to have a look round the library first.'

Eve groaned. 'I think I've just talked myself into another job, haven't I?'

As we were debating the merits of an early start to our treasure hunt in the library Tony ambled in. 'We're organizing a sledging expedition, we're all going up to the old quarry. There's a good slope there. We thought it might help to take everybody's mind of what happened to poor Beaumont. Would you care to join us?'

I explained our plans for the afternoon. 'I think it's important for me to try and start looking for a solution to the problem you set me. Normally I'd have loved to go along. There's also Eve's injured leg to think of. She wouldn't be able to go and it wouldn't be much fun for her stuck here alone.'

'No I suppose not. I'd forgotten about that,' Tony conceded. He thought for a moment, then added, 'I don't suppose you'd want to be bothered by Sammy in the circumstances, would you? The poor girl's sick as anything at missing out but her throat's worse, and Harriet's banned her from going. Thinks the cold air would be bad for her. But of course if you want to be alone, we could leave Sammy watching TV or something.'

I dare not look at Eve; I was trying too hard not to laugh and knew I'd never keep a straight face if I saw her expression. 'Tony,' I said eventually, 'I said Eve and I were going to search the library; nothing else. If Sammy's bored and on her own, she'd be more than welcome to help. There's a massive task ahead of us and the more help we get the better. There is one favour you could do for us though.'

'Of course, what is it?'

'Loan us your chair.' I pointed to the one behind the desk. 'It has castors on, and it would be great for Eve. She can't go climbing up and down those library steps, so if she and Sammy take the lower shelves I'll do the upper ones. If she has a chair with castors it'll help no end.'

'I'll get Rathbone to bring it through for you.' He ambled out.

I looked across the room at Eve; she was struggling with her laughter. 'I think Tony suspected we'd be having it off in the library,' she suggested.

'Damn, another plan foiled,' I said.

Sammy joined us only seconds after Rathbone had wheeled Eve's chair in to the library. 'Hello,' she whispered in a sort of croak. It was easy to see why Harriet had insisted she remain indoors. She looked flushed and there seemed little doubt she was running a temperature.

'OK, girls, we're looking for an old book,' – I looked at the long shelves that ran along three walls of the room – 'and it seems we have a few to choose from.'

Every shelf was crammed with books; the shelves stretched from floor to ceiling. The only breaks were for the door and fireplace. It was a daunting prospect. I didn't even want to speculate on the total number of volumes in that room. 'As I see it, we have two problems. One, we don't know if the book has a title or not, and even if it does the title may bear no resemblance to the contents. Two, we don't know what size or shape the book we're searching for is. Therefore, we have to take every book from the shelf, examine it, and put it back. The one we want will be about Mulgrave Castle and the Rowe family. Eve, whereabouts do you want to start?'

'To be honest I'm not sure I want to start at all,' she said with mock despair, 'but if we have to, why don't Sammy and I take one of the shorter walls each and you concentrate on the long wall. Then when we've finished on the lower shelves we can switch places with you.'

We had been at work a couple of hours when Rathbone entered bearing a large tray. In addition to a coffee pot and a mug of hot chocolate, Sammy's favourite, the tray contained a plate each of sandwiches and chocolate biscuits. 'With Lady Harriet's compliments,' Rathbone announced in pompous tones. He set the tray on the reading table and departed.

'Leave the last book you examined on its side on the shelf, Sammy,' Eve suggested, 'that way you'll know exactly where to start afterwards.'

Shortly before three o'clock, I decided enough was enough. I moved the last book I'd examined onto its side. It was a weighty seventeenth-century tome on astronomy. I doubted whether it had been opened since the day of its purchase. As I moved it, a smaller, much slimmer volume slipped from the shelf alongside and dropped onto the floor. I muttered a mild oath and climbed down. I picked it up and glanced at the cover. I whistled silently in surprise as I read *A History of Mulgrave Castle by Miles Rowe*. 'OK, folks, let's call it a day,' I suggested.

My colleagues needed no prompting. Eve swivelled round on her chair. 'I never realized a library could be such a filthy place,' she said inspecting her hands. 'I'm going to need a long hot shower after this. How about you?'

'I consider that a very generous offer,' I replied.

I ducked and narrowly avoided being hit by a low-flying copy of Chaucer's *Canterbury Tales*.

'What's that you've found?' Eve pointed to the book in my hand.

I showed her. 'I think we should have a look at it before dinner,' I suggested. 'The rest of the family should be back any time now.'

It was at that point that Tony burst into the library. 'Adam, we need your help,' his voice was high with worry bordering on panic. 'There's been an accident. It's Charlie. He's fallen down the cliff. I think his leg's broken. We can't get to him and it'll be dark soon.'

'OK,' I said, 'Tony, you take me to the spot. Eve, find Marsh. Tell him I want every inch of rope he can find and I want him out there as fast as possible. Tell him to bring every torch he can.'

Tony and I reached the quarry fifteen minutes later. The family was gathered round the cliff face, their expressions ranging from distraught to despondent. Harriet was being comforted by Polly. It seemed they'd been using the gentler slope away from the quarry. I strode past them and looked over the edge. The light was fading rapidly. We were running out of time. Tony pointed and I saw Charlie. He was in a precarious position on a ledge two-thirds of the way down the cliff. 'Charlie,' I called out. 'Can you move?'

'I'm scared,' he called back. His voice confirmed that.

'I'm not bloody surprised. Free fall is usually better with a parachute.' I tried to keep it light. 'Try and move your arms. I need to know if they're OK.'

I waited; then heard, 'I can move them.'

116

'Good lad, do you have any pain in your chest or back?'

'Everything feels sore,' he complained.

'Don't worry about that, as long as it's no worse than sore. Can you move your head and neck?'

'Yes, it's just my leg. That hurts all the time.'

'OK, as long as that's all. Now just lie still for a minute or two then we'll start work on getting you out of there, OK?'

'Please.' The cry was heart-rending.

Marsh came panting up the slope. 'I've got the spare bell rope from the chapel and a length of chain as well.'

I uncoiled the rope and flung one end of it over the cliff. I was relieved to see it reached Charlie, comfortably. I looked round for an anchorage. A sturdy looking oak tree was growing only a dozen or so yards away. 'Wrap that chain round the tree,' I told Marsh, 'and make certain it's secure. Then tie the rope to it and let me know when you've done it.'

'Charlie, I'll be down with you in a few minutes then we can get you out of there, don't worry.'

I signalled to Tony, his cousins and Marsh. 'When I call out, I want you four to haul the boy up, really gently. You're working against time – it'll be pitch black soon. As soon as you get him up here, get him onto a toboggan and take him back to the castle. Don't wait about for me. Leave Marsh to throw the rope down to me. Got that?'

They nodded. 'Right, here's hoping,' I wound the rope round my waist and under my arm, stuffed the torch Marsh had handed me into my pocket. Harriet was standing close by. I reached out and pulled her scarf from round her neck before I eased myself over the cliff edge. 'Pay it out slowly, Frank,' I told Marsh.

I hadn't abseiled in years, but the skill soon returned and within a couple of minutes I joined Charlie on his ledge. 'Hi there, Charlie,' I greeted him. 'Relax now.

We'll soon have you out of here. I'm going to fashion a harness to go under your arms. All you have to do is hold onto the ropes. Your Dad and the others at the top will haul you up. I'm going to tie your legs together with scarves to try and keep them straight. Try to remain as still as possible. The more you move or swing about the more pain you'll cause yourself, OK?'

'Yes, Adam,' he said through gritted teeth.

'What exactly happened?' I asked casually as I began knotting the rope.

He remained silent. I looked across at him and saw his lips were pressed tightly together as if he was in pain. 'Are you OK?'

'Yes,' he said easily enough. So that wasn't the problem.

'You were going to tell me what happened,' I prompted.

'I was waiting my turn on the sledge when I saw a peregrine falcon hovering over the quarry. I turned to watch it. I was standing near the edge,' he paused.

'What happened, did you slip?'

He looked at me and the anguish in his eyes had little to do with the pain from his leg, 'No,' he told me reluctantly, 'I didn't slip. Someone pushed me.'

I nearly dropped the rope, so great was my astonishment. 'Are you absolutely sure about that, Charlie? You didn't simply tumble and imagine the rest?'

'No, Adam,' his voice was steady now. 'Someone put both hands on my back and pushed me.'

'Did you see who it was?'

He shook his head. 'Can you remember who was near you at the time?'

'Everybody I think, apart from Becky. She'd just set off down the slope on the sledge.'

I needed a moment or two to think about this. 'Right, I'm going to put this rope over your shoulders and under

118

your arms. Do you think you can sit up if I help you?' I put the rope in place and tightened the noose. 'That won't let you down, so you don't have to worry about it. Now listen carefully. I don't want you to say a word about what happened to you. Not even to your Mum and Dad. Whoever did this will be expecting you to say something. If you don't, they'll be wondering why. I'll see you back at the castle later. Don't forget.'

'I won't.'

'Good lad; now get ready.' I turned to look upwards and raised my voice. 'OK, up there: start pulling.'

'OK, Adam,' I heard Tony answer.

Slowly, foot by foot, I watched the boy being hauled towards the top of the cliff. The sunshine had long since disappeared and there was a universal greyness to the last remaining light. Charlie's form disappeared into the gloom and I knew that when it came to my turn I would be climbing in total darkness. I felt something soft brush against my cheek. It had started to snow again.

After what seemed an age I heard Tony's voice; relief in every syllable. 'Adam, we've got him. He's safe. We're going to load him on the toboggan. As soon as we've got him on that, Marsh will throw the rope down for you. OK?'

'That'll be fine, Tony.'

It was a few minutes later when I heard a swishing sound that told me Marsh had thrown the rope down. A split second later I felt it hit my arm. I grabbed it and slipped the harness over my shoulder. I wanted to be out of the quarry as quickly as possible. I'm a good enough hand at rope-climbing but in the dark with snow falling, I wasn't relishing the challenge much. 'OK, Frank, I'm starting to climb now,' I called out. There was no response from above.

I began my ascent, hand over hand. I'd got no more than twenty feet when I suddenly felt the rope above me go slack. Then I was falling; sheer down the cliff face. I felt a buffet on my leg as I hit the ledge that saved Charlie. It didn't save me. It was the snow in the foot of the quarry that saved me; that and luck. I didn't appreciate the luck much at the time.

I hit the snowdrift and the breath exploded from my lungs as I was winded by the impact. Then my head hit something hard and I passed out.

Chapter Ten

I'm not sure how long I was unconscious. Not too long, I reckoned, because I'd not lost any body heat. I tried movement; slowly. My legs first, they felt OK. Then my arms, no problems there either. My chest and back felt sore but no worse than the rest, the shock of the impact and the winding were probably all they'd suffered. It was when I moved my head that the pain hit me. I felt as if I'd a wickedly bad hangover. I rolled cautiously onto all fours and waited for the pain to subside. It didn't. I got to my feet, moving like an arthritic eighty-year-old. I felt a bit like one too.

It was pitch black by now; what little light there had been was gone. I don't suppose the walls of the quarry helped much either. I peered around me, though quite what I expected to see, I've no idea. The pain increased but I was rewarded with the sight of a glimmer of pale yellow light a few yards away. I realized it was coming from my torch which had also survived the fall; probably better than I had. As I looked, the gleam of light from the torch became two; then three; then a whole kaleidoscope of amber reflections. I closed my eyes and shook my head to clear my vision. Mistake! Big mistake! Very, very big mistake! I waited for the pain to subside. If it did, I wasn't aware of it.

I opened my eyes again and looked cautiously towards the light. I was relieved to see only a single beam. Obviously, shaking my head had cured the problem. I still wouldn't recommend it. I moved again, this time trying to remove the harness from round my chest whilst keeping my head still. I'm a fast learner. It proved difficult and I had to pause to allow another surge of pain to pass. Its passage was dreadfully slow. I waded slowly towards my torch which was buried in about two feet of snow. Each step was an effort. I reached the torch, bent down, and plunged my hand into the drift to retrieve it. That was a double mistake. My trouser legs were already soaked by melted snow. Now I had collected more snow up the sleeve of my jacket, inside my shirt sleeve and clinging to my hand and wrist. That would soon melt and my arm too would be cold and wet. At the time I didn't appreciate the stupidity of what I'd done. I was busy trying to ignore the fresh pain in my head from bending over. I held the torch. Then I was holding two torches; then three. Then I blacked out again. I came to almost immediately. I was lying where I'd fallen and in falling I'd collected more snow that was already melting on me. As I moved I became aware that my foot was entangled in something. I groped around and my hand came in contact with the obstruction. It was the rope. I picked it up and held the torch to it. I worked a couple of feet along the rope until I reached the end of it. I'd been feeling pretty lousy already. The sight of the rope end made me feel ten times worse. The rope hadn't frayed or the knot untied. The end of the rope had been severed; cut straight and clean through with a knife.

My thoughts were chaotic. It didn't help much that I wasn't in the best shape for logical thinking in the first place. I took a deep breath. What could have happened? Well I knew what had happened, but how did it happen? Tony said he was leaving Marsh at the top of the cliff. Then the rope had been thrown down to me. I'd called out that I was going to climb up. I remembered being surprised there had been no reply. I was unwilling to believe that Frank Marsh was the killer, the idea seemed ludicrous. I went cold, or rather I went colder. I felt a sharp pang of fear for Marsh's safety.

Strangely, the knowledge that someone had attempted to kill me cleared my head; if only temporarily. I began to reason, for I knew my plight was still desperate. I might have survived the fall more or less intact, but I was trapped in a snowbound quarry in darkness. I was cold, wet, and aching and I had absolutely no idea how to escape from the hole I was in.

I glanced at my watch. 5.05 p.m. I wondered how Charlie had survived the pain of the journey back to the castle. I wondered again about what had happened to Marsh. I wondered who had cut the rope and tried to kill me. Most of all I wondered how the hell I was going to get out of that blasted quarry. It took a few moments, but eventually reason penetrated my poor aching skull and I began to think about the quarry. A quarry is a place where stone is dug out, I thought. Well, to be accurate, stone and aggregate. Once these products have been dug out they have to be transported from the quarry. Therefore the quarry had to have an exit road. I congratulated myself on the brilliance of my deduction. The only problem that remained was how to find the bloody road.

Whether or not it was from the effort of thinking but my vision went again. This time I didn't pass out but I felt an unpleasant nausea; like a severe case of seasickness. I waited for it to pass. It took its time. When I began to feel marginally better I tried thinking again. The dilemma facing me was that I had to move. I was feeling colder and wetter with every passing minute. If I didn't get some warmth soon I would be adding hypothermia to the suspected concussion I was already suffering. However, there was little point in moving for movement's sake. I needed to walk towards the exit road not away from it and how was I to find out where it was in the dark?

When Tony and I had left the castle we had walked

directly towards the setting sun: due west in other words. That meant the quarry face, down which I'd fallen, was the northern rim of the quarry. I was standing in front of that face, so I was facing more or less due south. The main road ran to the south of the castle, therefore it ran to the south of the quarry. If the operators of the quarry had been logical businessmen they would have put the track leading from the quarry on the side nearest the main road. Oh great, I thought, if my reasoning was correct that meant I had to wade the full width of the quarry, in the dark, encountering God knows what obstacles and all of them obscured by the snow.

As if the thought had prompted it, bad had just become worse: the falling snow was getting heavier. I shelved the thought that I might have got my thinking wrong, that the road might be on the east or the west of the quarry. Why think that? I didn't need depressing. I was depressed enough already. It took almost an hour to find that road, an hour of wading, slipping, falling, getting colder, getting wetter, getting angrier, cursing, swearing, and threatening vengeance. My journey wasn't made any easier by the load I was carrying. The rope was evidence; evidence that might be needed in a court of law. Alternatively, I could use it to hang the bastard who'd tried to kill me; who might still succeed if I couldn't get out of that place soon.

I paused for breath before tackling the exit road; but not for long. Although the exercise had warmed me slightly I knew I was beginning to lose sensation in the extremities of my fingers and toes. I thought about frostbite. I remembered with horror some of the cases I'd seen; gangrenous and evil-smelling obscenities that had once been healthy feet and legs. I tried to summon up amnesia on that subject. It didn't work. I needed to get up this track and across to the cliff top before I could consider returning to the castle. I wondered whether the castle's inhabitants had raised the alarm yet. Surely they would be aware I'd been missing far too long. Then I remembered Charlie's injuries. If my blood didn't run cold at the thought, it was because it was already cold enough. They would be preoccupied with Charlie and caring for him. Even if they'd noticed I was missing, who was there to come to my rescue?

The thought of the cliff top reminded me of Frank. I set off to battle my way up the track. Snow had drifted across it and the going was hard in some places; close to impossible in others. Eventually, I reached a point where the road that had been a cutting levelled out and I emerged onto flat land. I had escaped the quarry. I had surmounted the track. I was warmer from the exercise. I had completed half my journey. Or, to look at it from another point of view, I still had to make my way round the rim of the quarry from the south to the north side, to the cliff top, then I had to find out what had happened to Frank, then I had to get to the castle. I was wet, I was tired, I was feeling sick, and the headache was bad again. Oh, and the snow was falling heavier still.

I was lucky in choosing the first part of my route, for there was a large, flat expanse I later discovered was a patch devoted to grassland. That made walking somewhat easier. On the downside, I was now walking directly into the snowstorm. A phrase of the weather forecasters came to mind: 'drifting in a north-easterly wind.' The snow was being blown into my face. That raised the prospect of drifting.

I battled on and eventually reached a hedge. I looked at my watch and saw with surprise that it was 7.30 p.m.; to me it felt more like midnight. The hedge was a thorn one. It presented me with an interesting and different challenge – although those weren't the words I used at the time. I struggled through and emerged on the other side. The scratches it inflicted on every exposed part of me were a distraction from the pounding headache, sore chest, aching ribs, sore shins, sore knees, and sore temper. Not a welcome distraction; just a distraction.

The field beyond the hedge had been ploughed but not sown. That meant it was rutted, ruts I had to cross rather than walk along. More fun. I got across the field after countless more falls and prepared to do battle with another thorn hedge. It proved tougher than the first. I wondered if hedge number one had warned his colleague to be on the lookout for an attacker on the prowl. Then I realized I was becoming delirious; to imagine a conversation between intelligent hedges. I shook my head to clear it. Who said I was a fast learner? Tell him he's a liar.

I stood on the other side and regained my breath; if not my composure. I was muddy, bloody and angry. I was also wet and tired and aching from head to toe. I looked at my watch again. It was 8.15 p.m. I'd be late for dinner again, I thought, and began to giggle. I sobered up at the sound. This wouldn't do. Hysteria added to delirium added to concussion. I really wasn't feeling very well.

My sense of direction appeared to have deserted me. This didn't really surprise me as all the other senses seemed to have vanished along with it. After a few moments the snow slackened briefly and I was able to make out a darker line that I thought was in the general area of where I wanted to be. I hoped and prayed it had been in my eyesight rather than my imagination. I set off towards it, banishing the thought of falling over the cliff in the dark. Not again, I thought; once a day's quite enough.

I found the cliff edge. Then I found the oak tree. Then I found Frank Marsh. He was lying alongside the tree partially buried by the snow. I shook him gently and he groaned. That was one plus point. At least he was alive. I shone the torch on him. He was lying face down. At the base of his skull was an ugly looking egg-shaped lump. No wonder he hadn't replied when I called him.

I turned him gently on his side into the recovery

position. His eyes rolled up alarmingly in their sockets; then returned to a more normal position and I could see he was regaining consciousness. 'Marsh,' I said loudly. 'Frank, come on, wake up.'

He stirred and groaned once more. 'Don't try to talk yet,' I told him, although I didn't think he was about to. After I'd iced his wound with snow I helped him to his feet. The brief respite seemed to have alleviated my own problems slightly, which was as well as I knew I'd need what little strength I had left to help get Marsh back to the castle.

We reached our destination just in time to prevent a full blown row. Eve and Cathy Marsh were the protagonists on one side; ranged against them the other adults, apart from Tony, Harriet, and Charlotte, who were presumably tending Charlie.

I helped Frank along the corridor and opened the kitchen door, the room was empty. We staggered through and I opened the door into the dining hall. The bright light hit my eyeballs with searing force. I stood there supporting Marsh, both of us in a dreadful state. We must have made an impressive sight. Eve was the first to react. 'Adam, are you injured, what happened?'

I smiled weakly. I couldn't manage anything stronger. I helped Frank into a nearby chair. 'Sammy,' I called the youngster. I waited until she came over to me. 'Do me a favour, love. Run upstairs and ask your mum and dad and gran to come down, please.'

Cathy Marsh was fussing over her husband. 'He's had a nasty bang on the back of his head,' I told her, 'he needs to be put to bed. Watch out for concussion.'

I leaned against the back of a chair. It was all right me advising other people about concussion, but my own headache was back to full power. I felt nauseous and the room was flickering as if in an old movie. 'Evie,' I murmured. 'Help me off with this, will you?'

I pointed to the rope. As she was uncoiling it I said, 'Lay it down on the table, please.'

I was aware, in a detached sort of way that the others were eyeing me curiously. I didn't care. Tony and Harriet arrived, followed an instant later by Charlotte and Sammy.

'Adam, what happened, where have you been until now?' Tony asked.

'I've been very busy,' I told him, 'and I've got news for you. Not just you, Tony,' – I was beginning to feel light-headed – 'but for everyone; all except for one, that is.'

I paused and waited. Everyone waited. I'm not sure what they thought I was going to do or say. I was aware that I must look a strange sight to them, soaked through, scratched, bloody, and mud-bespattered; looking as if I'd been dragged through a hedge backwards. Well that was wrong, I'd gone through forwards. What had I been about to say? Something important. I remembered. 'How's Charlie?' I enquired.

'I put his leg in a splint as a precaution. I'm not sure if it's broken, it could just be badly sprained.' It was Charlotte who replied. 'He's resting now. He seemed very concerned about you, said you had something to tell us.'

'Yes I do. What was it though?'

I could feel Eve's arm around my waist, supporting me. I needed it. My brain cleared momentarily. 'I said I had something to tell you. I said someone in this room already knows what I'm about to say. The person who murdered Beaumont on Christmas Eve had a day off yesterday, but they've been extra busy today. Two attempted murders and a serious assault. I'd say that was a pretty fair afternoon's work.'

'Adam, what on earth are you babbling on about?' It was Polly Jardine who interrupted.

'Ah Polly, pretty Polly,' I chided her, 'don't you know? I hope you don't. I'll tell you, shall I? I mean whoever murdered Beaumont also pushed Charlie off the edge of the cliff into the quarry. That was attempted murder number one. Charlie told me about it whilst we were stuck together on that ledge. No, I don't mean we were stuck together,' I giggled, 'I mean we were on the ledge together. Not content with that, our murderous friend bashed poor Frank over the head and knocked him unconscious. I don't think that counts as attempted murder really, though; only assault. Then he or she sliced through the rope as I was climbing up the quarry side and sent me falling to what they hoped would be my death. That was attempted murder number two. But I foiled them; ha ha. Fortunately, I hadn't climbed very far when the rope was cut. They couldn't have counted on that, or on me landing in a snowdrift that broke my fall. Or on me spotting that the rope hadn't given way,' – I held up the end of the rope and the clean cut was visible to everyone. Everyone bar me that is, for the lights in the chandeliers were beginning to multiply and merge, merge and multiply and multiply and multiply …

I felt my knees buckle; then the lights went out.

I'm not sure what the time was when I passed out. The next few hours are only a hazy recollection of vaguely witnessed events. I came to some form of consciousness to find I was in bed. My first sensation was one of hearing. I listened; unwilling to try anything more active. I tried to identify the sound I could hear dimly. The noise was a gentle one and after a few seconds I was able to identify it. I knew there was someone nearby, someone extremely close. Otherwise I wouldn't have been able to hear the sound of their breathing.

Having established that, my curiosity was stirred. I was faced with a choice. I could either ask who was there or open my eyes and look. My head ached and the whole of my body felt sore but in spite of this I decided to risk it.

I opened my eyes. Ouch! I closed them again briefly, then tried once more. The second time the pain was marginally less intense. I waited; the room was in semi-darkness, the sole light coming from a lamp that was outside my field of vision. I was in my bedroom at Mulgrave Castle; that I could tell. I was pleased, not only did I know who I was; I also knew where I was. These were giant steps forward on the road to recovery. Recovery from what I couldn't remember until I moved slightly and the levels of pain jolted my memory. I listened once more. The sound seemed to be coming from my left. I gathered up courage and moved my head slowly. I did slowly very well. Although I was alone beneath the duvet I wasn't the only occupant of the bed. My companion was lying asleep and fully clothed on top of the duvet. I felt a vague disappointment.

I wasn't sure whether my next action was brave or rash. I turned over slowly to face my companion. The movement, slight and painfully slow as it had been, was sufficient to wake her.

'Hello, back in the land of the living?' She smiled.

'Hello,' I said wittily. My voice sounded strange, more of a croak than speech.

I cleared my throat and tried again. 'What happened; how did I get here?'

'You fainted, and no wonder after what you'd been through. You were unconscious until the early hours of the morning then you woke up briefly, before falling asleep.'

I felt the vague stirrings of a memory. 'What happened when I woke up?'

She smiled secretively. 'You don't remember?'

'Not really, no. I don't remember much to be honest. I don't even know how I got upstairs, who undressed me, anything like that.'

'Four of us carried you upstairs. You were soaked to the skin and freezing cold. I had to get you out of those wet clothes and towelled dry. I was petrified you'd get pneumonia or hypothermia. You're heavier than you look, especially when you're unconscious.'

I suppose I should have been embarrassed but it seemed unimportant. 'Thank you, that was devotion beyond the call of duty. I suppose you've been lying on top of the duvet guarding me all night?'

'Er, no, not all night,' she admitted. She blushed slightly. 'I packed you round with hot water bottles but they weren't doing the trick. You were shivering violently with cold. I was terribly worried. Your temperature seemed to be going down and your pulse rate was very sluggish.'

'So you took your clothes off, got into bed, and held me until I warmed through?' I suggested.

The blush deepened. 'I had to, I couldn't think of anything else,' she said defensively. 'You seemed to be unconscious. I didn't think you'd remember.'

'It certainly got my pulse rate up,' I said with a smile. 'I thought I was having a dream. A very pleasant dream,' I added.

'How do you feel now?' She seemed to want to change the subject.

'I've got a pounding headache, I'm sore all over, and I feel as if I've been hit in the chest with a sledgehammer. Apart from that, I feel fine.'

'That's hardly surprising, is it?'

'I suppose not. What happened after I passed out?'

'I'm not really sure. I was too busy looking after you to worry much about anything else. Cathy Marsh was fussing over Frank and the rest just did as Tony told them to.'

'What about Charlie?'

'He's going to be OK, I think. He's a bit bashed about like you but the only real concern is his leg. Charlotte said they need to get him to hospital as soon as they can so he can get proper treatment.'

She stretched out on the bed and I got a delightful view of her figure in silhouette. I smiled at the memory of what

I'd thought had been a dream.

'What's amusing you?' she demanded.

'I was just thinking what would have been said if anyone had walked in on us whilst you were keeping me warm.'

'I wasn't bothered about that. I was only concerned about you. Anyway, give me credit for a bit of sense. I locked the door.'

'I wonder what your sister would have said. She'd never have believed we'd been telling the truth about the night before, particularly if she'd walked in …' I paused.

'What were you going to say?' she asked challengingly.

'I'm not sure whether I dreamed it, or whether I actually did kiss you.' Her blush told me I hadn't dreamed it. 'I could do it again if you want.' I offered.

She laughed. 'Now I know you're feeling better.'

'Evie,' I said, seriously, 'thank you for everything.'

'Someone had to take care of you. Tony and Harriet were busy with Charlie and the rest of them were about as much use as a chocolate fireguard. Nobody seemed able to take control or get on with it. They're pathetic.'

'Maybe, maybe not.' I smiled at Eve's ferocity. 'One of them had a reason for not rushing to help.'

'True, I hadn't thought of that,' Eve was sobered by the idea. 'I'm going to sort out some breakfast for you. You must be starving by now. Then you're not to move from that bed today, understand?'

I smiled. 'I can't stay in bed all day.'

'Why not, what's so important you have to get up?'

'Actually, I need a pee.'

'Oh, yes, well that's different. Do you think you'll be able to manage getting to the shower room on your own?'

'I don't know until I try.'

She swung her legs off the bed and walked round to my side. Before I could guess what she was about she twitched the duvet back.

132

'Evie,' I protested. 'I've no clothes on.'

'Don't worry, I've seen it all before,' she paused, 'remember?'

'How about you; is your leg up to this?'

'My leg's fine, don't worry about me.'

I knew she wasn't going to yield. I moved my legs and swung upright to a sitting position. It wasn't as bad as I'd feared. Not quite.

'OK,' Eve told me, 'I'm going to put my arms round you. I want you to stand up on the count of three; one, two, three.' We stood up. I tottered slightly. 'Hold tight onto me,' Eve ordered.

I obeyed, murmuring, 'I love it when you talk dirty to me.'

'Behave yourself; or I'll drop you. Now, take your time, shuffle if you have to. I won't let you down.'

Eve was looking at me, her expression one of concern. I didn't feel embarrassed at my nudity. I felt too weak, too tired, and too ill for it to matter. 'OK, boss.'

I made it to the shower room and back.

'Right, I'm going to get Rathbone to bring your breakfast up on a tray.'

'On one condition, get him to bring yours up as well. I can't stand my nurse going off duty when I might need her.'

'Breakfast in your bedroom. Really, Adam, what would the neighbours say?' She grinned.

'Bugger the neighbours.'

Gradually, the protesting nerves that had disapproved so strongly of my visit to the shower room settled down and by the time Eve returned I was ready to take breakfast seriously. Rathbone followed her into the room and put a huge tray down on the table by the window. As far as I could see the tray contained almost everything from the kitchen bar the sink.

'There was a real scrum round the breakfast bar,' Eve

said as she prepared to bring me a plate of bacon and eggs. 'But Tony and Harriet ordered everyone to wait until you'd been served. They all look ravenous because they missed out on dinner last night. I pointed out that you'd missed two in a row. They didn't mind much, they were prepared to wait for the hero. To be honest, I think they're all worried stiff in case they get accused of murder and all the rest.'

'How is everyone this morning?'

'Apart from their hunger pangs everyone seems fine. They all asked after you and I reckon you'll have to brace yourself for a stream of visitors once they've eaten. I think part of that's genuine concern and part wanting to demonstrate their innocence. Harriet says Charlie's much brighter this morning but still in a lot of pain from his leg. From what Tony said it seems Marsh is also feeling much better, although he's got a bad headache.'

After we had eaten, Eve said, 'Unless you need anything else I'm off to my room for a shower. I still haven't had the one I promised myself when we were working in the library. I must stink.'

'Oh I don't know, you smelt fine to me during the night.'

Eve's a much better shot with a bread bun than she is with a book. As I was retrieving the missile I remembered something. 'What happened to that book I found; the history of the castle?'

'I've got it safe in my room. I'll bring it back,' she promised.

When Eve tip-toed back into the room I was dozing, but the soft click as she locked the door woke me. I opened my eyes fractionally and watched her move softly towards one of the armchairs, 'You smell nice,' I told her.

She poked her tongue out at me. 'Go back to sleep,' she ordered. 'I'm going to sit here and read.'

As she finished speaking however, there was a knock

on the door. As I expected, it was Harriet. 'Why did you lock the door?' she asked her sister.

'Adam was asleep, I didn't want him disturbed,' Eve said warily.

Harriet nodded. 'Very sensible.' She walked over to the bed. 'How are you, Adam?'

'I've felt better,' I admitted, 'but I'll live.'

'I'm not going to stay. I just wanted to thank you. I honestly think Charlie would have died if it hadn't been for what you did.'

'Glad to help,' I said. 'I just hope you can get him to hospital for treatment on that leg.'

'Tony's talking to the police now. He'll be up to see you in a few minutes.'

At that moment, there was another knock at the door and Tony walked in. His gloomy expression told us he'd brought bad news. 'The line went dead, but not before I spoke to Pratt, he's going to do what he can but apparently, there's more bad weather on the way. I suppose unless they get the roads cleared we're looking at a few more days of isolation, I'm afraid. I told him everything that happened yesterday. He wants statements from Charlie, Marsh, and you about what you remember. He also said he'd like to speak to you when you're up to it.'

'How do I do that without a phone?'

'The line to the castle is pretty antiquated, we're always having problems. It should be back in a day or so.'

I looked at the baronet and had I been able, would have shook my head in despair. It hadn't occurred to him that our only means of contact with the outside world was gone, that the occupants of the castle were marooned with a killer.

Chapter Eleven

Eve had threatened a stream of visitors, but what I got was a deluge. Cathy Marsh was next, accompanied by Polly Jardine. I noticed a sparkle of aggression in Eve's eyes when confronted by Polly and steered the conversation towards Frank and his condition. They left after a few minutes and they had barely got out of the door before the twins arrived. It was clear that Becky and Sammy adored their brother, and their concern for me was touchingly mixed with gratitude for saving him. After a while they were joined by Tony's cousins and their children. My bedroom was large but suddenly it felt crowded, claustrophobic. As soon as she could politely do so Eve asked them to leave so her patient could rest.

Before I was able to however, Charlotte arrived to add her thanks for saving her grandson. I promised to visit Charlie as soon as I felt up to it and she told me she would give him that message. Eve closed the door behind her and locked it. She pulled the curtains to. 'Rest now,' she ordered, 'you need to sleep, you've had more than enough for the time being.'

'Yes, nurse,' I agreed meekly. 'What will you do while I'm asleep? You must be as tired as me; you barely got any sleep last night.'

'Oh, I'll probably doze in the chair,' she said.

I patted the bed alongside me. 'Why not lie here,' I suggested. 'You'll be quite safe, I promise you.' I grinned. 'Whilst I'm in this condition at least.'

Eve eyed me and the bed with a mixture of wistful apprehension.

'Come on,' I encouraged her. 'I promise not to tell Harriet.'

She stretched out alongside me with the duvet decorously between us. I was asleep almost before her head touched the pillow.

I woke up several hours later. As I awoke I felt a curious numbness in my left shoulder. I turned my head slightly and felt Eve's hair tickling my cheek. I inhaled her fresh, clean scent. She was breathing softly as she slept. I wondered how her head came to be resting on my shoulder. It didn't matter. I enjoyed the pleasure of the moment. As if she sensed my thoughts she stirred in her sleep and her arm came across my chest. She moved once more, closer, and her arm tightened about me. I wondered what she was dreaming about; or whom? She wriggled her face against my neck. I didn't complain. We remained like that for a few minutes; then I felt her breathing change and knew she had woken up. I waited for her to move away. She didn't. In a subconscious movement I moved against her, softly to make her aware I too was awake. She raised her head and smiled at me. Her eyes were still heavy with sleep. 'Hello again,' her voice was little more than a whisper, 'how long have you been awake?'

'Not long.' I smiled. 'I didn't want to move for fear of waking you.'

She suddenly realized where her arm was and moved it down by her side. 'You were having a bad dream,' she told me. Her tone was defensive, 'I was trying to calm you down. You were agitated; calling out in your sleep.'

'What was I shouting?'

'Nothing much.' She gave that secretive smile again. 'Anyway, now you're awake why don't I go fetch us some coffee?'

She opened the curtains before she left and I could see

138

flakes of snow drifting lazily past the window. As DC Pratt had forecast; the weather had deteriorated again. 'Maybe we'll look at that book after our coffee,' I suggested.

'OK, Adam.'

Whilst she was away I reflected on the change over the three days. Not only the change in Eve; but the change in my attitude to her. At first I had been prepared to detest her; but then I'd found the real Eve behind the façade. Under the bluster and arrogance was a warm-hearted and loving nature. I spent several minutes cursing the man who had caused her to radiate such hostility. I'd been lucky; I'd got past that outer guard and seen the real person underneath. I liked what I saw.

The only practical way we could inspect the book together was if Eve curled up on the bed alongside me. Neither of us seemed particularly concerned about the proximity. 'I just hope I can concentrate,' I said softly.

'Because of your head, you mean? Is it hurting badly?' She looked concerned.

I looked at her and smiled. 'No not because of my head, because of you.'

She slapped my hand, but gently. 'Behave yourself.'

'That's no way to treat your patient.'

'Shut up and concentrate.'

I did as I was told. It took a few moments before she realized my concentration was on her, not the book. 'Adam,' she protested, 'you're supposed to be concentrating.'

'I was doing.'

'On the book, I mean.'

'Oh, all right, if I must, but I'd rather concentrate on you.'

She thought she'd conceal her smile by looking away but she reckoned without the dressing table mirror.

Miles Rowe's *History of Mulgrave Castle* was one of

those private publications that were popular during the nineteenth century by those who could afford them. 'I wonder who he was?' I said. 'Have a look at the date of publication.'

Eve opened the front cover. '1853,' she read.

'About when I would have expected. Let's have a look at what Miles has to tell us about Mulgrave Castle that we don't already know.'

As Eve turned the first few pages I could see Miles Rowe had traced the history of the castle from the earliest days, since its construction after the Norman invasion and subjugation of England in the eleventh and twelfth centuries. 'I reckon Miles had access to far more information than we might have,' I suggested.

Eve looked across at me. 'Why do you say that?'

'Look at the detail he goes into about the members of the Rowe family.' I pointed to one section. 'There for instance, Roland and William Rowe, those two old rogues Charlie told us about, the two whose tombs are in the chapel. I know Charlie told us a bit about them but Miles has devoted a whole chapter to their exploits.'

'What exactly are we looking for in this book?' Eve asked.

'I'm not really sure, but from the publication date I hoped there might be some reference to the first disappearance, that of Lady Elizabeth, if not the drowning of Sir Richard as well. On the other hand I'd not be surprised if neither of those tragedies got a mention.'

Eve looked puzzled and I explained. 'It all depends if the Rowe madness legend was in existence in 1853. If not, there would be no reason for him to omit those events. On the other hand, if the madness theory did exist in 1853 Miles might have been more inclined to exclude all reference to the disappearances.'

'In order for the past to become obscured, you mean?'

'Something like that. Let's read on and see what he

does put in.'

We continued to study the book for another hour but we could find no reference to either Lady Elizabeth's alleged elopement of the drowning of the young Sir Richard Rowe. By the time we had established these facts my headache had worsened and I declared I needed a rest. 'Why don't you read that middle passage to me? I must rest my eyes for a while,' I suggested.

Eve looked at me in concern, 'Are you sure? You don't want to sleep for a while and continue later?'

'No, I'll be fine if I just lie back and shut my eyes for a while.'

I settled back on the pillow and there was an immediate lessening of the pressure on my eyes, 'Go on,' I encouraged Eve, who was still watching me. 'Read me that part of the narrative about the destruction of the original building in a fire and the rebuilding. I wonder if that's part of the persecution Charlotte mentioned yesterday? I'd be interested to know if Charlotte's aware the castle had been burnt down and that this isn't the original construction.'

'Was that to do with Henry VIII, do you know?'

'Possibly, but it could equally well have been his daughter.'

'Elizabeth I?' Eve looked surprised. 'I wasn't much good at history. I didn't realize she was into persecution of Catholics as well?'

'You bet. Although in her case it was more self-preservation than religious fervour. Mind you, it had little to do with religion in Henry's case, more a question of him getting his leg over.'

'Adam, don't be coarse.'

'It's true,' I protested. 'Henry was desperate for a male heir. He couldn't get one from any of his wives so he either cut their head off or, when that caused a reluctance on the part of potential brides, he invented divorce as a more humane way of getting rid of them. The Catholic

141

Church opposed him so he told them to take a running jump and founded his own. One of the most amusing ironies in modern society is the Anglican unwillingness to allow divorced people to marry in church – when the establishment itself was founded on divorce.'

'There speaks an atheist.'

'Not really, but I don't like hypocrisy either.'

'Going back to Elizabeth, what was it about her and self-preservation?'

'You have to remember that when Henry died there was considerable opposition to her accession to the throne. There were a few others whose claims were as strong if not stronger than hers. Henry might have founded the Anglican Church and destroyed most of the monasteries that were an essential part of the Catholic power base, but the Anglican Church was a puny fledgling and a large proportion of the population was unwilling to relinquish the old ways. This was particularly the case amongst the nobles who were in a good position to form powerful alliances. They supported several Catholic contenders to the throne in the hope that they could re-establish the Catholic religion as the only true religion in England. I'm willing to bet the suitability of their chosen candidate for the role of monarch was secondary to their religious beliefs.'

'It all sounds rather shabby and underhand to me.'

'Of course, isn't all politics?'

'You're not an atheist, you're a cynic.'

'Maybe, either that or a realist; whichever you prefer.'

Eve had been leafing through the book whilst I delivered my diatribe and stopped suddenly. 'It sounds as if you're right,' said, without looking up. 'Listen to this bit.' She began to read.

'*The soldiers of Queen Elizabeth's army had been very active pursuing those of the true Faith within the region; attempting to enforce the policies of their sovereign.*

Thwarted in their attempts to apprehend a Jesuit Priest rumoured to be at large hereabouts they accused the Rowe family of conspiring to harbour him. They ransacked Mulgrave Castle, and despite being unable to find the priest or evidence of the family either giving shelter to him, or even of practicing the faith, the soldiers endeavoured to ensure the destruction of the castle. Perhaps their motive was precisely because they had been so thwarted. A simple act of spiteful vengeance in fact. To wreak their revenge the soldiers placed faggots of wood soaked in oil round all the castle walls and set torches to them.

'On the face of it, protestations to Queen Elizabeth appear to have done little more than ensure that permission for the rebuilding of the castle was granted. In effect it may have done more; for the sequestration of the estates was not enforced and the family was left in relative peace thereafter. It is difficult to judge at this distance in time whether it was royal intervention that prevented further persecution.'

Eve looked up. 'You were right then, it was exactly as you suggested.'

'It didn't take a genius,' I replied. 'Just someone with a decent education.'

Eve poked her tongue out at me. 'How's your head? Do you want me to stop or shall I read some more.'

'Carry on,' I said. In truth I enjoyed listening to her reading to me; enjoyed watching her too. I liked the little frown of concentration as she struggled with the slightly archaic phraseology of the book which she articulated brilliantly. I settled back once more and moved my left arm across the pillow next to me.

'OK, the next bit seems to be about the rebuilding of the castle and the people they employed. It sounds a bit dry, should I skip it?'

'No, read it, if anyone can make it sound interesting,

you can.'

She flashed me a smile. 'OK, here goes. *The rebuilding of the castle commenced two years after the destruction of the original building. When the work was set to commence the family engaged Craftsmen they knew would keep their plans secure and would undertake safeguards for the family's future security.*'

She paused. 'That sounds a bit odd. Why does he mention that? How does he know the builders were reliable centuries afterwards? Or is there something I'm missing?'

'If you're missing it, then I am too. As you say it seems a bit unnecessary. Read on a bit see if he explains his cryptic sentence.'

'*The family was aware that in order to ensure the successful completion of the special work they had commissioned they could only trust the undertaking to that most Secret of Crafts whose discretion could be relied upon completely.*'

Eve looked at me, even more baffled. 'What is he on about? What was so special about the builders and what was the secret work?'

'Hang on a second.' I sat up and my arm, from being on the pillow rested lightly around her waist. If she noticed, she didn't seem to mind. 'When it refers to 'craft' and 'craftsmen' does he use a capital letter?'

'Yes he does, why, is that important?'

'I rather think it is,' I said slowly. 'If I'm right it's not only important, it's got all sorts of significant overtones. It's also highly amusing in an ironic sort of way.'

'For goodness sake, Adam, stop dragging out the suspense. Tell me what it means, please.'

Without thinking I hugged her consolingly. She must have noticed that, but she bore it bravely. 'I think Miles is referring to members of the ancient Masonic Craft,' I told her. 'Although nowadays the Craft is little more than a meeting place and social club for businessmen, at one time it was a powerful secret society wielding enormous influence. Nowadays a Freemason who is actually connected with the building industry is the exception rather than the rule. In the past, Freemasonry was not only powerful politically, it was also the natural place to go for the finest builders, architects, and stonemasons in the world.

'The Craft is thought to have originated with the builders of King Solomon's temple. That work took so long that several generations were involved in the construction. To enable them to pass the secrets of their art from one generation to the next and to prevent them from falling into the hands of unscrupulous rivals the Masons devised a complicated series of signs and rituals that new members of the Craft had to learn. Once they were initiated into the mysteries of the Craft, there was no going back. They had sworn an oath of secrecy that was inviolate, even on pain of death.

'It's fascinating to learn they were still operating in England in their original guise as late as the Elizabethan era, but I suppose they would have flourished under a Protestant monarch. What's more relevant is the work they carried out for the Rowe family and the reasons they were chosen to undertake it.'

'What do you mean?'

'The irony is that a prominent Catholic family should employ Masons to work for them.'

'Why should it be ironic?'

'Because Catholicism and Masonry didn't mix. It wouldn't have been possible for a Catholic to become a Mason, nor would a Mason be allowed to convert to Catholicism.'

'Why not?'

'Simply because of the confessional. A Mason had to keep the secrets of the Craft. Therefore he would not have been able to seek absolution without revealing those secrets. And a Masonic Brother was not allowed to pass those secrets to anyone but another Brother.'

'Right, I can see that, it makes sense. But if that's the case why would the Rowe family use people whose very beliefs were diametrically opposed to their own.'

'For one thing, they knew they would get the best craftsmen to do the work. Even more important they knew that whatever they did would remain secret. Think about it, Evie; remember what Charlotte said about the family's passion for secrecy and wondering how it came about. If they wanted some part of the new building concealing, not only from view but even from rumour, if they wanted it to be the deepest, darkest secret, who better to use than someone they could rely on to keep the secret, even on pain of death.'

'You mean they asked the Masons to construct part of the castle that no-one else knew about? But where is it? What was the reason for it? Surely if they did, it would have become known by now?'

'Not necessarily, Evie, not if the Masons were as good as their reputation suggests. As to the reason for it, think of the unsettled times, remember the religious and political unrest I mentioned earlier. What more natural than for a family whose religion and the priests who ministered to them were proscribed, wanting to devise a way of concealing such clergy and keeping them safe. What the Masons constructed for the Rowe family would have been a fairly sophisticated form of priest's hole.'

'You're serious, aren't you? A hidden room or passage that has remained secret for centuries?'

'Maybe not entirely secret, perhaps some of the family knew about it from time to time, those who read the family journal, for example. One of those who obviously knew or suspected it was Miles; otherwise he would never have put it in the book.'

146

Eve settled back to consider this. My arm remained round her waist. If she didn't mind it being there who was I to object? My thought process seemed to have transferred itself down my arm to my fingers which tightened my grip slightly. She resisted for a second then relaxed and turned to look at me. 'Oi!' she said. 'What are you doing?'

'Obeying an old tradition. It's a well-known fact that patients fall in love with their nurses.'

'Oh, is it indeed? And do the nurses get a say in the matter?'

'That,' I told her, 'is for the nurse to decide.'

It was all rather light-hearted. If she thought I was joking, as I'm sure she did, then so be it. The declaration would have served its purpose if it did no more than plant the idea in her mind.

Chapter Twelve

'I don't suppose there's a sauna or Turkish bath anywhere in the castle, is there?'

My question took Eve by surprise, 'No, why do you ask?'

'I thought if I got in one it might help reduce the aches and pains.'

'Oh, I see, that's not a bad idea. I tell you what I can do. If I fill the bath with hot water alone and keep the shower room door closed it will create a similar effect. Then; when you get in the bath, keep topping the hot water up as hot as you can bear and soak in it.'

'I reckon it's worth a try as long as I can make it into the bath.'

I needed Eve's help to get there. In the process I knew she would see me naked again. I didn't care. I was feeling too lousy to bother. As she was helping me with the slow and painful process of getting into the bath she gave an exclamation of shock and horror. 'What is it?' I asked through gritted teeth.

'I've just seen the bruising on your back. It wasn't there earlier.'

'A pretty sight, is it?'

'Yes, if you like black, blue, purple, and yellow.'

'I prefer it to red,' I gasped. 'I can't stand the sight of blood, especially mine.'

I lowered myself into the hot water with some relief. Not much, but some. Eve was watching me, an expression on her face I found difficult to read. 'Give me a call when you're ready to get out. Don't try it on your own,' she ordered.

'Yes, nurse.'

If the bath provided a lessening of the pain I didn't notice it. I topped the hot water up twice; by which time the room was giving a passable imitation of a sauna. Eventually, when I'd had enough I braced myself for the inevitable. 'Eve,' I called out.

She appeared at the door immediately. 'Are you ready to get out?'

That was going a bit far but I agreed. 'As long as I can do it very, very slowly.'

If I'd thought getting into the bath was hard work, getting out again was ten times worse. Eventually, I made it and sat on the edge of the bath, dripping wet and with every nerve in my body protesting vigorously at this fresh abuse. Eve wrapped a bath sheet over my shoulders and began to dry me. I felt too wretched to protest. She did it with extreme gentleness. It hurt like hell. I watched her as she worked. My emotions as well as my nerve endings were all over the place. I'd started out by disliking her. Then the dislike had blossomed until I detested her. After I'd got to know her a bit better I found myself revising my earlier opinion until I actually liked her. I liked her more than I would have thought possible just a few short days ago. I wondered where the process would finish up.

She dried my upper body; then bent and dried my legs and feet. She straightened up and put the towel on top of the nearby linen bin. 'I'm going to help you stand up,' she told me unsmilingly. 'You can manage the rest for yourself.'

When I had finished, I said, 'OK, nurse, what now?'

'I want to get you into bed as quickly as possible before you catch cold.' She stopped as she realized what she had said and blushed. I pretended not to notice.

It was a relief to lie back down on the bed. Possibly the bath had done some good after all. I told her.

'In that case maybe it was worth me getting soaked,' she told me. 'Now lie there whilst I go organize some coffee and sandwiches.'

I leaned back against the pillows. Lethargy was an understatement for how I felt. I needed to try and exercise my battered body and get some movement back into it. I told Eve my plan when she returned.

'Starting tomorrow?' she said, incredulously. 'Adam you're barmy. You can't even manage the bathroom alone. No way will you be ready for that by tomorrow. Another week maybe, but no earlier.'

Missing dinner had become a ritual for me. That evening I didn't feel up to more than a bowl of soup and a roll. I watched enviously as Eve tucked enthusiastically into a generous portion of roast pork brought by Rathbone. The butler's habitually disagreeable expression seemed especially sour. I remarked on it to Eve.

'He's been told to get off his fat arse and do some work, that's why,' she told me. 'Tony told him to wait on Charlie as well as you and now Sammy's cold has got worse he's got to look after her as well.'

After our dinner was over, Eve told me her plans for the night. 'I'm going to sleep with you,' she said.

This time I was unable to keep a straight face. Her confusion was immediate and complete. 'I didn't mean that as it sounded,' she managed, eventually. 'What I meant was, I'm not going to leave you alone tonight.'

I laughed aloud and Eve realized she had just made bad worse. 'I'm going to stay here in this room tonight,' she said, or rather hissed. 'There, try and find a double meaning in that. If you need to go to the bathroom in the night you'll never make it on your own. That's only part of it. Twenty-four hours ago somebody tried to kill you. If it hadn't been for that snowdrift you'd be dead now.

151

Everybody knows you're in no condition to defend yourself. What chance would you have against a desperate and determined killer?'

Put that way there was no argument. I was touched by her thoughtfulness and told her so. 'Evie, I'm sorry I laughed, I really am grateful. But you need your sleep; couldn't someone else take over from you?'

'Who, for instance? Who do you trust enough? Who would I entrust you to? No, Adam, you're stuck with me.'

'I can live with that, it just seems unfair on you. Apart from anything else what would Harriet think, what would she say?'

'She already knows, she thinks it's a good idea, she said so.'

'OK,' I capitulated, 'but I'll only agree to it on one condition; that you lie on the bed and get some sleep.'

She smiled. 'We'll see about that.'

As previously she left one bedside lamp burning when she settled me down for the night then laid down on top of the duvet alongside me. Her regular breathing soon told me that she had fallen asleep. I did not find sleep so easy to come by. It might have been the aches and pains I was enduring that kept me awake; or it might have been the lack of exertion. The only other alternative was that I was distracted by Eve's presence so close to me.

Whatever the reason I was wide awake at 3.00 a.m. If not I'd probably not have heard the noise. It was the merest whisper of sound. Not a rustle or a scrape, not even a squeak but a gentle combination of all three. If I had to describe it I would say it was the sound of a key being turned very gently in a lock followed by the ultra-cautious turning of a door handle. I looked across the room. The fact that my diagnosis was accurate didn't comfort me in the slightest. I watched in a state of hypnotic terror as the door opened fractionally. I came to my senses; reached out and shook Eve. She sat up instantly. I pointed to the door.

'Who's there?' she demanded loudly and leapt from the bed. As she crossed the room I heard the light patter of footsteps down the corridor. Eve flung the door open and looked to her left and right. She closed the door again and turned. 'I couldn't see anybody,' she informed me then stopped.

I was laughing quietly, Eve frowned. 'What's so funny?' she demanded.

'You're a fine guard, forgetting to lock the door.'

She pointed over to the dressing table. The door key was there on the glass top. 'No I didn't,' she denied. 'I locked the door and took the key out, then put the key on the dressing table. Whoever tried to get in had another key.'

'Lock it again and leave the key in the lock this time, turned halfway to one side so nobody can poke it out of the keyhole,' I suggested.

She did so and returned to the bed. As she got onto the bed her arm brushed against mine. 'You're freezing,' I said, 'get under the duvet for goodness sake otherwise you'll catch pneumonia and I'd never forgive myself.'

She protested but I refused to take no for an answer. She settled down and soon fell asleep again. Unconsciously, she moved closer to me and I felt the warmth slowly returning to her limbs. Then I also fell asleep.

When I woke up it was daylight. Eve was already awake alongside me. I smiled at her. 'I'm glad you're awake at last,' she told me tartly. 'I'm going for a shower, I'll lock you in whilst I'm gone.'

She got up and walked over to the door. There was irritation in her every action. She opened it and I heard the scraping sound that told me she had locked it again behind her. The shower sounded a good plan. It was time I ventured forth on my own. Besides which I needed the bathroom. I made it, showered, and had just crept back into the bedroom to begin the task of dressing myself when Eve came back in. She stared at me; her eyes ablaze; not with passion but with anger. 'And just what would you have done if you'd fallen?' she demanded.

'Waited for you to pick me up,' I replied meekly, 'and would you mind closing the door please, I'm stark naked, in case you hadn't noticed.'

She slammed the door into the frame and stood watching my feeble attempts to dress myself with mounting irritation. The top half was painful but manageable. Underpants presented an insurmountable challenge; whilst socks were an absolute impossibility. She stalked over and snatched the underpants from me and helped me retain my balance whilst I put one foot after the other in them. She pulled them up; totally unembarrassed by so intimate an action. After that she helped me put on socks and jeans, then gave me her shoulder to lean on whilst I slipped my feet into a pair of casuals. 'Thank you, Evie,' I said gratefully.

'You're absolutely mad; you do realize that, don't you?' There seemed no relaxation in Eve's waspish tone.

'I'm lucky you're here to look after me,' I said, trying to ingratiate myself. It didn't work.

My entry to the dining hall on Eve's arm was greeted with great acclaim by everyone. That proved to me there was at least one good actor in the house. After breakfast I shuffled through to Tony's study, supported by Eve.

Tony joined us a few moments later. 'You're very lucky; both you and Marsh,' Tony said. 'How do you feel now?'

I smiled across the room at Eve. 'There's a lady present, so let's just say I've felt better. I think we should try and take more statements, try and find out who was near Charlie when he was pushed. See whether anyone noticed an absentee whilst you were carrying him back to the castle; someone might have dawdled behind long enough to attack Marsh and cut the rope.' A thought occurred to me. 'Perhaps that's why I survived. If they were keen to get back to the others without being missed, maybe they rushed it.'

We operated exactly as we had before, with Eve taking notes whilst Tony and I acted as interviewers. We questioned everybody who had been in the tobogganing party, whereas we had only taken statements from the adults concerning Beaumont's murder. When Eve put down her pencil following the exit of the final witness Tony shook his head in bewilderment. 'They all looked shifty to me,' he admitted. 'I reckon I'd be useless on a jury.'

'I think that was a combination of guilt and fear,' I suggested. 'Guilt that they were unable to tell us anything constructive, and fear that they might be accused.'

I refrained from telling Tony that although he had been right up to a point, there had been one witness who I'd noticed had seemed particularly uncomfortable whilst giving evidence. I wasn't prepared to mention the fact at the time, certainly not in Tony's hearing. I didn't think it was a wise move to suggest to him that his daughter was concealing something. I resolved to have a quiet word with Becky when I could catch her alone.

Snow had ceased falling the previous evening but the weather, far from improving had worsened. A slow thaw had begun and it was accompanied as was so often the case by dense, cold, and clammy fog. Any hope that help might reach Mulgrave Castle was dashed by the thick, swirling clouds that covered the whole county. According to the forecasters this weather seemed set to last for a few days. Nor, as Pratt told me somewhat despairingly, had road conditions improved noticeably. His opinion was that it would be the other side of New Year before they would reach us. I kept this information to myself as well. There was enough gloom and despondency amongst the family and guests without sharing this extra bit of less than cheerful news with them.

'What do we do now?' Tony asked.

'I don't see that there's too much we can do,' I pointed out, 'not until the police arrive. I thought Eve and I could go back into the library and resume our search for this elusive book. I still think the key to much of what's been happening might lie with that family ledger, if it exists.'

'In that case I think I ought to take my duty as host seriously. I'll go round up the rest of the party and see what we can organize to keep them amused, although that's going to be a bit limited as we can't go outside.'

He departed and I looked up to see Eve fixing me with a hostile glare. 'Since when have you started making decisions for me?' she demanded angrily.

I tried a disarming smile. It didn't work. 'You're not going to desert your patient, surely?' I pleaded.

'And your idea of exercise to help get yourself fit is scrambling up and down those library steps, I suppose?'

'It seemed as good as anything else. What's eating you all of a sudden?'

'I don't like being taken for granted, that's all,' she snapped. 'If you're going ahead with such an idiotic idea, you can do it on your own.'

She thrust her chair back with an angry gesture and limped out of the room. I stared after her. What on earth had provoked that outburst? I got wearily to my feet and began to shuffle towards the library.

The room was deserted. Without Eve's company it seemed cold and cheerless. My progress would have made a snail sneer with contempt. Each ascent of the ladder seemed to take an age. Descending again was no more rapid. I stuck to the task for most of the day in solitude. I didn't bother breaking for refreshment. My lack of activity and the pain I was suffering seemed to have banished my appetite. If I'd hoped my efforts, meagre as they were, might produce some results I was sadly disappointed. Neither did the exercise seem to be having the desired effect. Instead of loosening my muscles and easing the aches I simply felt weary, in pain, dejected, and a little dizzy.

The dejection was in part due to my lack of success and in part to my feeble condition. The major cause however was Eve's sudden tantrum and desertion of me. Although I pondered the possible reasons for her behaviour throughout my search, by the time I quit I was no nearer a solution than when I started.

After I left the library I decided to visit Charlie in his sick room. His room was on the second floor and by the time I reached his door I was panting for breath and felt a little sick. I didn't stay. I could hear the sound of a rugby league match on his TV, and knew he would be enjoying the game. And I was ready to return to my own room for a lie down.

I made it safely down the stairs to the first floor. I made it safely to my room. I made it safely to my shower room. I made it to my knees in front of the toilet. I put the seat up and was violently sick. The room or at least the small part of it I could see from a kneeling position was gyrating wildly. My vision blurred and I passed out.

I came to, briefly, and was aware that someone was bending over me, trying to lift me. I managed to get to my knees and was about to look round when I was violently sick once more. This time however my luck had run out and I remember nothing after that.

When I woke again I was back in bed. I considered lifting my head up to look round but the persistent feeling of sickness warned me off. There appeared to be just a single lamp burning. I wondered if this was because it was night time or in view of my obvious illness. I wanted to know if there was anyone in the room but dare not move. My throat felt sore, from the vomiting I supposed. I tried clearing it. My throat felt little better, but I succeeding in catching someone's attention for I heard movement across to my left. This was followed by footsteps then Harriet appeared in my limited field of vision. 'Hello, Harry,' I greeted her. My voice sounded little more than a pitiful croak. 'How did I get here?'

'Eve and I found you lying on the shower room floor. When you hadn't come down for dinner we came looking for you. At first we thought you'd disappeared or were still working in the library. This room was deserted and all in darkness. I went down to check the library and when I returned I found Eve trying to lift you up. You'd been sick and were in a dreadful mess. We managed to get you cleaned up and put you to bed. I've taken your clothing down to the laundry room and stuck it in the washing machine.'

'Where is Eve?' I asked.

'She was a bit upset by finding you in that state and she'd got herself in a bit of a mess trying to clean you up on her own so she decided to take a shower.'

Eve came in a few minutes later and Harriet said goodbye. 'I'm off on my ward round,' she told me with a smile. 'I can't afford to neglect my other patients, Sister will be cross. Do take care, Adam, and try to get some rest. You mustn't try to do anything strenuous until you're positive you're up to it.'

I watched her leave. So too did Eve. As soon as her sister closed the door Eve rounded on me. 'You are a selfish, thoughtless bastard. Don't you realize how worried I was, how everyone was? Don't you think poor Tony and Harriet have enough on their plate without you adding to their problems? First we thought you'd vanished. Then I saw you collapsed on the floor I thought you were dead. Do you realize how awful that feeling is? For a dreadful moment I thought the killer had attacked you again. Then you were sick all over the place. Harriet and I had to clean you up, undress you, and get you to bed. Then I had to scrub the carpet in the shower room with disinfectant. All this because you thought you were big and brave and tough. Well it wasn't big; it wasn't brave, and it certainly wasn't tough. What it was, was pig-headed, arrogant stubbornness that led you to think you could go dashing around the place as if you hadn't been seriously injured. I hope you're thoroughly ashamed of yourself.'

I closed my eyes. I really didn't need this. I felt too ill to cope with the fight Eve was obviously spoiling for. I felt the rising tide of nausea welling swiftly within me. I opened my eyes again and looked round in desperation. An enamel bowl had been placed on the bedside cabinet, its purpose obvious. I reached for it, sat up, and just got the bowl positioned in time. I fumbled the bowl back onto the cabinet and closed my eyes again. I hoped this would quell the nausea and stop the room dancing a jig. It didn't, or not for some time at least. The last thing I remember is muttering some sort of apology before I passed out once more.

The room was still in semi-darkness when I woke up again. I felt marginally better. Or to be more accurate I felt slightly less unwell. I turned my head and as soon as I moved Eve got up from her seat under the window and came across to the bedside. I watched her in some apprehension. Which Eve should I expect, I wondered? Would it be the ministering angel of the previous day or the raging virago of a few hours ago? I hardly dare speak. For one thing my throat felt terrible. For another I didn't want to provoke her.

'How do you feel now?' Eve's tone was neutral.

'Awful,' I tried to say. It didn't seem to register with her. I wasn't surprised. Even I could barely hear it.

'What was that? You'll have to speak up.' The tone convinced me; it wasn't the ministering angel.

I moved my hand, gesturing to my throat. If I'd

expected sympathy I wasn't getting any.

'What do you expect? You may have been asleep but your stomach wasn't. I've had to clean you up three times. Charlotte's been to look in on you. She says you've got delayed concussion.'

I don't know whether it was through shame at being sick and losing control or whether it was part of the effects of the concussion, but Eve's curt and angry tone was the last straw. A great tide of depression came over me suddenly. I could feel tears running down my cheeks. I turned my head away to hide this stupid weakness. Of course Eve took this for a stubborn refusal to accept the criticism she had doled out. The next thing I heard was the door slam.

As the minutes ticked by a great feeling of loneliness and abandonment swept over me. It was illogical but I was in no condition to argue logic. I wept unrestrainedly in great waves of self-pity. My emotional state was as feeble as my bodily condition. Eventually, some semblance of calm made the tears abate. It was then I realized with a shock that Eve had returned to my room and was standing watching me, her eyes wide with surprise. I turned away, mortified at being caught out in such weakness. She had expressed her feelings earlier without much by way of restraint. The contempt she must surely feel now was something I couldn't cope with. Unwilling to provoke yet more hostility, I began to drift off to sleep.

When I woke again daylight was etched around the still drawn curtains. I looked round. Eve was still seated in one of the chairs by the window. She saw I had woken up and crossed to the bedside. 'Hello, how do you feel this morning?' she asked, her voice sounded more like the Eve of earlier; the one I liked.

'I don't know yet,' I replied, or at least attempted to. The pitifully weak sound was barely distinguishable even to me. My throat felt as if I'd set fire to paraffin inside it.

My body seemed to have developed a trembling shakiness and I was cold. My headache had returned as strongly as ever. 'I don't feel very well,' I added.

'Can I get you anything?'

'Water,' I managed to croak. It was a success. Eve fetched me a glass from the dressing table then helped me to sit up and drink.

'You're cold and you're shivering,' she exclaimed.

She laid me down on the pillow and went out of the room. She returned a couple of minutes later with a couple of blankets and a hot water bottle. She piled the blankets over the duvet and put the hot water bottle under the duvet close to my feet.

She sat on the bed alongside me and watched me. I tried a smile. I'm not sure if it reassured her or not. 'I'm sorry I was such a cow yesterday,' she said quietly.

The water seemed to have done wonders for my speaking voice. 'I deserved it,' I told her.

She looked at me for a long silent moment then patted my hand, 'No, you didn't, Adam. Nobody deserves that sort of treatment. Please forgive me?'

I grasped hold of her hand. 'There's nothing to forgive,' I said. It was a long speech for me in my feeble state. It tired me so much I went back to sleep.

When I awoke the curtains were open. Not that it made much difference for the day was dismal and grey outside. What could be seen of the day that is, for there was a thick wall of fog clinging to the castle surrounds. I expected to see Eve but the room was empty. I felt a mild sense of panic, a slight pang of loss. As I struggled to recover from my fall I had come to rely on Eve. I sat up. At least I could do that without the nausea that had been my unwelcome companion for so long. Eve appeared at the shower room door; towel in one hand. 'Ah, you're awake,' she said and disappeared back into the room. There was a flushing sound and she reappeared. 'Sorry. I had to use your loo but

I didn't want to wake you by flushing it,' she smiled.

'What can I get for you?'

'Water, please. My throat still feels sore from being sick.'

'I'm not surprised.' She handed me the glass. 'Drink it slowly, I don't want a repeat performance.'

I sipped the water slowly, as instructed. Eve was watching me; her expression one of concern. The ministering angel was back. That in itself cheered me up. I preferred her to the virago. 'What time is it,' I asked. 'I've lost track altogether?'

'Just after three o'clock in the afternoon. You've been asleep or unconscious ever since we found you yesterday. Tony, Harriet, and Charlotte have all been to see how you were doing, Becky too. You slept through every visitor.'

'Good Heavens, I really did go out like a light; didn't I?'

'You did, and had everyone worried into the bargain,' Eve's expression turned fierce suddenly. 'Don't ever scare me like that again, do you hear?'

No sooner had she said it than she realized the significance of her words. A rich crimson blush flooded up from her neck to the roots of her hair. I pretended not to notice either her discomfort or what she had said. From out of the corner of my eye I could see she was panting slightly, as if she'd been running. As she thought I'd failed to take the hidden meaning of her remark on board she relaxed and her colour returned to normal. 'Let's forget about it, Adam. What we need to do is concentrate on getting you fit again.'

She smiled at me; a smile of radiant brilliance. 'How about something to eat? I'm afraid the menu's limited. For the time being you're rationed to light foods; soup perhaps, or scrambled eggs.'

I grimaced. 'Not scrambled eggs for sure. I dislike them at the best of times and at the moment they'd just remind me of what I've been getting rid of.'

'Don't be so revolting.' Although she reprimanded me Eve was smiling still. 'Can I assume soup won't offend you?'

She locked me in the room and returned fifteen minutes later with my belated lunch, or breakfast, or whatever it was. She was accompanied by her niece. 'Becky's going to sit with you whilst I take a shower,' Eve told me. 'She's a very experienced nurse. She's been looking after her brother and sister. I've told her to stand no nonsense from you.' Eve accompanied the words with another light-hearted smile. Her mercurial mood changes left me floundering, wondering which facet of her character she'd reveal next.

The soup bowl was the size of a young swimming pool. I sipped at the chicken and vegetable broth, cautiously to begin with. After my recent experiences I was uncertain how my stomach would react. The soup was obviously homemade. It smelt and tasted delicious. Hunger soon overcame caution, my stomach behaved itself, and I felt much better once I'd eaten. I offered the bowl to my new nurse with a smile. 'Thanks, Becky, I really enjoyed that,' I told her. I watched her place the empty bowl back on the tray. 'Since we're on our own, Becky, I want to have a word with you about your brother's accident.'

I saw the guarded expression descend on her face. 'Don't worry,' I reassured her, 'this is strictly between you and me. I promise I won't tell another soul, not even your mum and dad.'

She looked at me in silence for a long time. I could tell she was torn, wanting to speak; afraid of who to trust.

I prompted her, 'You saw something, didn't you, about the time Charlie fell?'

When Eve returned twenty minutes later I said goodbye to Becky. 'Thank you for sitting with me and don't worry, I won't break my promise.'

When she had gone, Eve asked, 'What promise was that?'

'If I told you I'd be breaking my promise.' I smiled. 'That soup has made me feel so much better. I wondered about getting up if that's allowed.'

I didn't really feel that good. I didn't really want to get up. I merely wanted to distract Eve's attention from my conversation with Becky. I only half listened to the reasons for me to stay put as Eve listed them. I was still trying to absorb the implications of what Becky had said. When Eve eventually paused for breath, I capitulated. 'OK, Matron, I promise to stay here and behave as long as you promise not to desert me as you did yesterday.'

'I couldn't help that; I wasn't well,' Eve said defensively, then saw I was teasing her. 'Just try and get rid of me,' she threatened.

'No, Evie, I certainly won't do that.' There must have been a ring of sincerity in my voice because she smiled; that secretive smile I liked so much.

I dined on chicken, rice, and broccoli that night. Soon after I'd eaten I went to sleep. I woke next morning feeling much better. Eve had opted to sleep alongside me. She had gone so far as to strip off to her bra and pants and joined me under the duvet. She must have been worn out because she fell asleep as soon as she got into bed and didn't stir even when I awoke. I looked at her lying there and marvelled at the resilience of women. Someone as scarred by experience as Eve still found the courage to stay in intimate proximity with a man little more than a stranger. I smiled at the thought of being so trusted.

'What are you laughing at?' she demanded sleepily.

'I wasn't laughing, I was smiling,' I corrected her. 'I was just thinking you're the prettiest nurse I've ever seen.'

She yawned and stretched. 'Then you must need your eyes testing, I bet I look a wreck.'

'Not from where I'm looking,' I said and again there

must have been a note of sincerity in my voice. This time her smile was cat-like. I found it irresistible. I leaned across and kissed her. For a moment I saw panic flare in her eyes, then some other emotion I couldn't fathom.

She laughed and swung her legs over the side of the bed. 'You're obviously feeling better. Do you feel up to taking a shower and going for some breakfast?'

'I certainly do; if it's allowed, Nurse.'

'In that case,' she told me with mock severity. 'I'd make it a cold shower if I was you.'

When we reached the dining hall most of the family had already eaten their breakfast and dispersed. Only Tony, Harriet, Charlotte, and Becky were seated round the large dining table. I responded to their questions about my condition and headed for the breakfast bar. Cathy had cooked kedgeree that morning. I adore kedgeree. I helped myself to a sizeable portion and sat down alongside Eve. Harriet was wearing a jacket of a very bright and distinctive combination of black, red, green, and yellow plaid. Apart from the gaudy check design and the garish mixture of colours the garment had another highly distinctive feature. The three silver buttons on the front of the jacket, each the size of a fifty-pence piece, were embossed with a large thistle pattern. I remarked in passing that the jacket was a good test for my improved health. 'If I'd seen that yesterday I might have been ill on the spot,' I muttered to Eve.

She gave me a baleful stare. 'Don't you like it?' she demanded.

'Yes, but it's not to be inflicted on someone with a weak stomach,' I replied.

'I'm glad about that, because I have an identical one upstairs so you'd better get used to it. Harriet and I bought them last summer in London.'

I decided it was time to change the subject. I asked Harriet about Charlie and Sammy. 'Charlie's not in so much pain now but I wish this wretched fog would lift so we can get him to hospital. Sammy's much better too. Her cold seems to have abated and her temperature's back to normal. She said her throat felt a lot less sore this morning so I've allowed her to get up for breakfast. In fact she should have been here by now; I wonder what's happened to her? Becky, when you've finished eating, go see what's keeping Sammy will you please?'

'Any news on the weather?'

'According to the forecast on the radio the fog could be lifting. If so, we might get a snowplough out this way.'

I smiled and said, 'It looks as if most of our problems might be on their way to being solved.'

I should have known better.

Chapter Thirteen

Becky left the table and went out in search of her twin sister. Ten minutes later, she and Sammy came into the dining hall together, chatting animatedly. Having greeted her nieces and enquired after Sammy's health, Eve rose and announced she was going to her room. 'I'm going for a shower,' she told everyone. 'Then I'm going to hunt through my wardrobe in the hope I can find something to wear that will not meet with too much disapproval from the style gurus round here,' – she eyed me balefully.

'I'm sure that you'll look devastatingly lovely whatever clothes you decide to wear,' I told her. I'm not too proud to crawl.

Eve continued to stare at me. I think she was trying to work out whether I was being sarcastic or not. After a moment or so she seemed satisfied and turned to walk out. As she was leaving the dining hall, Polly Jardine walked in. The effect of the encounter on both women was both instantaneous and visible. They passed each other with just the curtest of nods and I was reminded of two cats circling each other, hackles raised, claws unsheathed; ready for a fight. I half expected to hear hissing and spitting sounds coming from the pair of them.

Polly enquired politely about my health, without it seemed, being over concerned. I responded with equal formality and watched her as she disappeared behind the screen in front of the breakfast bar. I was intrigued by the effect Polly's appearance had on Harriet. Whereas a day or two previously Harriet would have greeted her old friend with open affection her attitude now seemed more guarded. Polly's scurrilous tales about Eve and me had rebounded on her, it seemed. I was glad of that as I considered Polly's influence over Harriet unhealthy.

I was feeling so much better I decided to visit Charlie in his room. I was fairly certain the boy would not be glued to the television set watching rugby at this hour of the morning. A brief visit might help alleviate his boredom and besides which I wanted to ask him a couple of questions. I spoke to Harriet before I left, 'I thought I'd look in on Charlie if he's up to receiving visitors.'

'I think he'd welcome that,' she said with a smile. 'He's going a bit stir-crazy up there on his own. Sammy and Becky visit him but another visitor would always be welcome. I just wish we could get him to hospital. At least there he wouldn't feel quite so isolated and left out of things.'

The effect of the cold, clammy, and decidedly miserable weather could be felt throughout the castle. I made my way slowly upstairs, for although I was feeling much better in myself I still ached in every limb. I paused when I reached the first floor and decided warmer clothing would be sensible. I had invested in some very stylish lambswool sweaters that autumn. One of those would be ideal for keeping the cold at bay. I turned and headed for my room. As I approached the door I could see it wasn't closed as I'd expected, but was slightly ajar. I stopped and thought about this fact for a moment. I was convinced I'd closed the door when Eve and I had left to go downstairs for breakfast, or had I? The more I thought about it the less certain I became. I approached the door cautiously as I didn't fancy another bang on the head, or anywhere else for that matter. I flung the door open wide and took a step back prepared for the worst.

No violently inclined intruders burst out of the room to

spring at me. There was no sound from within so I crept nearer and looked apprehensively inside. The room or at least the part of it I could see from outside the door seemed just as I had left it earlier. I moved step by step across the threshold and into the room itself. I sighed with relief and gazed round. I relaxed; it was obviously my imagination playing tricks. Nothing in the room had changed in the hour or so I'd left it vacant. Just to be on the safe side I swung the wardrobe door open. There was nobody inside. Not even a bank manager, I thought, with a rueful smile at my own hyper-active imagination. I also checked the shower room, going so far as to pull the shower curtain back. The room was as empty as the adjoining bedroom had been.

I took a sweater from the wardrobe and sat on the end of the bed to put it on. It wasn't easy for both my chest and arms were still sore and aching. As I struggled with the garment I berated myself for allowing the situation to affect my imagination. I thought about it and decided my mental state was still not back to normal otherwise I'd not have let a partly open door lead to such paranoid behaviour. I decided a body warmer would enhance the warming effect of the sweater and took one off its hanger in the wardrobe.

As I put it on I felt a gentle bump against my hip. I investigated and found it was the Swiss army knife I'd bought a couple of months ago. I'm a sucker for gimmicks and this neat little device in its own webbing case with everything a man could need built into a gadget little bigger than a penknife had been far too tempting for me to resist. I smiled at my own slightly childish delight in toys and replaced the tool in my pocket.

My wrestling match with the sweater had ruffled my hair into an unruly mess so I crossed to the dressing table to rectify the damage. After Eve's remark about style gurus I wasn't going to risk her sarcasm over my unkempt appearance. I picked up my hairbrush and tidied my hair. As I replaced the brush on the glass top of the dressing table I glanced down into the well where the stool was stored and where female guests would sit whilst doing their make-up. It was this glance that triggered a suspicion that something wasn't right. From the profusion of jumbled mental images of the previous days one picture slowly emerged as I stood there and I realized with a shock what it was. There was something missing. Something that should have been there had vanished. I remembered Rathbone arriving at Tony's command with a giant tray containing mine and Eve's meals. In order for the butler to have space to set the huge tray down on the dressing table Eve had moved everything off the glass top. The smaller items she had placed on the stool as a temporary measure. The largest item she had stored in the kneehole recess. That was the briefcase I had removed from Beaumont's room following his murder.

So when Eve and I left to go downstairs for breakfast I had closed the door properly after all. My feeling that an intruder had been inside my room wasn't the paranoid effect of the blow on the head I'd sustained, or the consequent concussion. Maybe I should have been comforted by these facts but I wasn't. I was as scared as hell.

Another mental image formed itself, that of the early hours of the morning, the castle in darkness and silence; with me lying in bed, unable to sleep because of the pain I was suffering. I recalled the attempted surreptitious entry into my room and Eve's foiling of it. At the time we'd both assumed it to have been another attempt on my life that she had frustrated. Perhaps there had been another motive for the intrusion. Maybe all the intruder had been after was the briefcase. That should have comforted me as well. It didn't.

I pondered matters for a short while. Just to be certain I

went over every square inch of the room again to ensure Eve hadn't moved the briefcase again to a more permanent resting place. I checked the wardrobe, lifted the lid on the ottoman, checked the chest of drawers, and even went down on one knee to look under the bed. This was a painful exercise in itself. After I got back to my feet, no mean feat, I stood for a moment to let my head stop spinning and the aches and pains in various parts of my anatomy subside. There had been nothing under the bed except a porcelain chamber pot and a considerable amount of dust. The latter caused me further distress as I began to sneeze. The pain this inflicted on my chest and back was excruciating. I sat on the bed until I had recovered somewhat then went to report the robbery.

I crossed the corridor to Eve's room and knocked on the door. After a few moments the door opened a couple of inches and Eve peered out. Through the gap in the door I could see she was clad in nothing more than a bath sheet. 'What is it, Adam?' she asked, her tone apprehensive.

'I've been robbed,' I told her dramatically.

'How do you mean, robbed?'

'I mean exactly that. Someone has been into my room whilst we were downstairs having breakfast. They've taken Beaumont's briefcase.'

'Good God. Give me five minutes and I'll come across.'

I went back to my room and sat on the bed. Five minutes passed slowly then another five dragged by before Eve appeared. She began a tour of inspection. After she had searched all the places I'd looked a few minutes earlier she agreed that I wasn't hallucinating. She sat on the end of the bed alongside me and put her hand on my knee. My pulse rate had been fine for a couple of days and didn't need raising any longer. I considered telling her this but opted against it. 'I reckon that explains the break-in a couple of nights ago,' I suggested, 'when we thought they

171

were coming to finish me off.'

'Maybe,' Eve's tone was reluctant, 'and maybe they intended to do both.'

I hadn't thought of that. I hadn't particularly wanted to think of it. 'Thanks, Evie,' I murmured, 'you're such a comfort. I'd just convinced myself I was no longer in danger until you made that remark. You realize what this means?'

'In what way?'

'If I'm still in danger, I'll still need a bodyguard to protect me.'

I have to admit Eve didn't seem too upset at the news. 'What do you suggest we do now?' she asked.

'I think we ought to tell Tony and Harriet what's happened. It is their house after all.'

When we reached the ground floor we bumped into Becky and Sammy. 'Hi, girls, are you two busy?'

'No, Adam,' they chorused, 'did you want us for something?' They looked at me hopefully.

I was mildly baffled by this sudden concern. 'I was going to go see your brother,' I told them, 'but something's come up that your auntie and I need to talk to your mum and dad about. Would you be angels and go sit with Charlie for a while? Tell him I'll be up to see him in an hour or two when I've sorted this other problem out. Would you do that for me?'

'Of course, Adam,' the twins chorused, and turned to set off upstairs.

I watched them go with mild bewilderment; then turned to see Eve smiling at me. 'What's with those two all of a sudden?' I asked.

Eve's smile broadened, 'Men,' she said disparagingly, 'you are supposed to be intelligent yet sometimes you can be as thick as two short planks.'

That left me even more baffled.

We found Tony in his study. 'We need to have a word

with you. Is Harriet about? She ought to be in on this as well.'

'She went through to the kitchen to sort out menus with Cathy and Polly after breakfast,' Tony said. 'I'll go get her if you like. Is it something serious?'

I nodded. 'Yes it is; both serious and disturbing.'

When Tony returned with Harriet I explained what had happened. 'Good grief!' Tony exclaimed. 'That's dreadful. What do you think we should do about it?'

'I've been thinking this over, and I reckon we ought to take expert opinion before we do anything. For myself, I'd recommend searching the castle from top to bottom. If we found the missing items I reckon we'd have a clue as to who's behind all this but do you need to ask Pratt if it's something we're allowed to do. I'm not sure what rights people have when they're staying in other houses than their own.'

'I don't much care what rights they might have,' Tony said with unexpected severity. 'I want this business cleared up and if we can find these things and get a line on the culprit I'll take the chance.'

'One thing in our favour,' Harriet added. 'I know the castle's a big place but you can't hide a briefcase easily. We should be able to find it without too much trouble.'

'I wouldn't worry about people's rights. Let's just go ahead with the search. It might be an idea to get everyone together and tell them what we intend to do. Watch their expressions and see if anyone looks guilty or frightened.'

Tony told the family after they had been gathered up and were sitting in the large drawing room. I watched everyone carefully. Eve watched everyone carefully. Harriet watched everyone carefully. After Tony had finished speaking and deputised various guests to different parts of the castle he sent them off in pairs to begin searching. Tony and Harriet, Eve and I were left alone with Lady Charlotte. 'Well,' Tony asked us, 'what did you think?'

'Nobody looked guilty to me. Nobody seemed in the slightest concerned that we might be searching their room. In fact they all looked perfectly innocent,' Harriet told him.

'I agree,' Eve added. 'Which seems to indicate they all believe we won't find out anything untoward.'

'I'm with both Eve and Harriet on that,' I said. 'And I'm afraid that means whoever took the briefcase has secreted it somewhere they're confident we won't find it; even with the most rigorous search.'

'That's what I like to hear,' Eve said, 'optimism at work; just what we need.'

Our search of the castle was thorough. It took the rest of the morning and most of the afternoon before we congregated once more in the sitting room. My downbeat assessment of our chances of finding the missing object had been proved accurate. Whoever had stolen the briefcase had been right to be confident that their hiding place was secure.

I felt tired and depressed by our lack of success. Too tired and too depressed to visit Charlie as I'd promised. I summoned my two allies and explained the position to them. 'Would you do another favour for me and go tell your brother what's happened?' I asked. 'Explain to Charlie that I'm tired and I'm going for a rest and that I'll see him in the morning.'

'Of course, Adam,' Becky said.

'You mustn't overdo it, Adam,' Sammy added. She sounded a lot like my mother used to.

After they left I turned to Eve despairingly. 'Don't look at me,' she said with a laugh. 'It's not my fault if you can't work it out. Now come on. You look as white as a sheet. Get up to your room otherwise you'll be fainting on me again.'

I let her take my arm to support me as we went upstairs.

I didn't think it tactful to point out that I didn't need the help. When we got to my room, I turned to face her. 'Thanks again, Evie,' I said.

I'd given her the chance to retire and get some rest herself. She ignored me. She pushed me through the door and watched as I kicked my shoes off and relaxed on the bed. Then she went over to the window and drew the curtains. She switched the bedside lamp on and sat in one of the armchairs by the window. She picked up the book by Miles Rowe then noticed me watching her. 'Go to sleep,' she ordered and opened the book.

I woke up feeling both rested and cheerful. I sat up and looked round. Eve was asleep in the chair, the book she had been reading lying open on her knee. She looked peaceful as she slept. There was a slight smile on her face. Eve, it seemed, was dreaming and by appearances it was a pleasant dream. I was loath to wake her, so I sat watching her for a while. Whether being observed in this manner disturbed her I'm not sure but she stirred, the book slipped from her lap, and landed on the floor with a gentle thump. 'Damn and blast,' she muttered then looked up to see me watching her. 'I thought I'd woken you up, dropping the book,' she explained. 'I didn't know you were already awake.'

'Yes, I've been awake for ages,' I teased her. 'Your snoring woke me up.'

'I don't snore,' she reacted sharply; then saw me laughing.

I got up and stretched. 'I must admit I feel lots better for that nap,' I admitted.

'Me too,' she agreed, 'Although I only nodded off for a few minutes.'

'Have you seen the time?'

She glanced at her watch. 'Golly,' she said, 'I didn't realize it was as late as that. We'd better go downstairs or we'll be late for dinner.'

175

'I can't do with missing another one or Cathy Marsh will get paranoia thinking I'm avoiding her food,' I agreed.

I remember that evening's meal not only for the novelty of my actual attendance at the dining table but also because it marked the culmination of the stalemate that had seemed to descend over events at the castle.

After it was over I opted for an early night and said goodnight to everyone. I went up to my room and closed the door. The room had been a haven for me whilst I had been recovering from my injuries, now it seemed a little less welcoming. It didn't take me long to figure out why. That gave me food for thought.

I was less than surprised when the door opened shortly after I'd got into bed. My night watchman had arrived. Suddenly the room felt warmer, brighter. I looked across the room. My eyes were already heavy with the prospect of sleep. 'Hello, Evie,' I smiled.

She appeared hesitant, reluctant almost. 'I came,' she said slowly, 'to see if you were going to be OK on your own or whether you want me to stay? In case the intruder returns,' she added, unnecessarily.

'I think it would be wise to avoid taking any chances,' I replied.

Her expression cleared. 'Oh, all right, in that case I'll go get a duvet from my room and curl up in the armchair,' she said.

'Whatever for?' I asked, 'Why not use the bed like before?'

'It was different then. You were ill and I didn't … I mean I wasn't …' The sentence petered out into uncomfortable silence.

'Evie,' I said gently. 'I won't harm you, I promise. You do believe me, don't you?'

She looked at me, her eyes a painful mix of emotions that defied guesswork. 'I've never been alone with a man since what happened to me. Not until I nursed you that is, and it was necessary then. What I mean is, it isn't you; it's me that's at fault. I can't explain it very well. I'm just plain scared, I guess.'

'You don't act that way most of the time,' I said ruefully, remembering our first encounter.

'Will you do me a great favour, Adam? Will you forget that ever happened?'

'If you prefer it, Evie,' I smiled comfortingly. 'If you will promise never to be scared of me?'

'That's asking a lot after what I've been through. I won't promise but I'll try my very best.'

'That's good enough for me,' I pulled back the duvet alongside me and after a moment's hesitation Eve turned her back and began removing her outer garments.

I watched her unashamedly. She had a delightful figure. I'd forgotten about the dressing table mirror. Eve turned round. 'Enjoying the view?' she asked sarcastically.

'Yes,' I admitted without a trace of guilt.

When she climbed into bed alongside me we both found sleep difficult. We talked for what seemed hours. It was that time of night where whispers seem to carry like shouts so we kept our voices low. Eve talked of her career with a major international trading group and the travels that took her all over Europe. 'It has been fun,' she said, 'but now I feel ready for a change. I'm sick of the travelling for one thing. Europe is interesting but I'd rather see it as a tourist. For me it has been one hotel room after another and one boardroom looks very much like the next whether you're in Rome, Paris, Madrid, or London.'

'I can understand that,' I agreed. 'Everyone thinks the life of a foreign correspondent is all glamour but in fact most of the time you're only called on to report man-made disasters such as shootings, bombings, or terrorist outrages. Alternatively, you get to report on air crashes or train accidents. For comic relief you get elections and a fair proportion of those are either dull foregone conclusions or rigged votes you can't tell people about.'

Later, Eve asked me gently if I'd like to tell her about Georgina. I did so with some reluctance because it was still a subject I avoided where possible. 'She was too gentle; too timid for the acting profession,' I said. 'The only way to succeed in that industry it seems to me is by battering people's door down to get the best parts. Georgina wasn't made that way. It wasn't in her nature to force herself onto people and she suffered for it. She had a mercurial temperament.' I smiled. 'A bit like yours in some way but nowhere near as violent.' I waited for Eve's protest, but strangely it didn't come. 'That was a joke,' I explained. 'What I meant was that Georgina would be full of fun and laughter one day, the next she'd be in the deepest depression. When the work got less and less so did the good days and the bad days became more and more frequent. I could do little to help. New York is a plum assignment for a correspondent but it also keeps you busy every hour you're prepared to spend working. You could work twenty-four hours a day in New York and not hope to cover all the stories going. You just have to be lucky and go for the ones you think will make the best headlines and trust to luck and judgement. Sometimes,' I added with a wry smile, 'you even manage to get it right.

'In the middle of all that I got a sudden transfer to Ethiopia. Georgina came to the airport to see me off and I could tell she was suffering but there was nothing I could do about it. I couldn't have foreseen she would get so far down she would just want to end it all.'

I stopped then and looked across at Eve. I could see tears in her eyes and from the marks on her cheeks I guessed she'd been crying a while. 'Hey,' I said. 'I'm sorry. I didn't mean for you to get upset.'

She composed herself. 'It seems such a waste,' she said, 'a waste for her and a waste for you. Do you think it would have been better if you'd had a family?'

'I don't really know,' I said heavily. The past was beginning to bear down on me oppressively as it always did when I dwelt on it too long. 'Georgina couldn't have children. It was something to do with a riding accident she had when she was at school. We did talk about adoption but just never seemed to get round to it. That was another problem with the job; being able to offer children a stable family upbringing when you could be posted anywhere in the world at the drop of a hat.'

'Would you have liked children? You would have made a good father,' she commented.

'I suppose so,' I thought about it for a moment. 'It wasn't to be, so I never thought of it at the time but yes, on balance I think I'd have enjoyed having children.'

'I can picture you with a daughter,' Eve said smiling, 'you'd have spoilt her rotten.'

'That's what fathers are for, isn't it? What about you? Don't you want a family of your own or are you happy enough as favourite aunt to Harriet's three?'

'Given my history I don't think the occasion will arise now,' Eve said sadly. 'I'm getting a bit long in the tooth for it anyway. Add that to the fact that I couldn't stand having a man near me let alone go to bed with one and I think the odds are pretty long; don't you?'

'You let me near you and as far as I can see from here you're in bed with me,' I pointed out.

'That's different, you're different, and I didn't mean being in bed that way.'

I smiled but refrained from any further comment on the subject.

We drifted off to sleep and the next thing I remember was waking briefly sometime in the early hours. Eve, who hated and distrusted all men; who was frightened to be alone with a man, was curled up against me, her head was on my shoulder and her arm was wrapped tightly round my chest. Anyone looking in would have taken us for lovers, which was far from being the case. But then again the situation was different and I was different and it wasn't at all like that. I knew this because Eve had said so.

When I woke a second time it was daylight. The pressure on my chest had eased and Eve's hair was no longer tickling my neck. I looked at her. Sometime in the night she had gone over onto her left side and was facing away from me. I had turned with her, it seemed. I had been given little choice in the matter for she was holding my hand in her sleep. I drifted back off to sleep. It seemed like only seconds later when I felt her stir and knew she had woken up. I decided to adopt a tactful approach and pretended to sleep on. She removed my hand gently from her waist and held it for a moment. I opened my eyes and looked at her. She looked confused; frightened, and alarmed. She said nothing but got straight out of bed and began pulling her clothes on. 'I'm going for a shower and then I'll meet you in the dining hall if you like,' she said when she was ready to leave.

I didn't want her to go. I realized it and knew better than to say it. 'OK, Evie,' I said, 'thank you for taking care of me again. You're a most efficient bodyguard.'

She eyed me dubiously, searching for the hidden meaning in my words. It was there but if she found it she didn't say so.

I beat her down to the dining room with ease and was talking to Tony and Harriet about a minor domestic crisis when Eve entered. She stood for a moment in the entrance, her expression defiant. She had obviously accepted the challenge thrown out by my remark the previous day and was wearing a close-fitting pair of black cords topped by a white polo-necked sweater and a plaid jacket identical to Harriet's. 'Wow, Evie,' I said, 'you look stunning.'

Like I said, I know when to crawl; but in this instance I wasn't exaggerating. She did look stunning. She smiled a little smugly and greeted her sister and brother-in-law. 'I was just telling Adam we appear to have mislaid our butler,' Tony informed her.

Eve gave a puzzled frown. 'Rathbone,' she said. 'Hasn't the old soak appeared this morning?'

'No, he hasn't,' Tony grimaced. 'He didn't seem in too bad a shape last night though. I was about to go check his room when Adam arrived then you came in.'

'I'd be tempted to check the wine cellar on your way past,' Eve suggested.

Tony reappeared ten minutes later. Rathbone's quarters were on the third floor of the castle and Tony was a little out of breath and pink in the face. 'There's no sign of him in his room. What's more it doesn't look as if his bed's been slept in.'

There was dreadful sense of similarity in Tony's words and I was reminded forcibly of Christmas morning when Beaumont had gone missing. I heaved a sigh. 'Another day; another search,' I said. 'When the rest of the family come down, I should get them to search within the castle. I'm going to have a look outside.'

Tony glanced at the weather outside and the others followed his gaze. 'You'll not be able to see far,' he suggested.

The fog that had descended after the thaw began was denser than ever. Our only hope of an early end to the isolation of the castle seemed to be if the roads had been cleared. On this however Tony had more bad news. 'I was listening to the radio whilst I was shaving,' he told us, 'and apparently the melting snow's caused a lot of flooding. The river has swollen to such an extent that it's washed away the bridge this side of Kirk Bolton. As that's the only route up the valley we might be marooned a while longer.'

'That makes it more urgent than ever to find Rathbone,' I suggested.

'Adam; sit down and get some breakfast before you go dashing off outside. You'll make yourself ill again if you

181

don't,' Eve ordered. 'I'll come and help you as soon as I've finished eating. My ankle is much better.'

'Eve's right,' Harriet added. 'If anything has happened to Rathbone a few minutes one way or another won't harm.'

The remainder of the family began drifting in as we were eating. They all seemed suitably shocked by the news of the butler's disappearance and agreed to begin searching the castle again after breakfast.

Once Eve and I had finished our meal we went out to get ready. 'We'll need to wrap up well,' I told her, 'this fog will be worse than the snow for making us cold. It's the damp that does it. I'm going to pick up the chapel key and have a look round Rathbone's pantry before we go. It might give us a clue to where he went and when.'

It didn't, however. I stuck the key in my pocket and we went into the corridor behind the kitchen to prepare for our walk outside. Hats, scarves, and warm coats were all essentials. Suitably attired, we set off. The fog had concealed an additional factor to the weather. Overnight the temperature had dropped below zero. What we were faced with was freezing fog in the air and sheet ice underfoot; particularly where the snow had been trodden down.

As we slipped and slid on our way round the outbuildings and castle surrounds it was all we could do to avoid falling. After Eve; who was less experienced in such conditions had nearly fallen for the third time I took her hand to steady her. I thought it was the least I could do as she'd volunteered to help me. She didn't seem to mind too much, so I maintained my grip as we continued our search. We concentrated on the outbuildings first but meeting with no success widened our search pattern in a slowly widening arc. We checked the greenhouses as we passed them but from what we could see nothing had been disturbed. Then we began walking towards the chapel. We made slow progress partly because it was treacherous underfoot and partly because I was unable to move quickly owing to the residual effects of my fall. We were totally enclosed within the blanket of fog that seemed to be thickening rather than dispersing. Nevertheless, the exercise was keeping us warm and the clothing repelled the damp. It was a silent walk but a companionable one and I swung Eve's hand gently as we marched along. She didn't object to that either. Indeed, when I glanced at her at one point it seemed to me she was smiling but I may have been mistaken.

We reached the chapel, eventually, and I let go of her hand to unlock the door. If the air outside had seemed cold it was positively Arctic within the chapel. We conducted a rudimentary search at first; then a more detailed one. Our quicker look around had established that Rathbone wasn't inside but I wanted to attempt to see what had attracted Beaumont to this building on Christmas Eve.

The detailed search yielded nothing of interest until eventually we stood looking at William Rowe's tomb. 'This is where we found the first trace of blood, remember?' I said to Eve. 'I still can't see what it was attracted Beaumont to this spot.'

I paused and looked at the tomb. The knight looked peaceful. As with all such ancient tombs an effigy of the inhabitant of the tomb had been carved from stone and laid on top of the dead man's sarcophagus. As I looked at it I noticed a tiny fragment of the hilt of the knight's sword had been broken off. The break looked relatively new. 'Hello, what's this?' I said and pointed to the break.

Eve peered over my shoulder. 'How do you think that happened?' she asked.

'I've no idea,' I replied. 'It almost looks as if something's been dropped on it but the chances of that happening when the chapel is used so little seem remote to say the least.'

I felt at the rough edge of the break and when I pulled my hand away I could feel something adhering to my fingers. I looked at them closely. 'What is it?' Eve asked.

'Grit,' I told her, 'remember when I washed my hands after I'd moved Beaumont's body and I found grit on the soap? I think I've just found out where that grit came from.'

'Do you think somebody pushed him over or banged his head against the tomb?'

'I don't think so. It wouldn't be sufficient to inflict the sort of injuries Beaumont had. His skull was smashed, remember. It would make more sense if someone had hit him with the tomb, or part of it, but it would be too heavy to lift.'

As I spoke, I put my hand on the slab of stone carved in the shape of a shield. To my astonishment the shield moved slightly at my touch. 'That's odd,' I looked at Eve puzzled. 'I didn't know they were meant to move like that.'

I looked at the shield again. It appeared to be firmly attached but when I grasped it with both hands it came away easily. I lifted the slab of stone. It took some doing; especially for someone in my weakened state. 'It's bloody heavy. Now this could have done the damage to Beaumont's head without any problem.'

'Try turning it over,' Eve suggested.

I did so and we stared at the back of the shield in astonishment. The first thing we noticed was the discolouration. Stains ran from the centre of the shield in all directions. Some of these looked darker than others. I touched one of the lighter ones and my fingers came away red. I stared at them for a long moment and my fears for the butler multiplied with every second. 'Is that blood?' Eve asked.

'I'm afraid it is,' I replied. I pointed to the centre of the reverse side of the shield. 'Look there; those two claw shaped pieces of stone fit around that bar on the effigy. That's what holds the shield in place. Or rather it would do but for the fact that one of them has been broken. Presumably that was done when Beaumont was hit over the head, hence the amount of grit in his wound.'

'But if the shield was used to batter Beaumont to death surely the blood would have dried by now ...' Eve's voice tailed off and she looked at me in horror. 'Rathbone,' she said. 'You don't think he ...?'

'I can't think of any other explanation. I reckon we should have a look around outside.'

I hadn't noticed as we'd approached the chapel that ours weren't the only footprints in the snow. That might have been because I was preoccupied. I blamed holding Eve's hand for this. Now I saw there were at least three sets of tracks, although it was difficult to sort them out into individual ones. I pointed these out to Eve then glanced to my left. 'See there, Evie, there's one set going off that way and another coming back. Now why would anyone head off in that direction?'

'They don't look the same either,' Eve said after inspecting them closely. 'Look Adam, the ones going out are deeper; as if they were made by a much heavier person than the ones coming back.'

'You're dead right,' I agreed after a close look at the prints. 'You'd make a brilliant detective. They could have been made by the same person though. Especially if that person had been carrying something heavy on the way out and returned without it.'

Eve stared at me. 'You mean if they were carrying something like a body.'

I nodded. 'Come on, let's look further.'

We'd only gone a few paces before we knew our assumptions were correct. Telltale red spots in the snow were sufficient to convince us. We reached the corner of the building and stared in horror at the sight before us. We didn't need to turn the body over to identify the victim. The formal clothing was sufficient clue. Ollerenshaw Rathbone had decanted his last bottle of port.

Chapter Fourteen

As entrances go ours was suitably dramatic. We looked to all intents and purposes like a pair of traditional country dwellers. Both us of wore Barbour jackets with scarves knotted in the approved fashion at the throat and both of us had wellington boots on; the latter items being green of course. Adding to the effect, Eve had a very stylish deerstalker on top of her red-gold locks whilst I wore a much less dashing but hopefully fashionable flat cap set at a modestly rakish angle. Our *Country Life* image was somewhat marred by the liberal quantities of blood staining our jeans, our waxed jackets, and our hands.

We walked through the kitchen to open-mouthed silence from Cathy and Frank Marsh and Polly Jardine. I hadn't realized we had been away as long as we had. Lunchtime was upon Mulgrave Castle and the family, no doubt with their appetites whetted by the search they had been conducting all morning, was gathered round the dining table. I'm not sure if it's a universal truth that the gravest events bring out the most macabre examples of humour but I seemed to be guilty of it in my opening remark.

'I'm sorry, Tony but I'm afraid your butler Rathbone got stoned last night for the last time,' I told him. I felt a giggle welling up inside me and knew hysteria was not far away.

'Adam; pull yourself together and tell them what we've found.' Eve's tone was sharp.

187

'Somebody hit Rathbone over the head with a stone shield and crushed his skull like an eggshell,' I told the family.

It was factual. Lacking in humour, macabre or otherwise but still Eve wasn't satisfied. 'We found Rathbone's body by the chapel,' she told them. 'He's been murdered, I'm afraid; and by the same person who killed Beaumont.'

That's what I'd been trying to tell them. Eve seemed to be doing it far better, so I let her get on with it. We got the stretcher out again and Colin Drake, Tony, Frank Marsh, and I formed ourselves into a pallbearer party. Marsh appeared to have recovered well enough from his blow to the head; better, on current evidence, than I had. We removed the aged butler's corpse to the stables and laid him alongside Beaumont. It appeared as if the morning's events had affected me more than I realized. This was apparent from my comments once we had walked out of the makeshift mortuary. 'If things don't improve soon, Tony,' I suggested helpfully as he locked the door, 'you might have to apply for planning permission to put up an extension.'

I caught him eyeing me as if I'd suddenly fallen victim to the Rowe family madness and realized the outlandish nature of my remark. I strove to regain some sort of mental composure, without a noticeable amount of success. 'When we get back inside we ought to ring that prat policeman,' I told him. 'No, I mean that policeman, Pratt.'

We were met by Eve, who summed up my condition with one glance. She made me wash my hands at the sink then sat me down at the kitchen table and plonked a plate of sandwiches and a balloon glass in front of me. She filled the glass with a liberal quantity of *Bisquit*, my favourite Cognac, and commanded me to eat up before I took a drink. The combination of the home-cured ham sandwiches followed by the mellow spirit had a splendidly recuperative effect. Shock receded and a measure of calm returned. 'Come on, Tony; let's ring Pratt,' I suggested.

We walked through to Tony's study accompanied by Eve and Harriet. Although the phone line was operational, speaking to Pratt proved more difficult than we'd anticipated. The telephonist informed me that he was unavailable and asked if my call was urgent.

'Yes; at least I think it is. My name's Adam Bailey and I'm calling from Mulgrave Castle. We've just had another murder. That's two in five days, plus three attempted murders and a robbery. I don't know if you consider that urgent, but we do. We want to stop it because we're worried it's becoming habit-forming.'

As I put the phone down, Eve thrust a steaming mug of coffee into my hand. 'Drink that,' she told me in a tone that brooked no argument. 'Then leave Tony to deal with the police when they ring back.'

As I was finishing the coffee, Eve spoke to her brother-in-law, 'I'm sure you can cope with the police. There's not much we can tell them about this murder that's any different from Beaumont's except we do know Rathbone was dumped outside the chapel. Adam's about at the end of his tether. After all he's had to put up with over the past week this has just about been the last straw. I'm going to take him upstairs and get him into bed.'

I leered at her. 'Oh good,' I said, 'but don't tell everybody.' They seemed to ignore me, with the exception of Eve, who went pink.

'Yes, I see what you mean,' Tony said. He turned to me. 'I'm really and truly sorry, Adam, everything seems to have fallen on you, I'm afraid.'

'Oh no,' I said. 'It fell on Beaumont and Rathbone.'

I'm not sure if it was the remark or the accompanying giggle that decided Eve. She dragged me out of Tony's study and pulled me to the staircase. She urged me upstairs holding me tightly all the way as if afraid I would collapse any moment. There wasn't any danger of that happening but I wasn't about to tell her so. Once we reached my room she helped me inside and sat me down on the edge of the bed. She removed my outer garments, my shoes and socks, then my shirt. 'Come on now, into bed with you,' she ordered, as briskly efficient as any hospital matron, 'I'll be back in five minutes, I promise you.'

When she returned she told me what she'd been up to. 'I've positioned two chairs outside your bedroom door. Your girlfriends are sitting there turning all visitors away until you recover.'

I stared at her in amazement, wondering for a moment which one of us had concussion. 'What girlfriends?' I asked, eventually.

She laughed. 'Sammy and Becky, of course. Didn't you realize they've both got a crush on you?'

'Good God, no,' I replied. 'I hadn't the vaguest notion.'

'Adam, they're teenagers. You come along with a glamorous past. You discover a murder victim, rescue their brother from an almost certain death, survive a murder attempt, and become an interesting invalid. How could they avoid it? At least it shows what good taste they've got.'

I stared at her in surprise and pleasure. 'Evie, that's the nicest thing you've said to me.'

'Ah well, you have to make allowances for an invalid,' she replied. 'Now; do you want to go to sleep or just rest?'

I opted for rest. It turned into sleep. The recurring concussion allied to the fresh and terrible shock I'd received combined to disturb my sleep. I was cold, I was shivering with the cold and with a dread I could not name and my brain was struggling to process a rapid succession of images; all of them unpleasant. Then I was in Eve's arms and she was holding me tight, holding me safe against the terrors in my dreams. Slowly the images faded, the shivering lessened then ceased, and the cold receded.

It all happened slowly. I hoped Eve hadn't realized it happened much less slowly than I made out. After a while she cottoned on and nudged me. 'Adam, you're OK now, you can let me go.'

I looked at her. 'What about relapses?' I asked hopefully.

She laughed. 'Now I know you're feeling better.'

She peeled back the duvet and stood alongside the bed. I had one last view of her superb figure in bra and pants before she began to dress. I tried my very hardest but somehow I couldn't achieve a relapse when I needed one most. I gave up the effort and suggested I should return downstairs. Eve agreed reluctantly but with stringent stipulations. I wasn't to go wandering off alone. If Eve wasn't available I would have to take Sammy and Becky with me. I was only allowed in the sitting room, Tony's study, and the dining hall and as soon as I felt the slightest bit tired I was to return to my room and rest accompanied by at least one of my minders.

I returned downstairs like a sultan with his harem; either that or a Chicago gangster with his bodyguard. As soon as I set foot outside my door Sammy and Becky jumped to their feet and ranged themselves protectively in front of me. With Eve one pace behind me as a rearguard I was protected from all but a missile attack.

We made our way in a phalanx down to the ground floor and continued in strict formation to Tony's study. Eve and I entered and as she swung the door to I saw the twins already in position outside facing away from the room. I smiled gently.

Tony and Harriet looked troubled. 'Are there problems?' I asked, 'apart from the obvious ones that is.'

'Pratt seems to be concerned that you're the one to find the body every time there's a murder,' Tony told me.

'What does he think we're doing here; playing some form of snuff Cluedo?' I asked.

'He wants to talk to you, anyway,' Tony said.

By the time Pratt rang back I was ready for him. The head of my protection detail was even better prepared. As soon as the phone rang, Eve intercepted the call. 'Detective Constable Pratt, this is Eve Samuels speaking, Lady Harriet's sister. Adam Bailey is my patient. When you speak to him I'd be obliged if you would bear in mind that he's been seriously ill with delayed concussion. Despite that he's been doing his very best to help you, by doing the work you wanted him to. That work and this latest terrible shock, combined with his severe injuries have almost done what the killer failed to achieve. I'll put you on to Adam now, but please take everything I've said into account when you speak to him.'

She handed me the phone and I talked with Pratt, who seemed not unnaturally subdued given the talking to he'd just been on the receiving end of. I confirmed everything that had happened which seemed to be as much as he wanted to know. 'All being well, I should be there some time tomorrow,' he told me, 'providing the flood water recedes and they manage to get a temporary bridge in place at Kirk Bolton. Don't try and do anything until we get there, just try and keep yourselves safe. Stay in the main body of the house and stick together. It seems to me this killer strikes when people are alone. You already seem to be a target, so you should be accompanied everywhere you go and at all times of day or night if that's possible.'

'I think that can be arranged,' I told him. 'I think it's very sensible advice and I'll ensure it's carried out to the letter.'

If the detective's words comforted me, his reassuring tone comforted me even more. Not that I needed extra comfort. Eve had remained alongside me and was holding my hand. That in itself was comfort enough.

When I left Tony's study the twins preceded me, Eve walked alongside me and Tony and Harriet followed me. I felt a bit like a wanted man being taken in by a posse. Dinner that evening was a surreal experience. The meal itself was a sketchy affair. Everything connected with it served as a reminder of Rathbone. Anything further removed from the festive season I have yet to experience. Immediately it was over, the party dispersed. I had eaten only sparsely and refused everything but water to drink. As soon as I had finished eating I declared my intention to go to bed. The moment I stood up my trio of bodyguards surrounded me. Escorted by Eve, Becky, and Sammy I went upstairs. When I reached the door of my room I was made to wait there until the twins had ensured it was safe for me to enter. They announced that it was all clear and I thanked them both for taking such trouble to look after me. You'd have thought I'd bestowed the VC on them from their reaction.

Eve shook her head. 'That's done it,' she told me. 'They'll be your slaves from now on unless you do something to upset them.'

I looked at her. 'I'll be OK alone if you want to leave me now,' I told her.

She eyed me and frowned. 'And what about Pratt's advice? You remember; the wisdom you agreed with and promised to stick to? The advice that recommended you shouldn't be alone at any time of day or night?'

'Oh that,' I said weakly. 'How did you hear that?'

'I was standing next to you, remember? Those phones are easy to eavesdrop on. I heard everything Pratt said to you. I suggest you get inside and then I can lock this door.'

I managed to conceal a smile of satisfaction. There was nothing I wanted less than to spend the night alone. I realized with a sense of mild shock that what I meant by that was I didn't want to spend it apart from Eve.

It was a long time before sleep came to me. For one thing the events of the day weighed heavily on my mind. For another the presence of Eve alongside me in the bed was having an increasingly disturbing effect. When at last I did sleep, it was a disturbed, dream tormented sleep. At first it was haunted by images of the two dead men. Later it switched and I was back in that recurring nightmare from the first time I read of the Rowe family curse. The five ancient corpses were there as previously but new ones had been added. I knew they were dead; although I could only see one of their faces. It was a face I recognized immediately. I should have done, I looked at it every morning when I shaved.

It was at this point; when the nightmare became so frighteningly real that my terror must have communicated itself to Eve. She held me in her arms whispering words of comfort until I settled and realized I was safe and holding Eve as she was holding me.

'Adam,' she whispered, 'are you OK now?'

'Yes thanks, Evie.' I was lying; she knew I was lying, and I knew she knew I was lying.

As I settled down I noticed out of the corner of my eye that Eve was still watching me. Her expression was another of those I hadn't learned to read.

Not unnaturally, I couldn't go back to sleep. My mind was in turmoil. To be fair I think it was in several. As if the events of the past few days culminating in Rathbone's murder were not enough to keep me from sleep; now there was the ever-present threat of the repeated nightmares and their significance. On top of all that I had at some stage to address the problem of my feelings for Eve. It was small wonder that the blackness that surrounded the curtains was already beginning to turn to grey when I fell at last into an uneasy sleep.

When I woke up, Eve was already awake. 'Did you sleep at all?' I asked her.

'Not much,' she admitted. 'How about you?'

'I was scared to because of the nightmares; and thinking about everything,' I said vaguely.

'It's still early enough to get some more sleep. We both need it; you in particular.'

'OK,' I agreed and settled down again.

Eve snuggled down alongside me and said, 'Sleep well, Adam, this time round.'

'You too, Evie,' I replied.

If I had scared away the demons in my nightmares I'm not sure but this time I did sleep well. When I woke for a second time I was alone. I looked round in panic but as I did so the room door opened and Eve appeared. She was carrying underwear and a towel. She smiled brightly at me. 'I'm taking my duties seriously,' she warned me, 'I thought it would be easier and safer to use your shower than mine. The girls aren't about yet to act as sentinels. Is that all right?'

'Help yourself,' I told her.

I watched idly as she stripped down to bra and pants with total lack of self-consciousness. She waved to me as she disappeared into the shower room. 'I'll leave the door open. Call out if there's trouble.'

'What will you do, squirt them with shampoo?' I teased.

She reappeared ten minutes later looking fresh and lovely. I smiled at her and murmured, 'You forgot about the mirror.'

Leaving the shower room door open had meant the mirror didn't steam up. 'Oh well,' she shrugged, 'it can't be helped. Are you going for a shower?'

'Yes, I will do in a few minutes when I've woken up a bit more.'

In truth I still felt jaded and a little unwell. Maybe a shower would help. I waited until Eve was busy opening the curtains then dived out of bed and into the shower room. I made sure the door was closed.

Immediately we left the room to go for breakfast our sentinels took up position alongside us. 'Good morning,

Adam,' they said in unison; then added, 'Good morning, Auntie Eve.'

I smiled at them and noticed they turned a shade pinker. 'Good morning, Becky. Good morning, Sammy. Still watching over me? Thank you. I feel much better with you close by.'

'No problem, Adam,' Sammy muttered; her sister joined in with, 'We won't let anyone harm you, Adam.'

Out of the corner of my eye I noticed Eve struggling to keep a straight face. I frowned sternly at her which merely seemed to make matters worse. We reached the dining hall and I noticed that for once all the family seemed to have gathered at the same time. Tony was looking rather glum and the reason for that became clear with his opening words. 'Morning, Adam, I've had a call from the police. Pratt got his sergeant to ring us. Apparently there's a big manhunt on and Pratt's leading it. Some bloke in Netherdale decided it would be a festive treat to kill his wife and chop her up with an axe. He ran off and until they capture him Pratt's going to be tied up with that. He hopes to have it wrapped up today but he can't be sure. To make matters worse the floods are up and because of it they've had to delay putting the temporary bridge in place at Kirk Bolton.'

Tony's expression got gloomier still if that was possible. 'The sergeant also said the weather forecast was bad. Apparently there's a chance that more snow will come our way.'

'Remind me never to say anything about our troubles being over soon; ever again. So we're stranded for another day at least. No sign of the fog clearing, I suppose?'

'That's one bright spot,' Tony said, 'although it's by no means certain. The forecasters say if the snow does return there would be a window of several hours between the fog lifting and the snow arriving.'

Chapter Fifteen

After breakfast I decided to pay my long overdue visit to
Charlie. Eve and I stood by the foot of the staircase
discussing the matter. 'If you're going to talk to Charlie
then I'm going back into the library to continue looking
for that book.'

I looked at the twins. 'Would one of you volunteer to
help Eve while I go talk to your brother? Then when I've
finished I'll join you in the library.'

They looked at one another and I wondered if I'd
provoked a mild disagreement. After a second's hesitation,
Sammy said, 'I'll go help in the library because I know
what to do and where I got to the other day.'

Becky duly escorted me upstairs and I looked in on
Charlie. Becky stationed herself outside Charlie's door and
I sat down beside the youngster. 'How's it going?' I
began.

'To be honest, Adam, I'm bored rigid,' Charlie told me.

'Is the leg still painful?'

'It's not so bad most of the time. Last night I must have
tried to move or something and it gave me hell. From four
o'clock this morning I've been playing on that thing.'
Charlie indicated the Atari VCS his parents had bought
him for Christmas. 'Do you know how maddening it can
be?'

'No, I must confess I don't,' I replied. 'Cryptic
crosswords are bad enough for me.'

'Anyway, how are you, Gran says you've been very

poorly?'

'I'm a lot better now,' I reassured him. 'Mainly thanks to your aunt. I had very bad concussion. Keeping finding bodies didn't help.'

'Yes I know. Poor old Rathbone. The girls came up yesterday and told me all about it. Gory was it; like Beaumont?'

I nodded. 'Very similar, I'm afraid.'

'How awful. I mean I know he was a sour-faced old p ... person,' I grinned as Charlie deftly changed the word. 'But I wouldn't have wished that on him.' Charlie thought for a moment then added, 'On anyone for that matter.'

'I suppose I ought to ask your mum or dad this question but tell me what Rathbone was like?'

Charlie may have been only twelve years old, but I had an idea he was shrewd in a way neither Tony nor Harriet were. He understood people better that either of his parents; he seemed to have an instinct for the way their minds worked.

'Rathbone wasn't the nicest person I know,' he told me. 'I realize you're not supposed to speak badly about dead people but he was mean and dishonest and nosy. He was always lurking around trying to find out things that were no business of his.'

'Big things or little things?' I asked.

'It didn't matter to Rathbone. He didn't gossip to the others but he wanted to know everything that was going on, whether it was to do with the house or not.'

'Right,' I said, 'enough about Rathbone. I've got a question for you about what happened at the clifftop. I came to ask you the other day, but you were too busy watching rugby on TV and besides which I felt rotten.'

'I know, I heard about it. Ma told me they found you unconscious in your room. She said they were very worried about you, her and Auntie Evie,' – he gave me a sly sideways glance – 'particularly Evie, or so Ma says. I think she reckons Evie has a bit of a thing for you; is that right?'

'If she has,' I told him, 'she hides it very well. She was concerned for me; that's all.'

'Of course she was,' he said cheerfully, 'we all were. Ma, Pa, everyone. It was only Evie who spent all that time in your room though; night after night; refusing help from anyone who volunteered.'

'She's just very kind-hearted and caring, and has a soft and gentle nature,' I said airily.

Charlie stared at me. 'We are talking about the same person, aren't we? The last two words I'd use to describe Auntie Evie are soft and gentle. Don't get me wrong, I love my auntie to bits; but soft and gentle – come off it, Adam.'

'Well that's how she was to me, Charlie. Probably because I was so ill and she felt sorry for me.'

Charlie shrugged. 'Anyway, what was it you wanted to ask about my fall?'

I was relieved to get off the topic of Eve. Like I said, Charlie could see through people. I just hoped he hadn't seen through me. 'OK, when we were on that ledge you told me you were pushed. I believed you then, and after I fell when I saw the rope had been cut through, I knew you were telling the truth. I'm trying to get to the bottom of who tried to kill us both, so I want to know everything you can remember; even if it doesn't seem important.'

'OK, but it isn't much I'm afraid.'

'Try your best. Let's start with who was near you before you went bird-watching.'

'Everyone, I think.' He pondered for a moment. 'Becky had just set off down on one of the toboggans and Sean Drake, my cousin, was pulling the other one back up the hill after his run. Apart from that they were all close by. Close enough to do what you're thinking about anyway.'

'OK, so we're making progress. We can discount Sean

as a killer and we know Becky's not a homicidal maniac.'

'She's a maniac alright,' Charlie agreed cheerfully. 'Both my sisters are, but homicidal; definitely not. Besides which, they love me.'

I was sidetracked momentarily. 'Charlie,' I asked him, 'do you know if they think alike; share each other's feelings and so on? I know they're not identical in looks but I've heard some twins have this power to sense if the other one is in pain; or upset.'

'Yes, they do,' he said instantly. 'It's quite uncanny sometimes. I tried it out once or twice. I sent Sammy out into the garden on an errand. I told her I wanted her to pick some yellow roses for Ma. Then I asked Becky what Sammy was doing. Becky thought for a moment then said, "She's picking flowers". No more specific than that but it made me feel spooky.'

'That's interesting; but she could have seen her through the window.'

'True, but the other time was two years ago. Sammy was off school with a cold. She was recuperating at the time and was downstairs in the sitting room. It was the second day of their school term and my school hadn't gone back. Ma and I were sitting with Sammy and she suddenly started to cry. Out of the blue; with no reason. Mum asked her what was wrong. Sammy said her arm was hurting really badly. She hadn't done anything to make it hurt; she was just sitting there reading. Half an hour later one of the teachers rang to say Becky had fallen playing tennis and injured her arm. They'd taken her to hospital for an X-ray. It turned out the arm was broken. The accident happened more or less at the exact time Sammy started to complain of the pain.'

'Now that really is spooky,' I agreed. 'But leaving that for a moment, we accept your sisters aren't trying to bump us off.' I saw Charlie's grin at the ridiculous idea. 'And you say you can't think of anyone in particular who might have pushed you. Let me ask you another question. When we were on the ledge you told me that all you felt was someone's hands on your back pushing you over the edge; is that right?'

'Yes, I didn't even get chance to look round it was so sudden. One second I was watching the peregrine falcon; the next I was looking at the quarry floor rushing towards me. Then I landed on the ledge.'

'Right, you didn't see anyone but you felt them. Felt their hands on your back; whereabouts?'

'Whereabouts on my back do you mean?'

'Yes. Was it on your shoulders, in the middle of your back or roundabout your waist? Can you remember that?'

He thought for a long moment and by his expression I knew he was reliving that dreadful moment. 'Around about my waist or just above,' he said at last. 'Certainly not on my shoulders or the top bit of my back.'

'OK, that's good. Now think about those hands and try to feel them on your back again. Were they small hands or big ones? Were they more like a man's or a woman's? It doesn't matter if you can't remember but it might be a little tiny clue.'

I had to wait a long, long time before Charlie replied. 'I can't be sure, but I think they were smallish rather than big.'

'OK, well done, that's all for now on the subject of your fall, anyway. I wanted to ask you one or two other things about the people who are staying here. Now this is just between you and me. I promise it won't go any further.'

Charlie grinned. 'You want to know the gossip and scandal don't you?'

'Is there any to tell?'

'Not much,' he said, his voice almost disappointed. 'There's the old stuff about you and Ma, of course.'

I looked at him in amazement. 'Who on earth told you

that?'

Charlie laughed. 'Ma did. When she was telling us about who was coming for Christmas. We wanted to know who you were and why you'd been invited. She told you you had been a famous TV reporter and that you were coming to find out about the curse. Naturally, we wanted to know how she knew a famous personality,' – his smile was a mocking one – 'even if we'd never heard of you. That was when she told us you and she had lived together when you were both at university. Then she told us the other things about you,' his voice became uncomfortable; hesitant.

'What other things?'

'About your wife and how she died. She said you'd given up on your old life after that.' It was plain Charlie was doing his best to avoid hurting me.

I smiled. 'Yes, that's all true, Charlie, but it's also a long time ago. Everything's different now.'

For a twelve-year-old, Charlie had a wicked sense of humour. 'I know,' he agreed, 'nowadays you're more interested in Auntie Evie.'

'Anyway – forgetting about me; it's the other guests I want you to tell me about.' My attempt to change the subject was only partially successful. I reckoned without Charlie's active and mischievous mind.

'OK,' he agreed, 'let's start with my Auntie Evie, shall we?'

'Charlie,' I asked him, 'when you were younger did you used to pull the wings off flies?'

He smiled triumphantly. 'I still do,' he admitted. 'Now, about Evie.'

'No, Charlie,' I said. 'Don't go there. If I want to discover anything about Eve, I'll find out for myself. Tell me instead about Edgar Beaumont.'

He grimaced. 'If you really insist, but like I said about Rathbone, you shouldn't speak badly of people when they're dead, should you? If that's the case I can't tell you anything about Beaumont. I didn't like him, the twins didn't like him; Ma and Pa didn't like him. We had to put up with him when he came here, occasionally. That wasn't too bad because it was usually just for a day and with a bit of luck the three of us would be at school and we'd miss seeing him altogether. When Mum told us he was coming for the Christmas break we thought she'd gone mad. Then she explained Pa was trying to get rid of him.'

Charlie stopped abruptly as he realized what he'd said. 'I didn't mean that like it sounded,' he explained carefully. 'What I meant was that Pa was trying to get Beaumont to sell his share in the business. Pa had been partners with Beaumont's father and they'd got on fine. Then when old man Beaumont died Pa was saddled with Edgar.'

'I never got chance to get to know him,' I said, 'apart from picking him up with Eve from Netherdale station that is. They never spoke to me much; thought I was the chauffeur,' I explained.

'I remember,' Charlie laughed. 'Aunt Evie was miffed, I can tell you. She's my godmother you know and she's always been my favourite. She was sad a lot of the time; sad and angry. Don't get me wrong, we loved her but she wasn't the same as she is now. It was like she'd had all the life taken out of her. These last few days, Sammy and Becky tell me she's like a different person. I noticed it too whenever she comes to visit me, in her spare time that is, when she's not with you. She sparkles with fun now.'

'Charlie, we were talking about Beaumont,' I reminded him.

'So we were,' – he grinned – 'but Eve's much more interesting, don't you think?'

'Charlie,' I pleaded despairingly.

'OK, OK,' he grumbled. 'But I have to make my own fun stuck up here.'

'Not at my expense you don't.'

'Right, Beaumont then. He's, well if you want to know he was everything Pa's not. Pa is not the world's biggest thinker. He's honest and kind and everything you want your pa to be. He's good at the estates and making money, but that's it. He loves Ma to death too. He was a bit worried about you coming to stay because of you and Ma, but he likes you. Beaumont wasn't at all like Pa. He was shifty and underhand, cunning and sly.'

'You really do study people and work them out, don't you?'

'I like to know what makes them tick,' Charlie agreed.

'Good. Because if I'm going to stand a chance of working this puzzle out I have to understand them all, and I don't have time. If it hadn't been for the days I lost to concussion I might have stood more of a chance. So your reading of the guests here might be very important.'

'I understand. Who do you want to talk about next?'

'Let's make a start with your cousin Russell and his wife.' In all my years as a reporter I'd have given an arm and a leg for half a dozen witnesses whose perception was as acute as Charlie's. As a character witness, his reading of people and situations was as good as any I'd come across.

'Russell's not my cousin, for one thing,' Charlie pointed out, 'he's my father's second cousin. Russell has always hung around the castle. I can remember him ever since I was little. Not that I know anything wrong about him. He's not exactly devious, but to be honest, Russell is one person I can't fathom out. You think you've got him tagged then you find out you're wrong.

'As for his wife, that's easy. She's a snob, through and through. She loves it here and doesn't she wish she was the lady of the castle. I reckon she wishes we'd all vanish then she could announce herself to all her committees as Lady Rowe. She joins everything that's going, charities, good works; you name it.'

'OK, that's her disposed of. I thought she looked at me

as if there was a dead fish under her nose.'

Charlie laughed. 'You mustn't take it personally, Adam. She looks at everybody that way.'

'What about their children?'

Charlie made a grotesque gesture of distaste and did a passable imitation of his father's cousin, 'Come along kids, come and play with cousin Charles.' Charlie switched voices and I knew it was their mother speaking. 'Yes do play with him, children; remember, he'll be *Sir* Charles one day.'

'OK, Charlie I get the message; you don't care for them?'

'Maybe it's not their fault. You don't get to choose your parents, do you?'

'So,' I asked him. 'What about Colin Drake and his ugly ducklings?'

Charlie giggled. 'Ah,' he said, 'I wondered when we were going to get to the scandal.'

'What scandal's that?'

'It's about his wife really, although Colin has to share a bit of the blame. The problem is she's a loony.'

'Charlie, to most twelve-year-olds all adults are loonies. Can you be more specific?'

'You have a point,' he grinned. 'Well, she has a couple of problems. One's to do with drink. She's an alky. She lost her driving licence a couple of years ago. She got smashed then the car got smashed. She was fined a thousand pounds and had her licence taken away.'

'Oh dear,' I said. 'That sounds bad. It's a hefty fine, is that, even for drink-driving.'

'I know, but that's not all she's been in court for. She's had a couple of shoplifting convictions as well.'

'Really?' I said. 'She doesn't look the type. What do your mum and dad say?'

Charlie laughed. 'When Pa told Ma about the fine for drink-driving Ma said, "She should be able to get the money easily enough", I thought that was pretty funny for Ma.'

'Is it a medical condition then?'

'Which one? The boozing or the nicking things? Both, I reckon. The shrinks are treating her for the theft; that was part of the terms of her conviction. She had to accept that or go inside. We were banned from making convict jokes.' There was a wistful tone in Charlie's voice and I could imagine some of the wisecracks. Children can be very cruel.

'She always swipes something when she's here. Ma and Dad know about it. When Colin gets home the first thing he does is search her case and handbag. He returns whatever's been nicked a few days later.'

'It must be difficult for him having to live with the potential problem all the time.'

'Yes, but you have to remember it was partly his fault.'

'You said that earlier; what exactly did you mean?'

'We all thought Colin was just a bit wet and hopeless, dominated by her until about three years ago. Ma and Pa were in a great flap about something they'd read in the papers. They wouldn't let any of us see them.'

'How did you find out?'

Charlie smiled triumphantly. 'I got a copy of the paper from Frank Marsh, even though he'd been told not to let us have it.'

'How did you manage that?'

'I threatened to tell Pa I'd seen Frank watching the girls sunbathing.'

'You didn't really, did you? Was it true?'

'No of course not, I made it up.'

'Charlie, that's blackmail; you shouldn't do that.'

'I know, I know, Sammy and Becky gave me a real telling-off about it.'

'What was in the newspaper that was so terrible?'

'Colin works for a bank and he'd been having an affair

with one of the cashiers. In the end she got pregnant and the whole business finished up in the paper.'

'I can quite see why your parents didn't want a nine-year-old to read that over breakfast,' I told him. 'I can imagine some of the lurid headlines.'

'Yes, they were quite funny. It was shortly after that when his wife's problems started to get worse. She never appears to be out of her tree, but she's never completely sober either. You'll have noticed she wears a fairly hefty perfume. That's to disguise the smell of the drink.'

'What about their children?'

'I feel sorry for them,' Charlie said seriously. 'From what I've gathered their mother and father are always rowing. It can't be much fun for Sean and Andrea.'

'OK, so that disposes of the family. What about your mum's friend, Polly?'

Charlie looked at me slyly. 'What do you want to know about Polly for?'

'Because I'm trying to get to know more about everyone staying in the castle,' I told him.

'Polly likes two things,' Charlie told me. 'She likes men and she likes money. She likes them both a lot more if they come together in the same package.'

'Is that it?' I asked.

'Just about. Except that I reckon she'd do just about anything to get her hands on either one.' I hesitated before asking Charlie my next question, but decided to go ahead. The boy had wisdom and commonsense beyond his years, which was what convinced me. 'This family curse business and the insanity that everyone seems reluctant to talk about: do you think there's any truth in it, or is it superstition?'

'Oh, yes,' Charlie answered nonchalantly. 'It's true all right – in the past, certainly. Do you know about Sir Henry, my great-grandfather, the one whose mother supposedly legged it with her lover?'

'I've read about him in that stuff your mum sent me.'

'I bet it didn't mention what happened to his younger brother, Albert?'

'No,' I agreed, 'his name wasn't mentioned.'

'I didn't think it would be. Albert was committed to an asylum when he was thirty years old and remained there for the rest of his life. According to what I heard he was absolutely off his trolley.'

'Do you know why he was put away?'

'He walked up to a complete stranger in the centre of York and beat him unconscious. They reckon it took five men to restrain him. When the time came to try him, they found he was completely gaga.'

'Oh, dear, that's sad.'

'Yes, I bet Sir Henry thought so too. He had to support Albert's wife and children for the rest of their lives. They became like permanent lodgers at the castle.'

'I suppose that is a bit of evidence, but you could find that in any family if you look hard enough.'

'Oh, that isn't the worst. Not by a long way.' It was clear Charlie was enjoying himself.

'How do you mean, Charlie?'

'A couple of generations before, another member of the clan topped himself. His name was Maximillian Rowe.'

'Do you know why he did that?'

'It might have had something to do with the fact that he was in prison awaiting trial. The prison warders went into his cell one morning and there he was, swinging in the breeze. He'd hanged himself from the bars with his sheets.'

'What was he being tried for, do you know that?'

Charlie did, but he was enjoying dragging out the suspense. 'According to the gossip, he took a fancy to one of the female guests staying in the castle and imprisoned her in his room until he'd had his wicked way with her. I'm not sure whether she enjoyed it or not, but her husband took great exception to what went on.'

'Charlie, how come you know all these obscure details that nobody else seems aware of?'

'I'm too young to be allowed to go shooting, but Pa started letting me go beating this season. All the other beaters and the loaders are either estate workers or live around Mulgrave village. They love telling me tales about the family; the more lurid the better. That's how I know so much about William and Roland, the un-heavenly twins. The guys think those stories are funny – I think they're great! Luckily, Pa doesn't know I've heard them. He wouldn't be pleased.'

Chapter Sixteen

I matched my guard stride for stride as we marched down the two flights of stairs from Charlie's room to the ground floor. We turned to the right; wheeling as correctly as ballroom dancers and headed for the library, where we knew we would find Becky's twin sister Sammy searching the bookshelves along with her Aunt Evie for the fabled Rowe family history.

I opened the door and we strode confidently into the room to find emptiness and silence. The library was deserted. Becky and I looked at other in consternation. 'Where are they, Adam?' Becky asked, perplexed.

'I've no idea,' I responded, 'let's go back upstairs. We'll try Eve's room first.' We tried Eve's room, then the twins' room, then their parents' room, then their brother's room but without success. Eventually, more from desperation than expectation we tried my room. Eve was sitting alongside her niece under the window, examining a slim blue volume.

'Where the devil have you been?' I demanded. 'Becky and I have been worried stiff! We've searched this house from top to bottom looking for the pair of you. I wish you would tell anyone when you're going to change your plans like that. You might stop people getting worked up into thinking the worst.'

'I'm so sorry,' Eve said, sarcastically. 'I didn't realize every move I made had to be reported to you and logged in. For future reference I intend going to the toilet in

211

seventeen minutes' time, if that meets with your approval.'

I flushed with annoyance. I could feel my cheeks getting hotter as the anger spread through me. I thought of several replies: a killer roaming loose, the history of the place, the recent murders, and rejected all of them. Instead I turned on my heel and walked out of the room. Even Becky was so taken by surprise at my sudden withdrawal that she failed to follow me. I walked downstairs, through the dining hall and the kitchen and out of the castle. I paused only to stick my feet into a pair of wellington boots, thrust a flat cap on my head, and collect a Barbour jacket. I knew there was something I had to examine urgently before it was too late. I didn't stop to think that I was now outside the building, alone. Only two others had ventured outside Mulgrave Castle on their own: and neither had returned ...

I owe my life to fortune; fortune and Becky Rowe. I reached the chapel after blundering through the fog for a while. To be honest I was seething with anger; anger at Eve for her unreasonable and careless attitude. It had provoked me into a recklessness I didn't know I possessed. I reached the chapel and began inspecting the footprints in the snow. This time I looked far more carefully. On the previous visit I had only looked at the prints to see how many people had come and gone from the chapel. This time I wanted to find out more. I wanted to know if the footprints were those of a man; a woman, or a child. I was kneeling down peering at the mass of interposed prints in dismay; the thaw had blurred the edges and they were now indistinguishable one from the other. The prints could have been those of a man, a woman, or a child; equally they could have been those of a Yeti.

It was as I was looking at the footprints that I heard Becky calling my name. That sound helped to save me. I looked up and saw a dark shadow swooping towards me. I ducked instinctively and the blow that was intended to kill me only glanced my temple. It was enough. In my weakened state I would have been defenceless against further attack had my bodyguard not appeared on the scene. I felt my senses swim and knew I was losing consciousness. As I crumpled to the ground I heard Becky close by, calling me; imploring me to answer. I felt hands on my body dragging me; and as if from far away I heard Becky's voice again. Then everything went black.

I felt myself returning to consciousness. Something in my poor, abused brain was sending out a warning against so rash a course of action. Unfortunately, the rest of my body ignored this sensible advice. Pain was the first sensation. Naturally; what else? I tried opening my eyes. They attempted to focus. They tried hard. I wished they wouldn't; but they did. When my surroundings came into some semblance of focus I realized I was in my room.

'Gran,' I heard a voice cry out, 'Adam's waking up.'

I recognized it as Becky's voice. I wished she wouldn't shout. Or, if she did shout, would she please shout at the person hammering six-inch nails into the side of my head and tell them to stop.

A face came into view, bending over me; then another. Becky and Sammy, I thought and congratulated myself on the feat. I thought it would be a good idea to speak. They looked worried and perhaps if I spoke it would reassure them, 'Hello Sammy; hello Becky,' I spoke. Or rather I shouted. Why was I shouting too? Why was everyone shouting?

Then I realized, they weren't shouting; it was my feeble condition that made it seem as if they were. My plan to reassure them by speaking didn't seem to have worked because both girls appeared more concerned rather than less. Then Sammy vanished and I saw Charlotte bending over me in her place. 'Hello, Your Ladyship,' I greeted her. 'How did I get here; what happened?'

'You were attacked outside the chapel,' she told me,

'you've got a bump the size of an egg on the side of your head; a goose egg,' she added. 'You're lucky to be alive.'

'I don't feel lucky,' I told her. Memory of the event began to return, though not in a flood, more in a trickle. 'Becky saved my life,' I said, smiling. 'Not once but twice. She called out and I looked up in time to see what was about to hit me and ducked. Otherwise I don't think I'd be here. After they hit me I felt myself being dragged along. I think they were planning on taking me somewhere out of the way to finish me off. The last thing I remember is Becky's voice calling out again. She must have been close by because they dropped me. Then I passed out.' I closed my eyes; after all it had been a long speech for me.

Harriet took up the tale. 'Becky set off after you, realized you'd gone outside, and followed. She found you unconscious and bleeding. At first she thought you were dead; then she saw you were breathing and started screaming for help.'

I looked up at Becky. 'You must have screamed very loud for it to be heard inside the castle.'

'It wasn't, not in that sense of the word,' Harriet told me calmly. 'Sammy sensed there was something wrong and insisted we set off to find you. You know how it is with twins sometimes.'

'Where's Eve?' I asked.

'She was upset; furious as well. She said she didn't see the point in trying to nurse you and get you better when you insist on continuously taking such foolish risks and breaking your own rules. She stalked off in a huff and was last seen heading for her room. To be honest, the girls told me what happened and I reckon she's feeling guilty because she provoked it. The problem is you'll never get Eve to admit she's guilty of anything, let alone apologize for it.'

I opened my eyes and smiled at Becky. 'Thank you seems inadequate,' I told her. 'I owe my life to you.'

'Perhaps that helps even the score,' Harriet said with a smile. 'After all, none of us believe Charlie would have survived had it not been for you, so Becky's just paying a bit of our debt to you back.'

'Would you help me sit up?' I asked them. 'I can't stay an invalid for ever.'

'Are you sure?' Harriet asked. 'Remember you've only just recovered from your last bout of concussion. What about a relapse?'

Strangely enough that didn't worry me. Apart from the headache I felt OK. 'I think I'll be all right. All I need is some painkillers for my head and I should be able to get up. It must have been no more than a glancing blow.'

'Some glance,' Harriet commented, as she and Becky helped me into a sitting position. I closed my eyes for a moment and waited for the pain to subside. After a moment or two I pretended that it had, and opened my eyes. My vision was clear and there was no lack of focus. I actually felt better for sitting up.

'I'm fine,' I reassured them. 'Just give me a few minutes and I'll get off this bed.'

'Do you really think that's wise?' Harriet was still dubious.

'Harry, I'm getting a bit tired of being the target for some maniac. I want to find out who's behind this and why, and I can't do that lying in a darkened room.'

Sammy had been sent on ahead to tell Tony we were coming downstairs. The twins mounted guard outside his study door whilst I discussed matters with their parents. 'The sooner we get to grips with our problems the better,' I told them. 'I'm more and more convinced that the secret of what's been happening is something to do with the old chapel. It's where Beaumont and Rathbone were killed and close to where I was attacked. Can either of you think of anything about the chapel that might provide some clue as to the reason for the murders?'

215

'Not unless somebody in this house has developed some form of religious mania,' Harriet suggested, 'and I for one, have seen no evidence of that.'

'There's nothing within the chapel of special significance or value, is there?'

'You mean a religious artefact of some description?' Tony asked.

'Something like that.'

'Nothing that I can think of. The chapel's only ever been used for private family worship from the time it was built.'

'Charlie told me about that,' I said with a grin. 'He said your ancestors were a pair of real villains.'

'Yes they were, according to the legends about them,' Tony agreed. 'Anyone less likely than William and Roland to sponsor the building of a place of worship it would be difficult to imagine.'

'I'm sure the other crucial key to the mystery lies within that family ledger, if it exists and can be found. So for now I'm going to concentrate on looking for that.'

When I left them I set off for the library with my two escorts alongside. Inside the room we were met by Eve. She was already at work searching for the book. She looked pale and there was a tight expression on her face as if she was containing some strong emotion. 'Hello, Evie,' I greeted her as if nothing untoward had happened between us. 'Great minds think alike; Sammy, Becky, and I were about to start looking for that book as well.'

Eve nodded distantly. 'Better get on with it, then,' her tone was cool to the point of aloofness. 'There's plenty to go at.' She indicated the long expanse of shelves we had not yet touched. With four of us on the job the work proceeded quickly. There was a tense, strained atmosphere between Eve and me. On previous occasions, I had attempted to defuse any potentially explosive confrontations. This time however, I was prepared to allow matters to take their own course. If Eve wanted a fight, she could have one. If she wanted to sever the close relationship that had been building up between us that was her prerogative. I wasn't about to force the issue.

By late afternoon we were almost through with the task and still we had seen no sign of the elusive volume. In deference to my less-than-perfect physical condition, Eve had assumed responsibility for the upper shelves. She had done this at the beginning with the tersest of comments. When I had prepared to climb the ladder she had almost thrust me to one side. 'I'll do that. You're in no fit state to go up and down ladders.'

I didn't attempt to argue, merely turned aside and started work on the lower shelves. Out of the corner of my eye however I saw Eve bite her lip in frustration. That strengthened my resolve to avoid a slanging match. It was as we searched the final set of shelves that near-disaster happened. Eve had positioned the ladder and begun work on the top shelf; positioned it badly as it turned out. I had completed looking at the lowest shelf on that section and was standing near the ladder easing the kinks out of my spine. I watched appreciatively as Eve climbed the five rungs that she needed to reach the top shelf. She really did have a superb figure.

It was as well that I was ogling her, for I noticed the ladder move sideways, possibly as quickly as Eve felt it move. Left with the choice of going down with the ladder or jumping overboard, Eve opted to leap clear. Towards me, as it happened – but fortunately, I was forewarned that she was about to throw herself at me, and braced myself to catch her.

I staggered back a couple of strides until my thighs came in contact with the table and I found myself lying across it with Eve in my arms on top of me. As I went down across the table the back of my head hit the far edge. I winced with the fresh pain, but the contact was slight enough to cause no more than momentary discomfort. For a moment we remained motionless, our eyes meeting from no more than a few inches apart. I realized my arms were clasped around Eve in an embrace any lover would have been proud of. I watched as a host of unreadable expressions chased across her face reflected in her lovely eyes. Tension built as the seconds passed with neither of us moving. 'Are you all right?' I asked.

It broke the spell and Eve freed herself from my grasp and stood up. 'Yes, I think so,' she said as she stood upright. 'How about you?'

I realized I was holding her hands. I didn't let go. 'Yes, I'm OK. I just banged my head on the edge of the table but it's nothing to worry about.'

'Thank you for being there,' she said; her tone as dispassionate as if she was talking to a stranger.

'No problem,' I replied. 'You can fall for me any time you like.'

She released her hands and turned away and I became aware of the twins watching us open-mouthed. 'It's a new acrobatic routine we're practicing. We thought we'd try it out here before we audition for the circus.'

Sammy and Becky grinned and we all returned to work. I remembered that brief few seconds when Eve had lain in my arms before I'd spoken. For one moment I thought she was going to kiss me, then the next I thought she had been about to slap me. That was the problem. I never knew from one second to the next with Eve; whether the passion that blazed in those beautiful eyes was love or hate. Then in the space of a breath she seemed totally indifferent.

The library search was over within half an hour. I was tired and ready for a rest. I declared my intention of taking a nap before dinner. My companions walked upstairs with me and I thanked them before I went into my room. Eve seemed as unapproachable as at any time since our first meeting and that disturbed me. It was so much at the forefront of my mind that sleep eluded me. Eventually, I decided I must resolve the situation. Becky was on duty outside my door. 'Where's Sammy?' I asked.

'She went to visit Charlie. Mum said he's a bit depressed so she thought it would cheer him up. I'll go see him after dinner.'

'OK, I'm just going to talk to your aunt,' I told her, 'so you don't have to follow me.'

'Adam, before you go, there's something I must tell you. I wanted to say it this morning, but because of everything else that happened I didn't get chance.'

'What is it, Becky?'

She explained, and although I didn't realize it at the time, her few short sentences handed me the key to who was behind all the grim events that had happened at the castle.

I knocked on Eve's door. 'Who is it?' she asked.

Her voice sounded heavy, sleepy, and slightly sensual. 'It's Adam,' I replied, 'can I have a word with you?'

'Come in.'

She had lain down wearing the clothes she had on to search the library, minus the polo-necked sweater. 'What is it?' she asked, drowsily.

I glanced about, for I'd not seen inside her room before. It was almost identical to mine even down to the furniture. At the bottom of the bed was an ancient-looking wooden chest, an ottoman. It was an exact copy of the one in my bedroom. I walked round this and stood alongside the bed. 'I came to apologize for this morning.' I hadn't intended to apologize. For all that I had been ruffled by her sarcasm I didn't believe I was totally to blame.

'I should hope so too,' she replied. 'Don't you realize people were very upset? Dashing off like that, putting yourself in danger. People do care what happens to you, you know. People do care about you, whatever you might think. People would be dreadfully hurt if you had been killed like those others.'

Her speech was disjointed, rambling, but her message was crystal clear. Even to me it was obvious. 'When you say *people* who do you mean?' I asked gently.

'Well, there's Tony and Harriet for a start. Charlie and the twins as well and ...' The sentence petered out.

'And?' I prompted her.

She looked at me and again there was that conflict raging in her eyes again. 'Yes, and me too damn it; yes I would be upset if you got yourself killed.'

She was breathing heavily, and I sensed the war within her hadn't ended even if this battle was over. 'I can't tell you how good that sounds,' I told her and she stared in amazement; her own emotions suspended.

I smiled. 'I truly am sorry. Please say you'll forgive me. The problem is it has been such a long time since I had anyone to care about what happened to me I'd quite forgotten what it was like.'

I wanted to kiss her, but dared not. For her, the war continued, its outcome still uncertain. Instead I took her hand. 'Can we be friends again?' I asked.

She looked at me for a long time and said, 'I suppose so.'

'Thank you, Evie. Now I must go try and get some rest.'

I fell asleep as soon as I got back to my room and almost at once I was plunged into another weird dream. I was searching the library again; together with Eve and all the time we searched I could hear Becky's voice, insistently in my ear. 'Look in the box, Adam, look in the box,' she repeated time after time.

Although I could hear Becky's voice in my dream I knew Becky wasn't there. Nor was there a box in the library as we searched. 'What do you think she meant, "look in the box"?' I asked Eve, but she was as unable to answer as I.

Chapter Seventeen

With the demise of Rathbone, dinner that evening was another buffet, and as I helped myself to a delicious-smelling pork casserole I was joined by Eve and the twins. The other members of the family were already seated and tucking into the meal. It was a reserved and muted atmosphere around the large table. I felt an air of suppressed tension too but possibly that was my imagination. By the time we finished eating most of the others had already dispersed. Eve seemed curiously changed from earlier; more relaxed and at peace with herself. She even smiled a couple of times which was a world record that day. She still seemed rather shy of me but at least there was no friction between us. She excused herself and pleaded tiredness when she had finished dining. 'I'm going to get an early night,' she told me, 'I need to catch up on my sleep.'

With that she left the dining hall. Tony had meandered off to play snooker with Russell and Colin, leaving Harriet and the twins with me in the dining hall. 'I sometimes wonder why Russell bothers,' Harriet commented, 'he can hardly see to the other end of the table.'

She saw my puzzled expression and explained, 'Russell's eyesight's very bad and it's getting worse. He doubts if he'll be allowed to drive much longer.'

Sammy and Becky said they were going to look in on Charlie but would be back down to escort me to bed. 'Don't worry,' Harriet told them, 'I'll make sure Adam gets to his room safely. You two turn in when you've said goodnight to your brother. Tell him I'll pop in to see him in a little while.'

She watched them go with a smile on her face; then turned to me. 'Adam Bailey,' she said accusingly, 'you really have set my daughters' hearts fluttering, haven't you?'

'Not intentionally,' I assured her. 'I didn't realize until Eve told me.'

'Don't worry, it won't do them any harm.'

'Harry,' I said, 'I'm glad I've got you on your own. I want to ask you a few questions. I was talking to Charlie earlier about the family. I'd like you to be absolutely honest with me. Forget any notions of loyalty or anything like that. Remember there's a double murderer loose somewhere in this castle. Someone who has not only killed twice, but made two attempts to kill me and one to kill your son.'

'Put like that, I can't refuse,' Harriet said slowly. 'The problem is, when you know people that closely you're reluctant to believe they could be capable of anything so wicked.'

'That may be so, but you listen to news bulletins, Harry. How many times have you heard neighbours being interviewed after a vicious killer's been convicted? They all say they can't believe it, what a nice person he or she seemed to be.'

'OK, Adam, I'll do what I can. Where do you want me to start?'

'Why not begin with Russell?' I suggested.

'I didn't like Russell to begin with. I first met him when I became engaged to Tony. I got the impression he was trying to put Tony off me. At the same time he warned me about Tony and the family madness thing. I didn't pay any attention to it. I was in love. When Russell saw that I wasn't going to be deterred he gave up and came round to the idea of my marriage to Tony. I like him well enough now; although I've always had that one reservation about him.'

'What about his wife, do they get on OK?'

Harriet grimaced. 'She's just the opposite and doesn't improve for knowing. She's a self-righteous snob and a dreadful prude. Tony says it's a miracle she and Russell have three children. Tony reckons she wears a padlocked chastity belt and has only forgotten to put it on three times. She's always busy sitting on committees and being awfully important. Don't get me wrong, she does a lot of charity work and helps out lots of good causes – but she likes everyone to know about it.'

'What does Russell do for a living?'

'He inherited quite a bit of money from his father and invested it in property. He picked a good time as well. When property values soared Russell was able to cash in with an enormous profit. He's been living off that ever since.'

'What about Colin Drake?'

'Now there's a good question,' Harriet said. 'Where would you like me to begin? Colin's got a miserable home life. Some of it's his own doing I'm afraid; although it's difficult to work out whether it's cause or effect.'

'You mean about his mistress and the pregnancy?'

'My son has a gift for scandal and gossip,' Harriet said ruefully. 'Did he by any chance tell you how he blackmailed poor Frank Marsh into showing him the newspaper article about Colin?'

'Yes he did, I told him he'd go a long way. Probably to prison.'

'That's Charlie for you,' Harriet agreed. 'Colin got a girl from his bank into trouble and the scandal got into the papers. But whether that was the cause of his wife's troubles or whether Colin sought consolation because home life was so difficult I can't be sure. Did Charlie say anything else?'

'He mentioned a drink problem and shoplifting, if that's what you mean.'

'Yes, her little foibles are too obvious to be hidden from the family, I'm afraid. The result of it all is that they are always at each other's throats. When she's here, she's either sloshed or hungover. That's when she's not slipping something into her case that Colin has to return later. Their kids despise her for being a thief and a lush; they despise their father for his affair and for being weak. Not the most pleasant of home lives, not for the adults or for the children. I know both kids have needed counselling after being tormented by other children at school whenever one of their mother's little problems hits the papers.'

'Tell me something, Harry, did Beaumont know either Russell or Colin before he came to the castle?'

Harriet thought it over. 'I'm not really sure. I believe he did have some business dealings with Colin's bank so possibly he would have known Colin; but I don't think he knew Russell.'

'Did Beaumont know any of the other guests?'

'I doubt it.' Harriet's tone was dry. 'We didn't socialize with him much. The only reason I agreed to him being invited was because I knew Tony was going to try and persuade Beaumont to sell his share in the business. As for who else he might have met – I did see him in one of Polly's restaurants once but whether he was ever introduced to Polly, I couldn't be sure.'

'Ok, that'll do for the grilling, Harry.' I yawned. 'I think it's time I went to bed.'

'I'd better do my escort duty, then.' Harriet smiled. 'Otherwise, I'll have two lovelorn teenagers to contend with for not taking care of you.'

'Just hope and pray they haven't inherited their aunt's temper,' I joked.

'Eve wasn't always like that, and to be fair she's been

much more like her old self these past few days,' – she shot me a sly sideways glance – 'which might be your doing. She was so messed up after what happened that I was really frightened she might harm herself, or worse.

'She came out of it to a degree, but it had warped her so much that until this last week I wouldn't have thought she'd trust being alone with a man again; let alone spending several nights nursing one in his bedroom as she has with you.'

'I owe her a lot, Harry. To be honest, I'm not sure I'd have recovered but for the way Eve nursed me. She didn't spare herself to make sure I pulled through,' I thought of Eve's warming me with her body. In view of what Harriet had said that became even more surprising.

Something in my tone must have given my feelings away, because Harriet looked at me suspiciously. 'Are you in love with her, Adam?' she asked.

'I think she's a lovely person who's had a raw deal,' I replied. 'I like and admire her a lot, Harry.'

'That's not answering my question, as you well know.'

'I know it isn't, but it's the best you're going to get for the time being. Look at it this way: given Eve's history, if there were to be feelings between us the initiative would have to come from her. The worst thing I could possibly do would be trying to force the issue or declaring myself. I reckon she knows I like her a lot and until I find out how she feels about me that will have to do.'

'For someone who wasn't prepared to state their feelings I think you've given yourself away totally,' Harriet said. 'I'm not sure what to think about it. Maybe Eve would be good for you. I know you'd be good for her.'

'In that case, you'll have to keep our conversation to yourself,' I advised her. 'The worst thing that could happen would be for Eve to think we've been gossiping about her.'

We walked upstairs and said goodnight outside my bedroom door. 'You can tell the twins you did your duty admirably,' I smiled.

Harriet nodded. 'That's the first question they'll ask,' she agreed ruefully.

I locked my door carefully, securing the key so it couldn't be dislodged. I undressed slowly as I was beginning to feel the effects of several new bruises, and climbed into bed.

It was the first night I had spent alone since Christmas Eve, I reflected as I settled down. The bed was comfortable yet sleep didn't come easily. For the last few nights I had found Eve's presence a distraction, and a disturbing one at that. Now, with her absence, I found it even more difficult to settle. I realized how much I missed her presence alongside me although I knew I had no right to expect it. I missed her laughter, her quick temper, and the mercurial mood changes that made her so exciting.

When I did fall asleep it was an uneasy rest. The dreams that had plagued even from before I arrived at Mulgrave Castle returned with even greater force. The frightening realism of the nightmare threatened to overpower me.

In my dream I was searching the castle yet again. This time there was a new, more vital urgency to my quest. It spurred me to greater efforts and it hastened my passage. As I ran from room to room I knew my mission was hopeless. I would not find what I sought.

I was helpless against the forces that I was fighting. They held all the cards. As I searched alone through the castle I knew this and yet I clung to a desperate thread of hope.

Why I should do this when I knew all along the reason for my failure, I did not know. My rational mind, if a dreamer can possess such a thing, told me to give up, to yield to the inevitable. Because of my stupidity, my vain, arrogant failure to spot the obvious, I had caused the death of Eve. If only I hadn't ignored what was there before me all the time I might have been in time to save her. What a fool I was to overlook it when it was there in front of my eyes waiting for me to discover it all along.

It was all right saying this, I argued with myself, but what was it I'd missed; what was it that had been so blatantly obvious only a fool could ignore it? What had I been looking in all the wrong places for? Even as I was questioning myself I realized the answer. Of course, I had spent fruitless hours with Eve, Sammy, and Becky ransacking the library for the Rowe family journal. If only I'd used my common sense instead of rushing into that wild goose chase. If only I'd paused to ask myself the rational, the obvious questions before starting the hunt. Who had hidden the journal? Answer: the Rowe family ancestors. What motive had they for hiding it? To avoid it being found, that was all so logical. Where is the first place to look for a book? In a library, of course. So why would they put something they wanted to conceal in the most obvious place for someone to search. The library would have been the last place they would have chosen. But in my blind, arrogant, stupid ignorance I'd totally overlooked that fact and now Eve had been left to suffer the consequences of my folly.

The castle was all in darkness as I dashed from room to room; from corridor to corridor; up and down stairway after stairway. All the time as I progressed in this Stygian black and ancient building I could hear the mocking sardonic laughter of my enemies. They had won and I had lost; the laughter told me so. They had won and they had claimed their prize. Their grim reward was the life of Eve. It was my price for failure.

All the time as I chased through the castle I retained the slim hope that perhaps I was wrong. Perhaps the laughter was challenging me. Perhaps after all I wasn't too late. Perhaps I would be in time to save her. There was still one enormous obstacle to overcome. I may have realized that the book would never have been concealed in the library but I still hadn't found its hiding place.

Again I knew that this was my fault. Something I'd overlooked held the key to the mystery, but what was it? Could it have been something I'd seen or heard? Was it something someone had done or said to me? My head was aching; nothing new in that, my head was always aching. This time however it wasn't merely the after effects of my injuries but the added strain of trying to recall what I had missed.

It was no good, I couldn't do it, I would have to give in. Nothing I tried would be of any use. I must face reality, the awful reality that I had lost this macabre game and with it, Eve would suffer a ghastly nameless fate. Just as I was giving way to despair a voice came to me out of the darkness of my dream, the blackness of my despondency. It was Eve's voice; clear and confident. 'Hurry, Adam,' she was pleading with me, 'hurry if you want to save me; I have so little time left, you must hurry.'

'I can't do this alone. I must know where to look. Why does it always have to be me? Why must I always be alone?'

Then in a really terrifying twist, my dream self was confronted with another figure; an accusing one. 'Georgina,' I cried out, 'what are you doing here?'

'I'm here because you asked a question. You asked why you always had to be alone. I'm here as an answer. You are always alone because you deserve no better than to be alone. You were too late then and you are too late now. Why couldn't you see I was desperate and needed you? Why couldn't you see that I was lonely? Why couldn't you have come back to me before it was too late?

'Now, when you'd been given a second chance, a

chance that isn't open to everyone, what have you done? Exactly as you did before. Ignored others, ignored what they were feeling, what pain and distress they were in, and gone your own sweet way until it was too late. You've lost her, Adam, exactly as you lost me, and for the same reason. Because in your foolish, blind, selfish arrogance you failed to see what she needed from you until it was too late.'

I woke up by sitting up. I was bolt upright in bed with a pounding headache, sweat pouring off me as if I was in the heat of a tropical rainforest. Although I was sweating I felt cold; chilled to the marrow by the ghastly nightmare. It was the coldness of fear; the icy desperation of terror that gripped me. As I strove to remember and rationalize the grisly dream that had haunted me I knew there was more than just a bizarre twisting of events in the nightmare. Somewhere within my fantasy lay a key I must try to use.

I glanced at the luminous dial of my watch. 2.15 a.m. I had slept barely three hours and felt jaded, yet I knew I couldn't rest any longer. I flicked on the bedside lamp and stumbled from the bed. I've no idea how long I paced the bedroom floor trying to shake the memory of my terrifying dream. It did not recede; rather it intensified. I sat on the ottoman at the base of the bed and began to think. It did no good, for all my puzzling I felt I was no closer to a solution than when I'd begun. My mouth felt dry and I needed a glass of water. As I stood up and turned towards the dressing table for a glass I bumped my thigh painfully against the corner of the ottoman. I stood for a moment cursing the Rowe family ancestor who had placed the ancient box in my room. I leaned on the lid for support. I stared at the box. Was this what had been under my nose and overlooked all along? I dismissed the thought as fanciful but it refused to be dismissed and the more I tried, the stronger it returned. I went and filled my water glass and sipped it slowly as I looked at the antique wooden blanket box. I set the glass down and approached the chest slowly; almost apprehensively. I had looked inside when we were searching for the missing briefcase; knew it contained blankets.

I reached for the lid. There was no creak, of the type so beloved of film-makers, as I opened it. The chest was too well-made for that. My imagination wandered to picture a line of movie directors arriving at the Pearly Gates only to be served with writs for defamation by Chippendale or Hepplewhite. I dismissed the notion and lifted the lid to find the blanket box still contained blankets. Nevertheless, my curiosity remained high and I lifted the blankets out of the chest one by one. I stacked them alongside on the floor until I was looking at them empty interior of the box. My fanciful imagination satisfied I stared at the empty receptacle. Despite my initial disappointment there remained a slight query in my mind. Something wasn't right.

I told myself I was clutching at straws, that whatever the meaning of my dream, if indeed there was any other explanation but the workings of an overwrought brain; this was not the answer. Such weird coincidences only happen within the covers of lurid thrillers or in the realms of Hollywood films. Despite my overwhelming sense of anti-climax the notion refused to go away. Something wasn't right about this chest. I looked again at the age-darkened, oak-panelled ottoman. What had I failed to spot? What was there to see? It was no more than a rectangular container without legs sitting flush to the floor, filled with blankets.

I had given up and picked up the first of the blankets to replace them inside the ottoman when I paused. I looked at the small pile of bedding; then at the chest. 'That's odd,' I told myself. I stared again at the chest; then at the blankets. I moved directly in front of the ottoman and sat on the floor. When I was seated, the top of the box was at eye level. It was when I viewed it from this angle that I realized what was wrong. When I'd opened the ottoman the pile of blankets had reached within half an inch of the lid. Stacked alongside the chest they only came halfway up the side. Obviously there was a difference between the dimensions of the interior and the exterior; a marked difference at that. To my mind there could only be one logical explanation for this. The base of the blanket container was not the base of the box. There was a hidden compartment below it.

I leapt to my feet and stared at the interior. The base and walls of the box were plain. No blemish that might be a device for accessing the hidden part of the chest. I suddenly realized I was cold. Before I began a detailed examination I decided it would be a wise precaution to get dressed. As I did so, I thought over the problem. Of course there wouldn't be access via the interior, I told myself; that would be too obvious for the cabinet maker. If the object was to create a secret compartment the way to open it would be hard to find or it would defeat the object.

As soon as I was dressed I resumed my examination. I pulled it away from the bed. That in itself wasn't easy, as the chest was extremely heavy. One significant fact occurred to me from my initial inspection. The box had been designed with a secret compartment in mind rather than a false base being put in later. Although, as I'd surmised, the way into the inner compartment would not be obvious; it would be visible if only one knew what to look for. I stared long and hard at the chest, studying it from all angles. I even tipped it on one end to see if the access might be through the base.

No success perhaps, but a faint thrill of excitement for, as I tilted the ottoman, I was sure I felt something move within it. I replaced the chest on the floor and paced around it once more, looking at the design. It was a long time before the solution came to me. It was an obvious one really, but all magicians' tricks are easy once they are explained. All the joints holding the sides of the box together were off the type known as 'tongue and groove'. They were exquisitely made, fitting perfectly together. Possibly the craftsman had used a little glue to help secure them initially but from the high standard of workmanship I thought that even that might not have been necessary. If the maker had used nothing but tongue and groove joints to build the chest, then why was there a screw hole complete with screw one-third of the way up the rear panel of the chest?

I reached into the pocket of my body warmer and removed my Swiss army knife. I opened the flat-bladed screwdriver and gave the screw a quarter turn. There was a soft click and the false bottom of the chest sprang open on beautifully made concealed hinges. I stared at the interior of the compartment. My excitement was at fever pitch as I reached inside and removed the heavy ancient volume from within. I was in absolutely no doubt that I had discovered the missing book; the Rowe family journal. What secrets would it yield? I wondered as I placed it carefully on the bed. I opened it at the first page and began to read.

Chapter Eighteen

The manuscript was old, the pages yellowed with age. The journal had been compiled in many different scripts; some of them impossible to decipher. There was obviously a marked variation in the standard of literacy of the many contributors. In parts the ink had faded so badly as to be completely illegible. I have to say that these sections, and those where the handwriting defied deciphering, were the only parts of the volume that I derived any pleasure from. My enjoyment was one of relief from a catalogue of crime such as I had never witnessed before or ever wish to read again.

I hadn't delved far into the volume before I became convinced that the legend of inherited insanity of the most terrible sort within the Rowe family was far more than a myth. It was an all-too-sickening reality that had been understated rather than exaggerated with the passage of time. The journal had not been started by William and Roland Rowe but their crimes had been faithfully catalogued by a descendant.

I wondered as I read the account of some of the twins' misdeeds whether they had been recorded out of some perverted sense of pride in their achievements or whether they served a more practical use? Had they perhaps been set down as a benchmark for future generations to follow – or even as a challenge for them to outdo the evils of their forbears?

If it was the latter, it soon became apparent that

William and Roland's successors had risen to the challenge with enthusiasm and alacrity. It seemed there was little or no crime or perversion the various generations of the Rowe family were incapable of committing. Nor, it appeared, was it only on the male side that this dark genetic fault had been passed down through the centuries.

Sickening tales of kidnap, rape, and murder were accompanied throughout the blood-bespattered pages by equally sinister accounts of incest, sodomy, nymphomania, and even necrophilia. In my entire journalistic career I had never seen or heard of anything so appalling, so lacking in any leavening aspect of shame or remorse at the horrors being so carefully set on record. I skimmed the pages, for reading in depth was impossible. I have a strong stomach, but not as strong as that.

My reason for wishing to find the journal had been twofold. To discover if there was truth in the legend of madness in the Rowe family for one thing: well, I'd certainly achieved that. My second motive was to discover if certain crimes had been committed and now I knew the truth of that also; not that it afforded me much comfort.

My last piece of reading was so horrific I closed the journal suddenly and threw it violently on top of the bed in disgust. My heart went out to the nameless, faceless victims whose torments had been so great. Their suffering had not been forgotten, it had never been recognized. I went into the shower room. I felt sick and dirty, as if I'd never be clean again, as if the mere act of reading this dreadful journal of sin had robbed me of every wholesome thought. I washed my hands; then as if that was not enough scrubbed them. The book had been musty with age and my hands were grubby but there was something rather more symbolic in the care with which I washed my hands. Once I had finished drying them I used the corner of the towel to lift the book. My intention was to replace it inside the secret compartment within the ottoman from which I wished it had never been disinterred.

As I picked it up, I noticed a tiny piece of paper, barely visible, protruding from the end of the spine, presumably dislodged by my violent treatment. I looked at it carefully. It appeared to be the corner of a folded piece of notepaper. My curiosity was roused despite a warning voice that cautioned me that I might find it contained fresh horrors. Using the tiny pliers within my multi-tool, I managed to obtain a grip on it. I pulled gently and eased it out. The paper had obviously been carefully concealed.

I unfolded the paper and inspected the contents with mounting interest. The date was the first thing to catch my eye. Once I realized the significance of that I turned the letter over to discover the identity of the writer and the addressee. My excitement mounted as I began to read the text of what was clearly a love letter.

I was in turn shocked and amused, enlightened and puzzled by the message contained within the letter. It was only after I had read the contents for a third time that the full implication struck me. Suddenly, it felt as if everything I had heard and read about Mulgrave Castle and the Rowe family, the curse, the madness, and the legends, had been turned on its head.

I paused for a long time, undecided what to do with this information. In the end I folded the letter carefully and secreted it, not back in the journal but in a hidden, interior pocket within my gilet. The contents of that letter were potentially explosive. I had to work out what relevance they had to the crimes that had been committed recently. Even if they were unconnected, the information within that letter would have far-reaching consequences if it became known. In any case, the facts had remained secret for a long time. A little while longer would not be harmful.

I replaced the journal in its hiding place and locked the secret compartment, pulled the ottoman into position at the foot of my bed, and replaced the blankets. I sat down on the chest to consider the facts I had learned from within the pages of that testament of wickedness.

Apart from the confirmation of the crimes that had been committed and the madness that had brought them about, the most significant fact within the journal had been confirmation of the existence of the secret room I had guessed at from Miles Rowe's history of the castle. It was now plain that Miles had read the journal. His careful avoidance of any mention of the misdeeds led me to speculate whether the omission was due to tacit acceptance or shame.

I glanced at my watch and was surprised to see the time was 6.30 a.m. I drew the curtains back. Although it was still dark, I could see the sky was clear and cloudless. I was relieved, for Charlie's sake as much as anything. At last he would be able to get transferred to hospital and receive proper medical attention. As well as that the change in the weather should mean that the police would be able to reach the castle and begin their investigation into the murders of Beaumont and Rathbone along with the attacks on Charlie, Marsh, and me.

If the police concentrated their efforts on the current crimes, the least I could do would be to attempt to solve the ancient mysteries and settle the issues raised by the legends for all time. In order to do that I would have to locate the chamber built ostensibly to house the fugitive priests. I was now aware that this could have a far more sinister purpose.

The corridors of the castle were deserted, as was to be expected at so early an hour. I reached the head of the stairs and paused. Whether it was the quietness of the old building or my reaction to the horrors I had recently been reading I wasn't sure, but I had a feeling that I was being followed or that someone was watching me. I dismissed the idea as fanciful and began making my way down the broad staircase towards the ground floor.

I paused again at the bottom. Had that sound been the echo of my footsteps or was someone else moving about close by? I glanced back up the stairs. Once more I felt a slightly uncomfortable sensation that I was not alone. I shrugged it off. I was obviously in an over-sensitive frame of mind.

I walked slowly across the wide hall, my nerves taut as piano wire. As I reached the library door the merest wisp of noise reached me. Had it been via my ears or was it my imagination playing tricks? I opted for it being my imagination. I opened the door slowly. When it was half open, the door creaked and so jangled were my nerves by this point that the sound made me shudder with apprehension and glance wildly round in all directions. There was nothing. Gradually, my nerves settled and my pulse rate reduced to a more acceptable level. I stepped cautiously into the library, casting darting glances to my left and right with every stride. The room was empty. I closed the door carefully behind me and paced slowly to the far end of the room, close to the huge fireplace. As I reached it I thought I heard that sound again and turned sharply. I looked around. The room was empty, nothing was moving and yet this time I was convinced it had not been my imagination. Although there was nothing to see and the door remained firmly closed as I had left it seconds before; something had made that slightest of sounds.

I was still pondering what to do when everything went dark. I was conscious for a split second but hadn't time to react to the bag being dropped over my head before the blow came and I felt nothing more.

I remember a blurred impression of consciousness, of being aware that my hands and feet were bound and of being dragged along a smooth surface. Then there was a pause and through the thick dark canvas hood that had been used to blindfold me I heard the faint muttering sound of indistinct voices whispering a short conversation.

The voices were too soft for me to make out the identity of the speakers. Before I could listen further I felt myself being hauled upright into a standing position. I was supported for a brief moment then I was pushed violently backwards. With both my ankles and hands tied I was incapable of saving myself. I felt myself falling then various parts of my body came in contact with a very hard surface, first my back, my elbows, and my head. Then I heard a snapping sound I didn't much care for, from my right leg. Then I was dragged for what seemed an eternity before I blacked out.

The first thing I was aware of was the pain. It was the pain that enabled me to establish that I was conscious. Although I was no longer blindfolded the darkness was as complete as when my assailant had placed the bag over my head. I tried to move and the agonizing pain level shot up. I tried to assess my situation and as the mists slowly cleared from my battered brain I realized with a fresh outburst of horror where I was. And that I was not alone.

I knew where I was by the darkness; yet those who were with me could no longer tell whether it was light or dark. I knew where I was by the coldness; yet those who were with me could no longer tell whether it was cold or hot. I guessed where I was by the lack of sound; yet those who were with me could neither see, nor feel, nor hear.

For them and now for me; this place was as silent as the grave.

For them and now for me; this place was their grave.

I tried to think but a wave of despair swept over me. Thinking had done me absolutely no good so far. Thinking had brought me to this dreadful place; but thinking would not get me out of it. Nothing would get me out of here. I knew beyond all doubt that those who were with me had tried to think; had tried to work out a way to escape. The truth, the brutal and unavoidable reality, was that there had been no escape for them and now there would be no escape for me.

I attempted to move and the pain became intense, unbearably so. I had experienced pain before, notably when I had been shot in Ethiopia, but this was different. This was pain layered upon more pain. It was at that point that my brain decided enough was enough and took the sensible option. It chose to shut down.

I came to again, slowly. I could not begin to guess if this happened minutes later, or hours or even days. Time had ceased to exist. As my brain began the slow process of adjusting to the situation and came to terms with a level of pain it was now forced to accept as the standard, I became aware of a fresh sensation. It was a sound; a sound in that silent place. I listened; and heard it again a gently rustling sound with sinister overtones. A slight but definite sound, but what was making it? What would make so insidious a sound? A fresh wave of horror engulfed me as realization dawned. I knew then what had made the sound. I knew then what would be at home in this cold, dark, damp, and foul place; this silent place where I was lying imprisoned. I knew what it was that would be waiting with infinite patience until I was too weak to resist.

I knew then that the one thing I feared and detested above all else in the world was there with me. I could cope with venomous snakes or poisonous spiders or wild and dangerous creatures; but not rats. I felt my loathing and nausea rise at the very thought that I was being inspected in the dark like a collection of gourmet diners eyeing up a particularly succulent steak.

I might have assumed that terror would have kept me conscious but obviously the pain I was suffering overcame the fear. How many times my brain performed its shutdown operation and sent me into unconsciousness before I came round again, I do not know. I had already lost complete track of the time I had been in that place.

At some point however; when I must have been semicomatose I heard a different sound. I had thought earlier that I had felt something brush against my leg. I had jerked in revulsion at the thought that it had been a rat and the pain that action generated had been enough to put me out again. Now as I listened I was not so sure. Through the blurring sensation of semi-consciousness I heard a mixture of sounds. One was the sound of breathing, of that I was certain. Someone or something was alive in there – but who or what was it?

I listened once more, willing myself to concentrate and it seemed to me that my earlier impression had been right. There had been two sounds. One was definitely the sound of someone breathing but mixed in with it was the noise of what could almost be quiet sobbing. It was a sound this dread chamber must have heard many times before but the shock of it sent my senses reeling. Was it my overworked imagination? Was I coming close to the end, to passing beyond this life? Was I hearing the sound of the ghosts of all those victims who had been here before? I summoned up what tattered remnant of courage I still retained. 'Who's there?' I asked.

The sobbing ceased and silence returned. 'Who is it? Please answer me. I'm Adam, Adam Bailey. Who are you?'

I had half convinced myself I was trying to talk to a spectre when a tearful, despairing voice answered me. 'Adam, it's me,' she said, her voice trembling with fear. 'Where are we, Adam? I can't see anything. Why have we been put in this place?'

'I don't know where we are exactly,' I replied carefully. 'Nor do I know why you've been put here. I've only a vague idea why I'm here.'

My reply was almost the truth. Too much knowledge would not have done her much good at this stage. Eventually I might have to tell her more. I faced up to the grim reality that we might have a lot of time to talk before the end. For the moment I put that thought resolutely to one side. 'Tell me what happened to you? Are you tied up like I am?'

Yes, Adam.' I could hear the sob in her voice. 'My hands and feet are tied together and they hurt.'

'Yes I know, mine do too. Keep talking for a while and tell me what happened before you were put in here. If you keep talking I'll try and come across towards the sound of your voice. Then we can sit together. Would you like that?'

'Yes, Adam, please.'

'OK, just sit still and keep talking.'

I listened carefully as she told me her tale. By the end of it I'd worked out not only where she was by the sound of her voice. By what she told me, I also knew the identity of the killers of Edgar Beaumont and the butler, Ollerenshaw Rathbone. I was also virtually convinced I knew the motive for the crimes and for my imprisonment. I only needed one more piece of evidence to complete the puzzle. For the moment though that was a secondary consideration. My first priority was our predicament.

I inched my way across the floor to where I thought she might be. I reached the wall and turned to lean against it. I could tell she was really close to me. 'Here I am,' I said gently. I heard her shuffle closer until her body was pressed against mine. I felt a quiver run through her slender frame and knew she was fighting against fresh tears. She put her head against my shoulder. 'Adam, are we going to die? I don't want to die.'

'I don't want you to think like that.' Of course I didn't. It was bad enough one of us thinking it. 'We must try and figure out how to get out of here.'

'Adam, I know this sounds horrible, but I'm glad you're here with me.' Her voice quivered again and I could tell she was on the brink of tears.

I didn't know if I was doing the right thing but it

seemed natural at the time. I turned my head and kissed her on the cheek. I felt her relax against me. I thought of our situation and desperation swept over me again. I knew what she didn't. I knew we were surrounded by other victims of the insanity that had afflicted the Rowe family through the generations. I wondered about the dreadful time the others had been through as they waited for the horrible and inevitable end. I knew that was to be our fate also. No swift bullet, no head crushed with stone, but a slow, lingering, and unpleasant waiting and wasting to death.

That was why I had been brought to Mulgrave Castle in the first place of course. I knew it now. I knew the mad cunning of the mind that had plotted and schemed this. The mind that had suggested I come to Mulgrave Castle whilst all the time scheming this end for me.

No matter how vile this seemed to me I was aware from reading the journal that far more wicked acts had been committed within the walls of this appalling dungeon. Unspeakable crimes committed by the most perverted minds. How many young girls had been brought to this place, this airless dark and terrible cell, to feed the insane lust of their sadistic captors. Then, when their pleasure was sated, what dreadful deaths had these poor innocents suffered?

She stirred against me as if my thoughts had disturbed her. The vile obscenity of our fate was a callous indication that the insanity at large now was as potent as that from ancient times.

The cruelty of the death sentence stiffened my resolve. The anger I felt coursed through my veins like fire, warming me to the thought of action. I knew I had to attempt something. I could not bear to lie here and meekly accept our fate. I must try to escape. I must try to get us out of this hell hole before it was too late.

I turned to communicate some of this to my

companion. As I moved, I felt something hard and bulky press against my waist. I realized with a mild sense of elation what it was. 'Are you awake?'

Her head was against my shoulder, she was breathing gently and evenly. It could almost have been a lovers' embrace we were in. I had to wake her; had to try to get free. I made my voice louder; more insistent, 'Wake up, we've work to do.'

She stirred, 'Adam,' her voice was reproachful. 'Why did you have to wake me? I was having such a lovely dream, we were ...' She stopped abruptly; then asked, 'Why did you wake me?'

'I'm sorry, but we must try to escape. First of all we need to get ourselves untied.'

'That's impossible, surely? Our hands are tied behind our backs. How can we hope to get them free?'

'There is a way, but it will be very hard and uncomfortable work for you. It will probably be very painful for me into the bargain, but that doesn't matter. Whatever it costs, however painful or uncomfortable it is we must try it, do you understand?'

I was still puzzled by one thing. Why had my companion been imprisoned with me? That was the only thing that didn't make sense. It was a while before I worked it out. 'Tell me something, what are you wearing?'

'What?'

I repeated the question. 'What does it matter?' Her tone was sharp, waspish. She was angry, and for once that was what I wanted.

'Humour me. Tell me what you're wearing?'

'If you must know, it's that jacket you were so rude about.'

That was it. The last piece in the jigsaw slotted neatly into place. 'Of course you are. You wouldn't be here otherwise.'

'Have you got concussion again?'

Despite our terrible predicament, I smiled. 'No, Evie. I'm not hallucinating. Now, could you for once do exactly as I tell you without argument?'

Chapter Nineteen

'Here's what I want you to do. First of all, can you shuffle round so your back is against my left side?'

It took a few minutes before she managed it. 'Good work; now see if by leaning forward a bit you can feel the pocket of my gilet with your hands.'

After a few minutes groping about, she said, 'Yes, I can feel the teeth of the zip with my fingers.'

'The next bit might be a bit trickier but see what you can do. I want you to try and get hold of the fastener and pull it across until the pocket is completely open.'

After a good deal of fumbling and a few false starts Eve managed to get the zip to move a little. Less than halfway across however, the zip caught in the lining of the pocket and refused to budge one way or the other. Eve swore, from frustration as much as anything, I guessed.

'I'm sorry, Adam I've made a mess of it,' she muttered.

I knew it was important to keep her morale high. 'No you haven't. It was my fault, not yours. I should have warned you the zip on that pocket is prone to sticking. I'm the one who should be saying sorry, not you. We'll just have to go about it another way.' I was guilty of a little white lie, the zip had never jammed before but I needed Eve's courage and resolve to be at its height.

'But you wanted the pocket open and now I can't either open or close it,' she insisted.

'In that case we'll have to make the best of it. There are two things we can try. Inside that pocket you'll find my

Swiss army knife. What I want you to try and do is get hold of the tool through the material of the pocket and slowly work it up towards the gap you've made in the zip. It might just be possible to squeeze it out through the opening. If that doesn't work we will have to rip the pocket. I don't particularly want to do that so try the other way first, and if you fail a time or two don't worry about it, just keep trying; we'll do it between us one way or the other.'

'You want me to get hold of your tool and work it up and down with my fingers?'

My laughter echoed around that chamber of death, probably the first time such a sound had been heard there. It was only in part down to Eve's smutty joke, more at the evidence of her returning courage. The joke and the uplift in morale seemed to act as a spur. Eve tried time after time to work the tool up the inside of the pocket but whenever she relaxed her fingers a little or met a fold in the cloth the tool slipped from her grasp and slid back down to the bottom of the pocket.

I sensed that she was getting more and more frustrated by her inability to complete what was, on the face of it, a straightforward-sounding task. After the fifth attempt had ended in failure, Eve let slip a string of extremely unladylike words.

The incongruity and shock of hearing what would have been totally unremarkable in a man made me laugh out loud. I sensed my amusement had a relaxing effect on Eve too, for after leaning back against me for a moment she began to try again. 'Don't worry if you can't manage it this time, we can always use plan B if we need to.' My refusal to be panicked by our repeated lack of success and the calm measured tone of my voice seemed to act as an additional spur to her determination.

'I'm not going to be beaten by this,' she said through teeth I could tell were gritted. The tone as much as the words themselves heartened me immensely and after a long struggle she eventually succeeded in getting the tool through the gap and passing it to me.

'Well done, Evie; that was brilliant!' I didn't need to exaggerate. She had done really well. I certainly didn't want to dishearten her by telling her that what she'd achieved had been the easy bit.

Eve was bubbling with excitement after her success. 'What do we do now?' she asked.

'Before we start on the next phase I want you to rest for a short while. Are your arms aching?'

'Yes, they are a bit, but I don't mind, honestly.'

'Try to relax them. The next part is down to me in any case. When the cramp in your muscles eases off we'll start again.'

'OK, whatever you say.'

Now there's a first, I thought. Wisely, I didn't give voice to the thought. She leaned back against my shoulder and I knew it was for comfort as much as support. 'Once we've got our arms and legs free,' I told her confidently, 'things will be much better. When that's done we can start trying to figure out how to escape from this place.'

'How can we do that, when we can't even see?'

'We'll have to do like blind people and use our other senses. We still have our hearing, our sense of smell, and when our arms and legs are free we will be able to move about and touch things. There is one entrance into this place that we know about. I have a feeling there might be a second one. I can't be sure, but I reckon if there is a second entrance the people who put us here might not know about it. Either that, or they are confident we would never be able to escape through it. If we can find it and get out then we'll be able to escape and keep clear of danger.'

'You know why those people have done this to us, don't you?'

'I have a pretty good idea.'

'Will you tell me, please?'

'I will do when the time is right. Just at the moment I want us to concentrate on getting ourselves free from these bonds.'

I didn't want to tell her at that stage. I waited patiently until she said, 'My arms feel OK now. What do we do next?'

While we had talked, I had managed to open the knife and find the saw-edged blade. 'I'm going to give you the knife back. I want you to hold it firm whilst I start rubbing the tape holding my wrists against the blade.'

'It sounds impossible.' I heard renewed despondency in her tone.

It did sound impossible but I wasn't about to admit the fact. 'It might be difficult but I'm sure we'll manage it given time. Are you ready to give it a try?'

'Yes, of course I am.'

I was beginning to appreciate the extent of her determination and strength of character. I was glad because I knew she would need every ounce of those qualities if we were to stand even the remotest chance of escaping. I was also aware that I would have to match them and more.

I started shuffling into position. As I moved my legs, my foot brushed against something, and I heard the sound of an object rolling across the chamber floor. Eve heard the noise as well. 'What was that?' she asked.

'I've no idea,' I told her. I could not; I dare not say what I thought it might be. The only object I could think of that would roll across the floor of a cell such as this had to be round in shape – round like a skull.

Once I had shuffled into place, I leaned back against Eve and grasped her hands with mine. Fortunately for me, the person who had tied me up was an amateur at the job. For one thing, they had used tape. That might have been all they could lay their hands on, of course, but it isn't the best method of securing someone. Far more likely that they felt confident I wouldn't be able to free myself. Secondly, they hadn't bothered to search me. If they had done, they would certainly have removed so useful a tool as a knife; particularly one with a saw-edged blade. Their greatest mistake of all however was the way they had secured my hands. They had bound my wrists together instead of leaving them crossed. This meant that with a little effort I was able to get a reasonable amount of movement in my wrists.

'When I put the knife in your hand, hold it firmly while I move the tape across the saw edge. Once the tape begins to fray I should be able to get free easily enough.'

It sounded simple. It sounded quick and it even sounded painless. It wasn't simple, it wasn't quick, and it certainly wasn't painless. Eve dropped the knife several times. Locating it on the floor and picking it up again was both difficult and frustrating. Each time it happened I sensed her growing despair. 'Cheer up,' I encouraged her. 'I said it was going to be the tricky bit. I guessed this was likely to happen. Don't worry. We'll make it.'

I hoped my words sounded more convincing to her than they did to me. I lost count of the number of times the saw sliced into me rather than the tape. My hands felt like a pair of pincushions and I could feel one or two trickles I knew to be blood on them. I thrust the thought of what the smell of the blood might attract resolutely away and continued with grim determination. At least this new pain in my hands and wrists was having the effect of distracting me from the howling agony of my leg.

Suddenly, when I'd all but given up hope of a positive outcome, I felt the saw bite into the edge of the tape. I rubbed hard and cried out with delight as I felt the tightness against my wrists easing fractionally. 'It's working, Evie, keep holding it tight for a minute longer.'

Three more strokes and a large strand of the tape

parted. I was now able to get my hands several inches apart, a couple of strokes more and my wrists were completely free. I moved my arms gently to ease the ache in my shoulders then brought my hands in front of me. I removed the remnants of tape and leaned across to take the knife from Eve.

She waited in patient silence as I felt carefully for the tape securing her wrists and sliced effortlessly through it. She cried out joyfully as she felt her bonds loosen. We hugged one another in mutual delight and self-congratulation. Then we freed each other's ankles. We had achieved a minor miracle. Unfortunately, it was a very minor one. We were still held prisoner in that dark and gruesome cell. 'Let's take a rest before we begin exploring,' I suggested.

I reached across and gently pulled her towards me. We sat for a while, close together, holding hands. 'What happened to you?' I asked.

'I was restless, couldn't sleep, so I got dressed and went downstairs to make myself a drink. There was nobody about apart from Cathy and her husband in the kitchen. They made me a drink and from there I went through into the library to see if I could think of another place that book might have been concealed. Then something hit me on the head and that's the last thing I remember until I woke up in here.'

'Can you remember what time it was roughly when you went into the library?'

'It was early, I do know that. Before seven o'clock.'

'I was still baffled. 'I suppose it was just getting light at that time?'

'Not really; why, does that make a difference?'

'Yes and no. Tell me something, was it quite gloomy in the library or did you put the lights on?'

'No. There was a little bit of reflected light from the snow outside I went in looking for you and I suppose by then I was a bit het up so I went charging down the room without thinking. I'd got almost to the far end when I thought that I could have saved myself a lot of trouble if I'd just flicked the light switch by the door.'

I smiled grimly to myself. I was glad at that precise moment that we were in total darkness so nobody could see my expression. Eve had just provided me with another piece of very useful information. Unfortunately, the problem was that once again it was an item I was unable to share with anyone else.

It would do her absolutely no good to learn that she had been taken prisoner in error, that the real target had been her sister, that the killers had seen the plaid jacket and jumped to the wrong conclusion in the half-light of the library. It had been a fundamental error, but what was worse it signalled that to all intents and purposes their plot was in ruins. It had foundered on a simple case of mistaken identity. This was the latest instance of their bungling inefficiency. They had made one mistake after another. What would they do now?

Even as I realized the extent of their blunder I was aware that the comfort it brought was cold. Their plan may have been scuppered but that didn't make our situation any better. We represented as great a threat to them as ever. There was no way they could afford to release either of us. Whether their plan was doomed to failure or not, one thing was certain; we were doomed. We were condemned to remain in this cell. It would become our crypt.

My thinking halted abruptly at that point. I must have remained quiet for too long because Eve was beginning to become agitated. 'Are you alright, Adam?' she asked.

'Yes, I'm fine, sorry I was thinking,' I reassured her. 'Just keep quiet a moment or too longer; this might be important.'

It was the word 'crypt' that had arrested my train of thought as abruptly as if I'd pulled a communication cord in my mind. For the first time since I regained consciousness, I looked up towards the ceiling; although what I expected to see in that all-pervading blackness I will never know. At first I thought my eyes were deceiving me; then I thought it was some form of wish-fulfilment but when I looked again I was convinced that away to my left and high above me there was a fractional lessening in the depth of the blackness.

I turned my thoughts back to the chamber into which we had been brought and at the same time returned my eyes to the darkness immediately surrounding us. I would look upward again in a while but first I had to allow my eyes to adjust and also I wanted to check out my theory.

I broke the silence. 'Can you remember anything after you were tied up? Anything that happened before you were dumped in here?'

'They put a bag over my head and I felt myself being carried down some stairs. After that they carried me on the level for a long while and then put me down. After a couple of minutes they picked me up again and dumped me here. The next thing I remember was hearing your voice.'

'This long walk on the level when they were carrying you; could that have been along a corridor or passage like those inside the castle?'

There was a long pause before she replied. 'I suppose it might have been something of that sort but it was much longer. It seemed to take them ages.'

'Would you care to take a guess at how long? Was it say, five minutes or ten? Or even longer perhaps?'

'I can't be sure. If I had to guess I'd say fifteen or twenty minutes. Is all this important?'

Eve's voice sounded drowsy and her speech had become a trifle slurred.

'It could be very important, Evie; how are you feeling? Are you all right?' I was concerned by her detached almost dreamy tone.

'My head aches awfully and I feel ever so sleepy,' Eve confirmed.

That didn't sound at all good to me and the last thing we needed in our cell was more bad news. 'I want you to keep talking to me. It's very, very important, do you understand? Evie you must try and keep from falling asleep. You've had a nasty bang on the head and the worst thing would be to fall asleep.'

'OK, Adam, I'll try my best but it's very hard.'

'I'll kick you or pinch you to make sure you stay awake,' I threatened.

'Try that and you could get a boot in the balls.'

I grinned. 'Right I'm going to leave you now. I want to have a look around.'

'A look around?' she echoed. 'Adam, you may not have noticed but we're in total darkness, what's there to see?'

I was delighted, the sarcastic tone was more the old Eve. 'OK, wise guy,' I conceded. 'I mean a feel around. I'm going to see if I can find a way out of this place.'

I began the slow and painful process of crawling across the floor, my right leg dragging behind me until I reached the wall where we had leant when we were going through the process of freeing ourselves. I inched my way along it and headed to my left; towards where I'd seen the impression of a lighter patch above our heads. I knew I had a long slow crawl ahead of me as I needed to reach the opposite corner of the chamber or at least that was where I judged it to be. The darkness was disorientating which didn't help.

I glanced at the luminous dial on my wrist watch. It showed 3.15 p.m. If there was to be any light above us, it would not last much longer on a short winter day – and my crawl across the floor of the chamber seemed to be taking an age.

I was not making spectacular progress when I was slowed by something I hadn't reckoned on. That was the chance of meeting unwelcome obstacles in my path. I had been crawling for some time when I felt something move under my hand. I felt about. It was narrow and hard. At first it felt like a stick. As I moved my hand further I felt another; then more and more. I almost cried out aloud with horror when I realized what it was that I was touching.

It was without doubt the bones of a human skeleton.

Chapter Twenty

I sat for a long moment; shivering with revulsion at the grisly reminder of the dungeon's terrible past. As I struggled to retain my composure some measure of my distress must have communicated itself to Eve. Although I had managed to check my impulse to cry out aloud at the abhorrent manifestation she asked me almost immediately if I was all right. The tone of her voices mirrored the depth of her anxiety. 'Yes, I'm OK,' I told her, although this was far from being the truth.

I may have been able to avoid any audible expression of dismay; I hadn't been able to stop myself from recoiling from the awful thing before me. The unstoppable reflex action had communicated itself throughout my body and the involuntary movement set up a fresh howl of protest from the nerves in my injured leg.

I gritted my teeth and tried to concentrate on the task I'd set myself. This was in part down to a wish to be out of this abomination of a chamber, and in some measure to free my thoughts from the recent encounter and the pain it had generated. The attempt wasn't an unqualified success but with the passage of time the discomfort eased. 'How are you doing?' I asked with as much cheerfulness as I could manage. From my tone of voice it didn't sound much.

'Adam, I'm cold. So cold that I can hardly feel my fingers and toes.'

So was I, but I hadn't wanted to admit the fact. The

penetrating cold was only part of the problem, and not the worst part by any means. The other concern that was uppermost in my mind, despite my determination not to dwell on it, was certainly something I wasn't prepared to tell Eve unless I absolutely had to. By now I had realized that the dungeon was sealed off to the outside world and that meant sooner or later the oxygen within that small chamber would run out as we consumed it.

The question was whether it would be better to wait in the hope of being rescued and thus remain inactive to conserve our precious dwindling supply of oxygen, or whether to risk using up what we had in trying to find a way to escape. No contest. After only the briefest of time spent thinking it over, the solution was obvious. The only people who knew we were trapped within the dungeon were certainly not about to raise the alarm and head up a rescue party. Even if our absence had been noticed, they would be far more likely to distract anyone searching for us by sending them in the wrong direction. An additional worry was that anyone commenting on our absence might jump to completely the wrong conclusion as to why Eve and I were not with the main party. To onlookers, it must have appeared as if we had grown extremely, intimately close over the previous days. What more natural than to assume we were locked in each other's arms, locked in either my bedroom or Eve's rather than being locked in this chamber of death.

It was all very well me facing up to these unpalatable facts, but my dilemma was whether I should share them with Eve, or spare her the worst of the danger we were in. After agonizing over the problem for several minutes I decided I had to be up front with her. If we did manage to escape from this place, I knew that any hope I had of furthering our relationship could only be built on total honesty. Having come to this decision, I braced myself for the task of how to tell her. I turned back to where I had left

256

her.

'Call out to me, Evie,' I encouraged her. There was no reply. Panic set in. 'Evie, Evie darling. Are you awake?'

Her voice was low, husky with the tears she had obviously been shedding. 'Adam, I thought you had gone. What did you call me?'

She was close, close enough for me to reach out to her. I found her hand. It was as cold as ice. I pulled her to me. She came, unresisting, and I could tell she was shivering even before I embraced her. A fresh worry assailed me. Hypothermia. I wrapped her in a tight embrace, and after a few moments felt her hand creep round the back of my neck, pulling my head forward, my lips close to her cheek. 'I won't hit you this time,' she whispered.

The kiss was no passionate encounter, rather an acknowledgment of what might be, or given our perilous situation, what might have been. We would have to be lucky for that not to become true. 'You called me "darling",' Eve whispered after a few moments.

'I did, and I meant it.'

'Are you serious?'

'Never more so.'

'I can't believe you called me that. Not here. Not in this awful place.'

'It's this awful place that convinced me I had to let you know how I feel. If we're ever going to get out of here, I need something to try for. I can't think of a better reason for wanting to escape than having you to look forward to. I just don't want our time together to end too soon, but if it has to, I want you to know there is no one I would rather have with me at the end than you.'

There was a long silence in that perennially silent room, before eventually Eve said, 'In that case, I don't mind.'

'You don't?' I pulled her closer and kissed her passionately. This time the response was all I could have hoped for and more. I felt her tongue moving against mine as she murmured my name over and over again, the sound like a caress that stoked the fires of my need for her. I made no attempt to disguise my arousal and Eve noticed it with a sound I could best describe as a purr of satisfaction. She moved against me, and her leg collided with my knee. The injured knee.

I gave a sort of strangled yelp of pain, but although I'd tried to, I could no longer hide the fact that I was injured. Eve had nursed me over too many hours to be fooled by my lame explanations, so I offered none, simply told her the truth. 'I don't know what's wrong with it. I don't think the leg's broken, but my knee hurts like hell when I move it.'

'Then don't try to move it. Just hold onto me and we'll wait together.'

Eve's calm, level tone worried me. It was as if she had accepted the inevitable. Not good news. If so, she would be tempted to give up, to give in. That was the last thing I needed. I searched around in my mind for something to tell her, the slightest scrap of positive thought to set against all the horrors she had learned over the past few hours. Then I remembered. I glanced at the luminous dial on my wrist watch before I spoke. 'We can't tell at the moment, because it's dark outside, but earlier on, I thought I saw a gleam of light overhead, almost as if there was a gap in the roof of this place. Maybe there's a way out of here after all. A way they don't know about.'

'How long will it be before daylight? How long before we know one way or another?'

'A few hours.' I didn't tell her exactly how long. I was trying to encourage her, not depress her.

'What shall we do whilst we're waiting? Any ideas?'

'I had one, but I don't think my knee would stand up to it.'

'Men! All you think about is sex.'

'That's not true. Sometimes we think about cricket, or football.'

'Very funny. Getting back to my point, how are we to spend the time until daylight?'

'I suppose I could tell you why we're here, and who did this to us, if you want to hear it.'

'You know?'

'Yes, I do, although proving it might be difficult.'

'Go on then, tell me.'

The explanation didn't take as long as I'd hoped, even though I dragged it out. At the end, Eve thought for a moment, before turning her head towards me. We were lying in each other's arms, and I could feel myself becoming drowsy. 'That can't be right,' Eve said after a while.

'Why not?'

'I took everyone's statements, if you remember. When Rathbone was killed, both of them had alibis. Cast-iron ones at that.'

'We don't know when Rathbone was murdered. Not precisely. There could be a gap in those alibis.'

'I don't think so. We know the approximate time to within an hour or two.'

'I know, but I still think I'm right. It has to be them. It's the only explanation that fits the facts.'

Eve yawned, and a second or two later I followed suit. It acted as a danger signal. My alarm translated into movement and I sat upright, ignoring the protest from my knee. 'What's matter, Adam?'

'We can't wait for daylight. We have to try and find that way out before then.'

'Can't I just have a nap first. I'm so tired.'

'That's precisely why you can't take a nap. That weariness means the oxygen in here is running short. If we go to sleep we might never wake up. Come on, Evie. We have to do something – now.'

It is strange that sometimes the actions of people or animals have the opposite effect to that they intend or desire. Our urgency to escape might have come to nothing had it not been for what happened next. I was still trying to persuade Eve to stay awake when she screamed. The sound was ear-piercing in the confines of the small dungeon. As the last echoes died away, I pleaded with her to tell me what was wrong.

'Something touched my hand. Something warm and furry. Then I heard it. There's something alive in here. Something moving.'

Rats! That was all it could be. Made bold by our lack of movement they had approached, no doubt thinking that this was their Christmas dinner. Over my dead body, I thought; which would more than likely be true. But not if we could help it. I'd seen the aftermath of them feasting on the corpse of a mountain goat in the Ethiopian hills. The idea of that obscenity happening to my lovely Eve was too much to bear. 'Come on then, Evie. Let's foil their plan. Let's get out of here.'

That was all very well, but first we needed a plan of our own unless we were going to become rat meat. My brain started to work. Desperation, rather than necessity, being the mother of invention. I took hold of her hand, using it to point a direction in the dark. 'It was over there that I saw what I thought was a little light. If there is an entrance there, in the roof, there has to be a way of getting to it; a ladder, for instance. What I want you to do is stand up, very slowly and carefully, then help me up. You're going to have to support my weight, I'm afraid.'

'I don't care what I have to do as long as it gets us out of here.'

I heard her move, and seconds later she reached down to me. In the darkness her aim was somewhat awry. I began to laugh. 'That's not my hand,' I told her.

'No, I can tell that, now.' She released her hold on the

crotch of my trousers and began feeling my upper body. I grasped her hand, noticing how cold her fingers were. 'If we do find a way out, you'll need to warm your hands before you try to escape, otherwise you won't be able to grip.'

'And how do you suggest I do that?' her voice was full of suspicion.

'You could do worse than putting them back where they were a few seconds ago.'

The slap was no more than a caress. Knowing how hard Eve could hit, I took this as a compliment. Next minute she had hold of my arms under the shoulders. 'Come on, lover boy, up you get.'

The pain when I got to my feet made me dizzy. I clutched at Eve for support. My aim was no better than hers. 'No time for that,' she whispered. 'If you behave yourself I might let you play with them later. Much later.' Another good reason to escape.

Slowly, painfully, and fumbling our way in the darkness, we made our way, step by cautious step across the room until we came to a wall. As we did so, Eve's foot collided with something. We heard it roll away. 'What was that?' she asked.

'I think it belongs to one of the other inhabitants,' I said, as tactfully as I could.

Tact didn't work. 'You think that was a skull?'

'I certainly don't think it was a football. At least we've found the wall. I need to rest against it for a minute.'

Chance, once again. We could have searched for hours without locating anything. As I leaned back against the cold, damp stonework, I tilted my head back. My neck came in contact with something cold and hard. Cold and hard and oblong. Cold, hard, oblong and horizontal. Something like a block of stone set at right angles to the wall. Or like a stone step. 'Evie, give me your hand.'

She obeyed, and I guided it to the object. 'It's a step,'

she said. 'Hang on a second.'

I heard a shuffling, scraping sound as she moved her hand to and fro along the wall. 'Yes, there's another one above it and a bit further along. That means you were right. There must be a way out, and it has to be above our heads.'

The discovery was significant, not least as a morale boost. However, we still had no way of telling how to get out of the cell. And that might have to wait for several hours more. The only good thing was that our burst of activity seemed to have discouraged the hopeful diners.

I stared upwards towards the roof above me; or at least into the darkness where I imagined the roof to be. The vague impression of light I'd seen; or rather thought I'd seen from the far side of our cell had been no trick of my imagination. As I looked up, I could definitely make out a lighter shape in the ceiling above me. I waited as it took my eyes a few seconds to focus on the change. I wanted to be certain that what I could see wasn't a trick, that I wasn't hallucinating or fooling myself into believing what I wanted to be there was actual.

When my eyesight had adjusted to the altered light value, I was able to determine that I was looking at a large rectangular patch of light. The edges of the rectangle were sharper than the middle. I guessed the size of the patch to be about eight feet by four feet. My first impression was that it was similar to looking at the underside of a trapdoor such as might lead to an attic. I was about to point it out to Eve when she spoke. 'Adam, can you see what I can? Is that really a line of light?'

'I think it must be, darling, because I was about to mention it to you, so we can't both be imagining it, can we?'

It took a while before realization of the significance of the dimensions of the shape of light came to me. If Eve's memory of being carried for a long time down a passage had been correct, the cell in which we were being held captive was beneath the family chapel. We were quite literally in a crypt. There was nothing hallowed about this chamber, however. I considered the motives behind the building of the chapel. Charlie had told Eve and me about the evil career of the twins William and Roland Rowe. He had told us of their being barred by the church establishment from worship and that had been their supposed reason for building the chapel.

All along I had thought this altruistic gesture incongruous. If their career of vice had been accurately reported down the centuries, such an act as building a chapel was totally out of character. Now I knew that their motive was a cynical disregard for anything holy. Instead of building a place to worship God, they had ordered the construction of the chapel merely to conceal this chamber; the cell where they could indulge in every perverted, sadistic, and degrading practice their evil, twisted minds could devise.

The light above us had to be the surround of the tomb of one of the twins. The tomb itself was a sham, merely a hollow container. No repentant sinner lay within. The tomb was merely an empty shell to house and conceal the entrance to their sordid lair.

These were all merely my assumptions. If they were correct, I would need to prolong my search a little. I would have to grope around in the dark until I found a way to reach the base of that tomb. There had to be a way, of that I was sure; or almost sure. If I could find it, then Eve and I stood a faint chance of survival. It was, I knew, a remote chance and the odds were still stacked heavily against us. But it was a chance and it represented one more chance than we had previously even dared to think of, or hope for.

'I think I know where that is, Evie. I think we're under the old chapel. And that is the shape of one of the tombs.'

Chapter Twenty-one

Desperate situations call for desperate remedies, the saying goes. Our situation was about as desperate as I could imagine. I knew what the first part of the remedy had to be, and that alone appalled me. In order to find out how to reach the tomb entrance and get back to Eve as quickly as possible I would have to do something desperate. I would have to do the last thing I wanted to do, the one thing guaranteed to cause me the greatest possible pain. I would have to attempt to climb up that set of steps. Not content with the suffering that would cause, I would have to attempt to put weight on my injured leg.

Faced with this appalling option and knowing it to be the only choice open to me, I wasted no time thinking about it. If that sounds courageous, believe me, it wasn't. I knew if I started to dwell on the possible outcome of my proposed action my resolve would weaken. 'I'm going to try and go up there,' I told her.

'No, Adam, don't. Let me go.'

Ignoring Eve and my various aches and pains, I turned and felt along the wall and soon found a third stone, then a fourth. All were at right angles to the wall, jutting out about a foot from the wall itself. Each was at a different height and they seemed to run diagonally up the wall.

So great was my surge of elation at my discovery and the fresh hope it generated for our deliverance from this awful place that I ignored; or failed to grasp the significance of their position. It was only when thinking about it a few moments later that the location of the steps and the meaning to me in particularly dawned.

The wall was on my right-hand side; with the steps running up it from right to left. This meant the open void of the crypt would be on the left of anyone attempting to mount those steps. This also meant the climber would need to rely on his right leg more than his left leg. And it was my right leg that was causing me so much pain. Oh, bugger!

I took a deep breath and banished the thought of the pain and damage the climb would cause. At that point I think I would have happily sacrificed the leg itself in order to effect our escape. Well; perhaps not happily, but I reckon the sacrifice would have been worth it.

'Right, I'm going up.'

Eve reached out and gripped my hand. 'Be careful, Adam.'

As I turned away I noticed something significant. Although Eve had been cold earlier, her hand felt warm to the touch now. She had been as warm as I was; as warm as the air in the chamber itself. We were below ground level in a crypt that was unventilated apart from the minute gap round the tomb entrance. It defied logic that the crypt was getting warmer, but how else could we be gaining body heat instead of losing it?

The explanation was simple, terrible, and frightening. We were running short of oxygen. The clean air we had breathed in was replaced by the carbon dioxide we exhaled. The process had been going on for several hours. With no means for air to enter the chamber, we were using up the oxygen and when it was used up we would start to breathe carbon dioxide. Sooner or later we would suffocate for lack of oxygen in our lungs.

I knew the dangers of this happening would be enhanced and speeded up by increased activity, yet a higher level of activity was just what I had in mind. To some that might have seemed an impossible dilemma. To me, it was no contest; if we didn't get out we were going to die. The cause of death was immaterial.

'Evie, these steps are very narrow and quite steep. If I can support my weight on your shoulder until I get out of reach that would make it easier.'

'Don't worry, Adam, I won't let you down.'

'Right, here goes then. Give me your hand so I can rest my weight on you when I put my right leg down. I need so see how much it will bear.'

'Please be careful, Adam.'

I inched myself slowly to one side until my right shoulder was brushing against the wall and groped for the first step with my left foot. I found the stone slab and put my foot on it; talking through each move with Eve as I went along. 'OK, I'm going to balance on you until I can find the next step. Then I'll put my right foot on it and we'll see if I can move up to the next level.'

That method didn't work. I should have realized the effort of swinging my full weight to bear on my right leg would be more than it would stand. If it hadn't been for Eve's support I would have fallen and I dreaded to think of the consequences to my leg had that happened. 'I'm going to have to do it differently. My right leg won't do all I want it to so I'm going to have to try going up one step at a time. It will take longer but hopefully won't be as painful.'

It was much easier doing it that way. Not exactly pain free but just about bearable. I climbed until I had reached a point where I was no longer able to bear my weight on Eve's shoulder. 'Hang on, Adam, I've had an idea,' she told me.

I waited for a few moments listening to the sound of her movement then she braced my back with her left hand. 'I'll keep on the step behind you, and if you tell me when you're going to move I can use both hands to steady you.'

'Evie, you're terrific,' I told her.

I'm quite honestly unsure whether I'd have made it without her help; not only steadying me but encouraging me.

'We're there, Evie,' I exclaimed at last. 'I'm on the last step. My head's almost touching the roof. Hang on tight, while I have a feel around.'

For the only time in my life I got something of an impression of what it would be like to have blindness cured. Admittedly the hairline strip surrounding the tomb entrance could hardly be said to provide much in the way of illumination, but to someone starved of the least vestige of light it was as water in a parched desert.

I began cautiously feeling with my left hand round the sides of the rectangular shape above me. I was soon convinced that my earlier surmise had been correct. The floor and walls of the crypt that had become our prison were of rough, undressed stone. Knowing the region I would guess that they were most probably limestone. The slab of stone contained within the rectangle of light however was smooth and cool to the touch. To me that meant one thing: marble, the stone which was only used by those with the means to afford it, and usually for headstones, effigies, or tombs.

William and Roland Rowe; the original sinners of the Rowe family, had been commemorated in marble. I was certain the space above my head was the tomb of one of the twins.

'Evie, I want to try and check out what's overhead. Can you manage to hold onto me a minute or two longer?'

'I'll try, Adam, but make it as quick as you can. My arms are starting to get very tired and my legs are beginning to shake.'

If there was a way to unlock the tomb entrance from below, and that was by no means certain, I reasoned it had to be along one of the edges of the lid. I felt my way cautiously with one hand along the short side nearest to me. I tried to put as little pressure on Eve as I could. I found nothing significant; nothing that would be of any use to help us effect our escape. I shuffled slightly and began work on one of the longer edges. Again the effort proved unsuccessful.

'Adam, I can't hold you any longer,' there was a note of desperation in her voice.

'OK; you lean against the wall. Let go of me, I'll try and manage on my own.'

'I'm so sorry, Adam,' she said, tearfully.

'Don't fret about it.' I reached carefully to my left for the farthest edge of the tomb lid and felt along. My finger end caught hold of something different, something I needed to check out carefully.

'Adam, are you OK?' There was real concern in her voice. Not merely the concern she had shown before, when she'd nursed me in my room. This was the worry of someone who regarded me as special. Nothing could have spurred me to action more certainly than the desire to rescue Eve. If I failed in this attempt it would be too late. It would be too late for Eve – and too late for me. When daylight returned the next day we would already be far beyond escape; far beyond rescue. I knew that. I hoped that Eve didn't know it. I was also well aware that the rats knew it; or sensed it at least. They were already becoming bolder. Soon they would be gathering; their razor-sharp teeth at the ready; napkins tucked under their chin ready for their squarest meal in a century.

There appeared to be a horizontal bar of stone across the centre. The purpose of this puzzled me and as I couldn't think of a reason for it being there I concentrated on the far end of the rectangle. I could feel three claw-shaped objects; one at either side and one in the middle of the slab of stone. As my fingers groped around them I felt movement under my hand. My earlier impression had been correct.

I groped slowly along the edge. There seemed to be a long cylindrical rod running horizontally along the shorter edge of the tomb; held in place by the claws. The movement I'd sensed was only fractional as it was a very tight fit. What I'd found was in effect a primitive but highly efficient bolt.

Instinct told me that if I could dislodge the bolt it would leave the tomb lid free, and I would be able to slide it open. As I was pondering how to go about this I remembered the effigy of the ancient sinner that lay on top of each tomb. That led me to realize the purpose of the horizontal bar across the middle of the lid. It was an end stop; designed to prevent the lid from careering free of the sarcophagus. The weight of the marble was obviously too great for it to be stopped by any other means.

I struggled with the marble rod but try as I might with my fingers in varying positions, I couldn't get the bolt to move. I wondered how many others had tried over the centuries; tried and failed. My hopes that had been so high just moments ago began to wilt under this discouragement. Eve, bless her, came to the rescue. I reported the problem to her.

'What about your knife, Adam? Have you tried with that?'

'Of course not, it takes someone clever to think of that. I'll give it a go.'

My hopes rose again; bobbing up and down like a yo-yo on a string. No wonder the prisoners from bygone days had failed to escape. The Swiss army knife hadn't been invented in their day. Added to which they hadn't had Eve with them.

I opened the flat blade of the knife and groped for the rod. I felt for the far end and managed to get the blade behind the marble claw. To my delight I felt a fractional sideways movement; then another. I felt around with my finger and encountered the end of the cylinder.

I attacked the rod with renewed vigour and enthusiasm. Slowly, painfully slowly for my excited state of mind, I managed to work it sideways until I could get my fingertips behind it. Eventually, I got it all the way across the end of the tomb and pushed hard to free the rod from the last of the claws. It dropped clear and I seized the horizontal end stop and heaved with all my remaining strength.

The speed with which the stone slab moved surprised me. It was quite phenomenal to see so heavy a piece of masonry move so rapidly after one sharp push. It shot open; I heard a dull thud and then the slab was arrested by the end stop. It was only when I examined it later that I found it ran along a series of cylindrical pieces of marble that acted as rollers and accelerated the motion of the slab far beyond that of my body's strength.

The shock of the movement and the ensuing brightness almost dislodged me from my precarious perch. I tottered for a moment before grasping the edge of the tomb for support. As I struggled to maintain my balance I heard a cry of joy from behind me.

'Come on, girl, get yourself up those last few steps as quickly as you can, but take care you don't fall.'

I heaved myself over the side of the mock tomb and watched Eve climb to safety and freedom. As she made her way up the steps I could see she was smiling; it was at that point I realized I had a big idiotic grin on my face.

I reached my hand down and helped her over the side. We stood there; hugging one another in sheer elation and relief. Eve was crying; and I don't mind admitting I was crying just as much.

I glanced round. Now our ordeal was over I saw we had been imprisoned under William Rowe's tomb. Freedom had been achieved, but almost immediately I began to suffer the consequences. The leg I had abused so violently during our period of captivity was beginning to seek its revenge. Nausea and pain swept over me in waves.

'Adam, you've gone as white as a sheet. Come on, I'l help you, sit down here.'

She guided me to the nearest pew which happened to be next to the overhanging slab of the marble tomb. I lay back along the pew staring at the slab. 'Go get Tony,' said. 'Get everybody you can find. If the police are here fetch them as well.'

'I'm not leaving you; not after all you've done for me.'

'You must do. I'll be all right.'

'How will I get out of the chapel? The door's always kept locked.'

'If you can't get out through the door smash a window whatever you need to do.'

I heard her footsteps clicking loudly on the tiled floor and turned to watch her go. That was when I saw the blood. I sat bolt upright, staggered to my feet and hobbled to the rear of the tomb. Lying on the floor, his head smashed to a bloody pulp and surrounded by a rapidly widening pool of blood, was the body of Russell Rowe. stared in amazement. Every theory about the events a Mulgrave Castle had just been shot to ribbons by the discovery of Russell's body.

Then, as I looked around, I began to realize why Russell had been killed; and by whom. 'Evie,' I said; my voice low, 'come back.'

'The door's unlocked,' she said as she walked back towards me. When she saw the body, her scream was piercing enough to awaken the sleeping ancestors. She clung to me. 'Adam, what's going on? Why Russell?'

'I'll tell you later, just get out of here as fast as you can Get back to the castle for help. Go now!'

'Yes, but, will you be OK?' Eve gestured to the body.

'Just do as I say. Oh, one more thing, whatever you do please don't leave Harriet alone. Make sure you stay with her; don't let her out of your sight. I know it's unlikely but she could just be still in danger.'

She caught the note of urgency. I heard her footsteps in the porch outside then the door swung to and the chapel fell silent once more. I groped my way back to the nearest pew and sat down to wait.

I knew I was now alone with Russell Rowe's killer.

Chapter Twenty-two

I waited in silence, staring at the killer. Neither of us spoke. I blinked a little in the light after so long in the oppressive darkness of the crypt. I willed the pain in my leg to lessen. Freed from any distractions or counter irritant it refused to listen to my request. Time passed slowly. If I'd thought it had dragged during my captivity; these last minutes before help arrived seemed like an eternity. The silence was oppressive, for I knew that when help arrived I would be able to provide answers to every question hanging over Mulgrave Castle. I would be able to prove the existence of the Rowe family curse; the truth of the inherited madness that had plagued the Rowe family for centuries; and I would be able to identify those who had carried out the killings of Edgar Beaumont, the butler Ollerenshaw Rathbone, and finally Russell Rowe.

When Eve returned she brought Tony and Harriet, together with a string of strangers. Two of the men carried a stretcher; another carried a doctor's bag. Tony introduced the others as Detective Constable Tom Pratt and his boss, Detective Inspector Hardy.

The doctor made a fleeting inspection of Russell Rowe's body before pronouncing him dead; which by that time we all knew. He transferred his attention to me. I pleaded for a pain-killing injection, but he insisted on examining me thoroughly first. Eve had come to stand by me and held my hand as I went through ordeal by triage. When he had done with me I had an additional reason for needing the injection.

'You're lucky the ambulance and doctor were here,' Harriet told me. 'They were just about to set off with Charlie when Eve burst in demanding they come over here for you first.'

'I don't suppose Charlie will mind waiting a bit longer,' I said. 'He's waited long enough already. I'd like to get this over and done with though before I go.'

'Only if you feel up to it,' Eve said.

I smiled at her. 'I'll manage.' To be honest the effects of my ordeal; the various injuries I'd sustained and particularly the damaged knee were beginning to tell; but I was keen to let the police know what I'd learned, or most of it at least.

'To start with,' I began, 'the legend of the Rowe family curse; the legend of inherited madness is true. If you need proof, all you need to do is take a look in that crypt where Eve and I were kept prisoner. In there I think you will find several sets of human remains. The ones I feel certain you'll find are those of Lady Elizabeth Rowe and her lover Sir Robert Mainwaring who were murdered by Lady Elizabeth's husband three hundred years ago. Sir Richard Rowe was murdered by his younger brother, Hugo, two hundred years ago, and Lady Amelia Rowe was murdered a hundred years ago, along with an extremely unlucky gentleman by the name of Ralph Aston. Her husband, Sir Frederick Rowe, killed them in the same way as his predecessors disposed of their victims; by leaving them in that foul place to die. There you are, Inspector; that's five murders already solved and you've only been here a few minutes.'

I wasn't sure whether elation at our freedom, a return of my concussion, or the pain-killing injection was having the effect of making me light-headed. 'That was what was supposed to happen to us. But, due to a combination of inefficiency and bad luck, the plot went sadly wrong. For a start, it wasn't supposed to be Eve who was imprisoned in the crypt, but her sister, Lady Harriet.

'Unfortunately for the killers, Eve and Harriet look very much alike and they both own a distinctive – not to say garish – plaid jacket. In the half-light of the library it would be easy to mistake one for the other; particularly for someone whose sight was less than perfect.

'Harriet was the intended victim; or should I say one of the intended victims. I was the other. When the idea of getting me to Mulgrave Castle was brought up, it was done during a family discussion and nobody seems able to remember whose suggestion it was. The plan was simple. Harriet and I were to be entombed alive in the crypt and left there to die. Charlie would also be killed in a rigged accident and when Tony was killed, it would be made to appear that he had done away with his wife and her lover, much as his ancestors made a habit of doing. Then, in a fit of remorse over our deaths and that of his son, Tony would have taken his own life.'

I paused, took a deep breath and continued, 'I have no doubt the police would be given "clues" to enable them to discover the crypt, but by then it would be too late. All very well, but in practice it went horribly wrong. It didn't help when I foiled the murder attempt on Charlie, nor did it help when Rathbone discovered part of their secret and attempted to blackmail them. There had been three plotters in the first instance. Edgar Beaumont was one of the three. Whether he got greedy for a bigger share of the spoils or whether the others decided a half-share was better than a third I don't know, but Beaumont was disposed of. He was lured to the chapel on Christmas Eve, perhaps by Polly, who seems to be good at that. When he got here, one of them, probably Russell, smashed his skull in with the shield from William Rowe's tomb. Unfortunately, although the plotters knew about the entrance to the crypt via the chapel, they only discovered the other entrance –

the one somewhere in the library – in the last day or two
That meant they had to sneak out of the castle. I had a look
at Rathbone's pantry and noticed there was a system o
signal bells so whenever anyone went in or out of any or
the castle entrances, Rathbone knew of it. He must have
confronted them and paid the price for it. We found blood
on the shield after his death, and it hadn't dried sufficiently
for it to have belonged to Beaumont.

'I think the idea behind the scheme was that with Tony
and Charlie dead, and Beaumont too, all the wealth o
Tony's business interests, the castle and the estates, and a
five-million-pound life insurance policy would go to the
remaining plotters. Not a bad motive for murder,
suppose. As I said, they were very clumsy and inefficient
When I saved Charlie, one of the plotters tried to kill me
out of anger. That was a huge mistake. What they didn'
know was that whilst Becky was careering down the slope
on her toboggan she looked back and was able to see the
one person near enough to her brother to push him over the
edge. When I asked Charlie about the hands on his back he
said they were small; like a woman's hands. They
belonged to Polly Jardine, who was in league with Edga
Beaumont and her lover to murder their way to a smal
fortune. Beaumont's motive was greed; for although he
had a half-share in the business he wanted it all. Polly'
was money, to a certain extent believe she coveted
Harriet's status. But it was more likely passion for he
lover.

'That was another piece of bad luck for the plotters
They weren't aware that Eve had recruited two persona
and highly efficient bodyguards for me, and it was Becky
who spotted Russell Rowe leaving Polly Jardine's room
early one morning and sneaking back to his own room
Russell was the one who hatched the plan, I guess. He
used to insist he stay in the room I was allocated. He mus
have found the family journal there, just as I did, an

learned of the existence of the crypt. The journal contains a sickening record of the appalling crimes committed by some members of the Rowe family over the centuries. The victims in that crypt are just a few of the unfortunates who fell foul of the insanity that ran through the generations. I'm guessing, but I believe he was the one who suggested inviting me here to spend Christmas investigating the curse. The plan being to set me up as Harriet's paramour.'

I looked across at Tony. 'Can you remember who first brought up the subject of the curse? And in particular, who drew your attention to the fact that it recurs every hundred years?'

Tony didn't even pause as he replied, 'It was Russell, I'm absolutely certain of that.'

'Hang on; are you saying Russell Rowe and Polly Jardine were plotting all this? If that's the case; who killed Russell Rowe? Was it Polly Jardine?' Inspector Hardy asked.

'No,' I confessed. 'You could say I killed Russell Rowe. Or at least, that I was his murderer's accomplice.' I looked round my audience and saw they were open-mouthed with shock.

Pratt was the first to recover. 'Who did murder Rowe? Whose accomplice were you?' he asked.

I smiled. 'Someone you will never be able to charge,' I told him. I pointed across the chapel. 'There's the killer: William Rowe.'

Everyone stared at the effigy. 'Would you mind explaining?' Pratt sounded baffled.

'It was the act of our escaping that was responsible for Russell's death. You have to understand this part is purely guesswork, but I think when I slid the bolt out of its slot, Russell was here in the chapel. That's why the lights were on. He must have guessed what was happening and panicked. I think he bent down with the intention of pushing the marble bolt back in place when I shoved the tomb lid open. Several tons of marble were sufficient to crush his skull like an eggshell.'

I stopped at that point. I could have added more but felt it better to omit one or two other facts I'd learned during my stay. Besides which I was beginning to feel extremely unwell. As the ambulance men put me on a stretcher I passed out.

I learned later that the concussion had been so severe I'd been sedated for over a week for my own safety. Not that I was going anywhere. From my hospital bed I saw one or two vaguely familiar faces from time to time, people I felt I ought to recognize, but everything seemed blurred, as if I was looking through a bathroom window. In any case, everything seemed too much of an effort. Added to my other troubles there were severe complications with my leg. It wasn't broken, but I had a dislocated kneecap and torn ligaments. I'm not sure what the pain level from a broken leg is, but the injuries I had were bad enough. When the hospital eventually released me I was handed over to an expert in the art of torture who introduced himself as a physiotherapist. It was late February before I was pronounced fit enough to drive again. I would have to go to Mulgrave Castle once more to collect my car and belongings.

Tony picked me up from Netherdale station and we drove to the castle in reflective mood. Tony told me the police had got a full confession from Polly Jardine. They had also removed a total of nine sets of human remains from the crypt.

He seemed a bit gloomy, so I asked him what was troubling him. 'To be honest, Adam, it's this family insanity business. You said yourself: it's as potent now as it was centuries ago. We're all worried Charlie or I might have it.'

I smiled gently. 'Don't worry, Tony, I might be able to set your mind at rest on that score as well.'

My welcome at the castle was a hero's one. I fielded all the questions about my health and was relieved to find Charlie fit and well and a dab hand at using crutches for his severely sprained leg. We sat down to a superb lunch cooked by Cathy Marsh and served by the new butler, a young Swede whom, Charlie told me with glee, was gay and had a boyfriend in Netherdale he visited whenever he had a day off.

After lunch we adjourned to the sitting room. Tony produced a box of cigars and passed me one. Not any old cigar but a *Romeo y Julieta*. I removed it from its cylindrical foil container and put my hand into my gilet inner pocket. I removed a piece of paper and folded it into a spill, went over to the fire and lit the edge of the paper. I waited until it was burning and lit the cigar. I dropped the paper into the grate and turned to face the Rowe family. I smiled at them. 'Tell me about Eve,' I asked Harriet, 'how is she?'

'I think she's pining for you, Adam. She tells me she's fed up with London, fed up with her job, and fed up with life in general,' Harriet told me with a smile. 'She's been on the phone almost every day asking after you; but I'm not supposed to tell you that. I suggested she rang you but I don't think she's got the courage to, after what she went through in the past. She did tell me how much she misses you; but I'm not supposed to tell you that either.'

I smiled with genuine pleasure. I felt in my gilet pocket for the rail ticket I'd bought. The last train for London was at 6.00 p.m. 'OK, I'll have to be going soon, but before I do I want to tell you something. It's something that must never go outside this room. Tony, you don't have to worry about the family insanity. Neither you nor any of the children could possibly be affected by it.'

'How can you be sure, Adam?'

I smiled at him, at Harriet and Charlotte, at Charlie and ast, at the twins; my two personal guardian angels.

'Because when I found the journal, I also discovered a letter hidden inside the spine of the book. It was addressed to Lady Amelia from her lover, and was dated shortly before her disappearance. It is obvious to me that Lady Amelia must have found the journal and secreted the letter inside it. The letter proposes that they elope together taking her elder son with them. The writer acknowledges that the child is his, not Sir Frederick's.

'The writer uses the telling phrase, "you must escape as soon as possible from that place, now that you have discovered the evil that lies within". That suggests to me that Lady Amelia not only found the journal, but that she read it and told her lover of the sickening catalogue of vice it contained.

'I feel certain that Sir Frederick never discovered the whole truth. He must at the very least have suspected that Lady Amelia had a lover; even that she planned to elope but I am sure he could never have lived with the knowledge that the heir to Mulgrave Castle wasn't his son but the illegitimate child fathered by his wife's lover.

'Possibly the bitterest irony in all this is that Lady Amelia should have chosen that journal of depravity in which to hide the letter, only to fall victim to another member of the Rowe dynasty carrying the curse of insanity. Anyway, as a consequence, although Russell undoubtedly inherited the family insanity; you couldn't have done, and nor can Charlie; because your grandfather hadn't a drop of Rowe blood in his veins.'

'This is dreadful.' Tony cast a look around. 'That means I'm not really entitled to all this.'

'I shouldn't worry about it,' I told him cheerfully. 'If you were able to go back through most aristocratic family histories you'll probably find the same thing had happened; in some cases probably more than once. The ironic part is that if Russell had found that letter when he was examining the journal, he could have simply produced it and demanded blood tests or this new-fangled-DNA which everyone is talking about, and none of this whole mess would have been necessary.'

'But I can't simply ignore it. What about the letter?' Tony objected. 'That proves it surely. What if someone gets hold of it and makes it public? The whole sordid business will come out.'

'They couldn't do that,' I told him calmly. 'I've just lit my cigar with it.'

'So you're telling me that I'm actually descended from Ralph Aston?'

'No, that's not true either. Do you remember that day in the chapel? I referred to Aston as being extremely unlucky. He wasn't Lady Amelia's lover. The signature on the letter wasn't Aston's. Sir Frederick murdered an innocent man.'

'Who was her lover?'

'A man by the name of Bradley. He was the estate manager. I got DC Pratt to do a bit of digging whilst I was in hospital, but he couldn't find out much about him.

'What happened to Bradley?' Charlie asked.

'He quit his job, or was fired by Sir Frederick. After that, there seems to be no record of him. One other thing that I was pondering whilst I was laid up was the irony that if Tony had got his way over the library and had converted it to a rumpus room, you'd have discovered the entrance to the priest's hole and connecting passage to the crypt behind the panelling.'

'It's all been bricked up now, Adam,' Lady Charlotte informed me. 'Tony got a firm to bring one of those big mobile mixers on the back of a wagon and they filled the whole of that dungeon with concrete. After that we removed the effigies of William and Roland Rowe and had them smashed to pieces. Finally, we got a priest in to re-consecrate the chapel and hold a mass for the souls of the departed. It seemed the right thing to do.'

'Have they held the inquests yet?'

'No,' – Tony leaned forward in his chair – 'I got a phone call from DC Pratt the other day. Apparently, they have to wait for an expert to establish how old the remains are before they can hazard a guess at their identities. Some, of course, we will never know, but hopefully we can put a name to five of them. They will all be buried in the consecrated ground alongside the chapel where the rest of the family are. It seems the least we can do.'

It was almost 9 p.m. when I rang the doorbell of Eve's flat. I was carrying a bottle of wine and a bunch of flowers. She stared at me in astonishment.

'Hi, Evie,' I said with a smile that reflected a confidence I didn't feel.

'Adam, what are you doing here?'

'During the time I was in hospital, all I could think of was you, how much I missed you, and how desperate I was to see you again.'

'In that case, you'd better come inside and we'll talk. I don't want my neighbours seeing you there.'

Typical of Eve, I thought. Her less-than-rapturous greeting seemed at odds with what Harriet had told me. It left me wondering what her reaction would be to the question I'd come to London to ask her …

End

Other Accent Press titles you may enjoy:

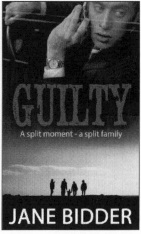

For more information about **Bill Kitson**
and other **Accent Press** titles
please visit

www.accentpress.co.uk

10648714R00170

Printed in Great Brita
by Amazon.co.uk, Lt
Marston Gate.